Other Ti

TO KILL A WARLOCK (E

The murder of a dark arts warlock.
A shape-shifting, ravenous creature on the loose.
A devilishly handsome stranger sent to investigate.
Sometimes working law enforcement for the Netherworld is a real bitch.

Dulcie O'Neil is a fairy. And not the type to frolic in gardens. She's a Regulator—a law-enforcement agent who monitors the creatures of the Netherworld to keep them from wreaking havoc in the mortal world.

When a warlock is murdered and Dulcie was the last person to see him alive, she must uncover the truth before she's either deported back to the Netherworld, or she becomes the next victim.

Enter Knight Vander, a sinfully attractive investigator sent from the Netherworld to work the case with Dulcie. Between battling her attraction to her self-appointed partner, keeping a sadomasochistic demon in check, and fending off the advances of a sexy and powerful vampire, Dulcie's got her hands full.

As the body count increases, Dulcie finds herself battling dark magic, reconnoitering in S&M clubs and suffering the greatest of all betrayals.

Other Titles by H.P. Mallory:

FIRE BURN AND CAULDRON BUBBLE
(Book 1 of the Jolie Wilkins series)

A self-deprecating witch with the unique ability to reanimate the dead.
A dangerously handsome warlock torn between being her boss and her would-be lover.
A six hundred year old English vampire with his own agenda; one that includes an appetite for witches.
The Underworld in a state of chaos.
Let the games begin.

Life isn't bad for psychic Jolie Wilkins. True, she doesn't have a love life to speak of, but she has a cute house in the suburbs of Los Angeles, a cat and a quirky best friend.

Enter Rand Balfour, a sinfully attractive warlock who insists she's a witch and who just might turn her life upside down. Rand hires her to help him solve a mystery regarding the death of his client who also happens to be a ghost. Jolie not only uncovers the cause of the ghost's demise but, in the process, she brings him back to life!

Word of Jolie's incredible ability to bring back the dead spreads like wildfire, putting her at the top of the Underworld's most wanted list. Consequently, she finds herself at the center of a custody battle between a villainous witch, a dangerous but oh-so-sexy vampire, and her warlock boss, Rand.

Other Titles by H.P. Mallory:

TOIL AND TROUBLE

(Book 2 of the Jolie Wilkins series)

The Underworld in civil war. The cause? A witch who can reanimate the dead.
A sexy as sin vampire determined to claim her.
An infuriatingly handsome warlock torn between duty and love.
Who says blonds have more fun?

After defending herself against fairy magic, Jolie Wilkins wakes to find her world turned upside down—the creatures of the Underworld on the precipice of war.

The Underworld is polarized in a battle of witch against witch, creature against creature, led by the villainous Bella, who would be Queen.

While Jolie has one goal in mind, to stake the vampire, Ryder, who nearly killed her, she also must choose between the affections of her warlock employer, Rand, and the mysteriously sexy vampire, Sinjin.

And as if that weren't enough to ruin a girl's day, everything Jolie knows will be turned inside out when she's thrust into the shock of a lifetime.

A Tale of Two Goblins

by
H.P. Mallory

A Tale of Two Goblins

A TALE OF TWO GOBLINS

H.P. MALLORY

Acknowledgements:

To my fabulous mother, as always, thank you for all your help—none of my books
would be what they are without you!

To Dia Robinson: Thank you so much for entering my "Become a character in my next book" contest—I am thrilled with your addition to the book, Diva!!!

To my husband and my son: I love you

To my beta readers: Sofia Oberg, Belinda Boring, Evie Amaro, Mary Genther, Sally Arnold, Laura Gibala, Jennifer Widener, Meagan Mize and Val Averill, thank you so much for wanting to read this book and for all your comments. You were all a huge help!

To all my readers: I cannot thank you enough for your continued support—I never would have made it this far without all of you...thank you.

ONE

I yawned but forced the desire to crawl back into bed out of my mind. Exercise was important in my line of work, and although it was only five in the morning, it was my favorite hour to jog. I grabbed my iPod and glanced down at Blue as he pawed my toes, only to lean back on his haunches and stretch. Guess it was early for him too.

Pushing an ear piece into my ear, I opened the front door of my crappy apartment and inhaled the cold Splendor air. The chirping of insects was as loud as the finale of any symphony and I shivered as a cold wind assaulted me. I wasn't a big fan of November in California—give me hot, sunny weather all year long and I'd be as happy as a pixie on a bliss potion.

I leaned over and grabbed my ankles, stretching my quads and stood up, pulling my arms over my head and stretched my triceps. One should never exercise with cold muscles. Blue started groaning and circled me as if to say "hurry up already." Feeling limber enough, I stepped outside, locked the door and started my jog while Katy Perry sang "Teenage Dream" into my head.

Maybe five minutes into our run, Blue slowed and cocked his head to the side, but I didn't need his canine sixth sense to know someone was following us. I swallowed the anxiety in my throat and went into autopilot or auto cop, as the case may be. Turning the volume down on my iPod, I didn't remove the ear buds, not wanting to alert my visitor to the fact that I knew he was there. Rolling my arms in tight circles, I waited—well figuratively, I was still jogging, still giving the illusion of everything being hunky dory in the life of Dulcie the fairy.

Before I had the chance to think, a shadow flickered from between the trees. My breath caught in my throat, and I paused, bending over to pretend to tie my shoelace. Even though I was doing my damndest not to give anything away, Blue wasn't quite so stealthy. Instead, he stood as if in rigor mortis, his hackles raised and his lips curling back to reveal an impressive set of sharp teeth. His growl interrupted the otherwise still night, and I glanced back at the tree line, watching and waiting for whatever was out there to make itself known. When it did, I'd be ready to take it down with a palm full of fairy dust—my weapon extraordinaire. I stood up and braced myself, feet shoulder width apart.

I didn't have to wait long. My assailant made himself known, jumping out at me with a huge...smile?

"Knight!" I leaned onto my knees, breathing out the angst that just seconds ago would have dictated I use my fairy powers to take him out. "You bastard," I breathed, refusing to look at him.

Blue wasn't as polite. His growl sounded like a large truck driving over rocks. The dog must have thought growling wasn't threatening enough because he then broke into a deep and angry bark. I petted his head and tried to calm him with "it's okay, boy" but the dog wouldn't back down. Instead, he lunged for Knight and much as I was annoyed with Knight myself, he didn't deserve to get bitten. Not that I thought Blue would bite him, but better to be safe than stuck in the emergency room. So, I grabbed Blue's collar and held him back with a none too subtle "No!"

"Nice dog," Knight scoffed as Blue continued to growl. Hmm, maybe I hadn't socialized him well enough. Come to think of it, I hadn't socialized him at all, which shouldn't have been much of a surprise as I wasn't a very social person myself.

"What do you want?" I demanded.

"Morning, Dulce," Knight said, completely disregarding my less than friendly greeting. Unable to avoid looking at him for more than a few seconds, I finally brought my attention to his face.

Knight Vander was a *Loki*, a creature from the Netherworld who also happened to be an investigator working for the Association of Netherworld Creatures otherwise known as the ANC. And he also happened to be the hottest thing in Splendor.

"What the hell are you doing outside my apartment at five am?" I insisted, and patted Blue's head so he'd stop growling. He finally obeyed and sat silently at my feet, wearing a happy dog smile.

"Technically I'm not outside your apartment," Knight said and flashed me a beautiful smile. Holy Hades, the man was sexy.

"So, we're going to play word games?" Rather than waiting for an answer, I started jogging again. Not that I disliked Knight but he was a cocky SOB and there wasn't any room in my life for cockiness or SOBs or, for that matter, Knight. "So, what, you just hang around my house waiting for me to come out?"

"I needed to get in touch with you," he said in his alto voice, as rich as a piece of dark chocolate cake.

The moon was still in full effect, and the milky rays glowed against Knight's white tee shirt. His shorts ended just below his knees, and I couldn't help but notice how muscular his calves were, muscular and evenly covered with black hair. Realizing I was checking his legs out and very obviously, I brought my attention to the road and tried to increase my pace. Knight easily kept up with me which wasn't hard considering I was five-one and he was at least six-two, maybe six-three. To me, he looked like a giant.

"Have you heard of this pretty cool invention called the phone?" I asked, keeping my attention straight ahead. "Through a series of wires and electrodes, my voice travels to you and you never have to leave your house! Imagine that!"

"Haha, Dulce, I've called you countless times over the last two months, and I've lost track of how many messages I've left." He didn't sound angry, merely conversational.

Okay, so I was guilty about not calling him back, so what? "I've been...busy," I said, though it was farthest from the truth. Having recently given Knight my letter of resignation (he'd been my boss), I now had lots of free time but not a whole lot to fill it with. Course, Knight didn't need to know that.

"Busy?" he repeated, his tone just as dubious as his smile. "I see you've got a dog but other than that, what's been occupying your time?"

The sound of our footfalls against the pavement echoed my shallow breathing. I hadn't been on a jog in at least a week and it was making itself known in every section of my body.

"Writing," I answered succinctly. And it was the truth. I'd been spending all my time working on a book, the second in a series. I had aspirations to be a full time writer, and it seemed those aspirations might actually be headed somewhere—recently a literary agent had requested the full manuscript of my book, "A Vampire and a Gentleman."

Knight just nodded, and I felt my breath becoming more and more shallow. It wasn't easy to run and talk at the same time. I glanced at my companion, the *Loki*, and found he didn't seem to be huffing or puffing. Instead, he just wore an amused smile and looked me up and down appreciatively. I frowned and glanced back at the road, feeling the need to slow my pace. But, I wouldn't give in—not yet.

"Where'd you get the dog?" he asked, eyeing the subject all the while.

"He was a gift," I answered and felt like I was going to pass out with the effort.

"Who from?"

Hmm, this was a question that wouldn't get an honest answer, or at least not a full honest answer. Blue had been given to me by my ex boss (the one before Knight), Quillan, who was now a wanted potions smuggler. Quillan...just his name left a bad taste in my mouth—he'd been my boss, yes, but also my friend, and I'd sort of lusted after him...just a little. But, when it came down to apprehending him, when I was still a cop, aka Regulator working for the Netherworld, I'd failed. And so far, I hadn't been able to forgive myself for failing, for allowing my emotions to get in the way of my position as Regulator. It had been a sign that I wasn't the Regulator I'd thought I was or needed to be. So, I'd resigned.

I didn't like to think about Quillan, and I really didn't like to talk about him.

"Just a friend." I made the mistake of glancing up at Knight. The cock-eyed expression he wore made me look away quickly. He seemed to always know when there was more to a story. Course, I was also a terrible liar.

"A friend?" he inquired.

Not able to continue on, I stopped jogging and faced him, irritation seeping into my gut as I fought to catch my breath. "Didn't your mother ever tell you it's rude to put your nose in other people's business?"

Knight also stopped jogging, that same smile still hanging from his lips. "Can't recall that she did."

I crossed my arms against my chest, trying to ward off the cold night air and wished I'd worn something over my sports bra. Maybe my annoyance with Knight would be enough to keep me warm. "Let's cut the crap, Knight, what are you doing here?"

"I need your help."

That could mean many things but due to the fact that I'd promised Knight I'd be available to work as a consultant whenever he had a tough Netherworld case, the playing field was narrowed. "What do you need my help for?" I asked, watching Blue arch his back and pee against a bush. He still hadn't mastered the art of lifting one leg but I wasn't sure how I was supposed to teach him.

"There's a case that's been baffling us all."

Before I decided to hear anymore, I turned around and started walking back toward my apartment, rolling my arms in big circles. No use in discussing ANC business while we were standing in the middle of the road. Knight was beside me momentarily and threw me another disarmingly handsome smile. With his black hair, blue eyes and tan complexion, immense height and broad build, he looked like a God. And, boy, wouldn't he have loved to know that.

"Let's talk about it in my apartment," I started.

"I was hoping you'd say that."

"Don't get any ideas," I grumbled, watching Blue scout the bushes and trees before us. I never took him on a leash because we never met anyone on our five am excursions. Guess I couldn't say that anymore.

"Dulce, I've been getting ideas where you're concerned since we met," Knight said, his voice heavy.

"Well, keep them to yourself," I snapped. I'd already made up my mind not to get involved with Knight.

"Why do you fight your attraction to me?" His tone wasn't clipped or otherwise pointing to a hurt self esteem. Course, he was never anything other than sure, and his infallible confidence was one of his character traits that bothered me the most. I mean, didn't everyone succumb to self doubt once in a while? Ha, not if you were a *Loki* who answered to the name of Knight.

"Who said I'm attracted to you?" I insisted, wishing I could wipe the cocky and proud smile right off his mouth.

"No point in denying it; I'm fully aware of your real feelings for me."

I laughed, but it was an acidic sound because I was suddenly worried that he could sense it. Even though I'd pledged never to develop feelings for him, I couldn't deny the fact that I was attracted to Knight and always had been. But, I tempered that attraction by keeping him at arm's length.

As a rule, I didn't get involved with men. Now, before you question that statement—I also didn't get involved with women—I just didn't get involved period. After a pretty crappy breakup two years earlier, my heart still hadn't fully mended and Knight was the type of man who would break it again, into tiny little shards that would be impossible to glue back together. If he ever got the chance, that is.

"Hmm..." I started, really not knowing what else to say. Even though as a fairy, I had the innate ability to detect creatures just by looking at them, Knight had thrown me for a loop from day one. Course, the reason had been that I'd never come into contact with one of his kind before—a *Loki*. Furthermore, the unfortunate thing about Knight's being a *Loki* was I had no clue what his powers were. Unlike my ability to create magic from fairy dust, Knight's abilities weren't quite so straight forward. I'd actually been keeping a list of the types of powers he'd demonstrated so far. Guess I could add attraction detector to the mix. Unless he was full of it...

"You just know?" I asked doubtfully. "What, is that another of your *Loki* character traits?"

"Nope," he said in a self-satisfied sort of way. "It's just Vander instinct, one hundred percent."

"Well, your Vander instinct is confused by your Vander cockiness," I snapped.

He laughed, but his eyes were hot, hungry and I felt consumed just by his wolfish stare. I dropped my attention to the ground and mumbled something under my breath, trying to keep Knight from noticing the red flush currently overtaking my cheeks. We reached my apartment and could now talk about ANC business and not the fact that I was lusting after Knight and furthermore, that he knew it.

I jammed the key into the lock and nearly lost my focus when I felt the heat of Knight's body just behind me. The iciness of the air seemed doubly cold in front of me while Knight's heat penetrated my back. I closed my eyes at the feel of his hands massaging my forearms. Thank Hades my back was to him and he couldn't see my reaction. Course, the goose bumps on my arms could be compared to a big arrow sign pointing at me with the words: "she's hot for you" emblazoned on it.

"You have goose flesh," he whispered and caused a seizure in my stomach.

"I, uh, it's...it's cold out here."

He chuckled and lifted the heavy curtain of my honey blond hair over one shoulder, trailing the back of my neck with his index finger. I couldn't help the shudder that raced through me.

"I haven't stopped thinking about you, Dulcie." His voice was a mere breath whispering against my skin, and I closed my eyes, reveling in the feel of him. The touch of his lips against my neck brought a hiss of air from my mouth, and before I lost all sense of reason right there, Blue walked over and pawed my toes, as if reminding me I'd been attempting to unlock the door and more so, that I was acting like an idiot.

I opened my eyes and silently praised the dog for bringing me back to my senses. Cranking the key to the left, I pushed the door open with such strength, I nearly lost my footing. But, I was inside and away from Knight...things were looking up.

Turning on the light, I flung myself into my computer desk chair, making sure to sit somewhere Knight couldn't sit beside me. I wheeled around and faced him, finding the air in my tiny apartment considerably stuffy. Knight closed the door behind him and lumbered into my living room, seating himself on my couch.

"One of these days, Dulce, you aren't going to be able to deny there is something between us."

Irritation bled through me. I didn't like people telling me what I could and couldn't do. "Regardless of what you think, I'm not interested."

Knight cocked a brow and chuckled, but said nothing.

"So, let's talk about the reason you're here," I said.

"There have been quite a few cases recently of comatose victims, both here in Splendor but also in Estuary and Moon." His tone was suddenly all business, and I breathed an inward sigh of relief. All business Knight I could handle.

Estuary was in our district—we provided police work for Splendor, Estuary and Haven. Moon, though, was out of our district and had its own ANC force. But, back to the comatose victims... "So, why should I be concerned?"

Knight shrugged. "All victims were otherwise healthy, according to their friends and family. Then one night they go to sleep and never wake up the next morning."

I nodded, feeling a cramp building in my calf. I propped one leg over my knee, leaned forward and started my after exercise stretch routine. "Has anyone died?"

"One death."

Stretching my calf, I winced against the pain.

"Cramp?" Knight asked. "I can do wonders on sore muscles."

"I'm fine," I started and, not wanting to appear so out of sorts, added: "Thanks."

Knight, apparently not used to hearing no for an answer, stood up and approached me. "Lay with your back on the floor and I'll show you a good one for leg cramps and for stretching your quads."

The cramp in my calf suddenly started pounding as if it wanted nothing more than to be massaged by the incredibly handsome *Loki*, and before I knew it, I was lying on the floor, looking up at him. He reached for my right leg and cradled it against his thigh as he massaged my calf, kneading my sore muscles with his large hands. Little by little, the cramp stopped throbbing and eventually went away. Hmm, another Knight Vander *Loki* ability?

"When did these comas start?" I asked quickly, trying to pull my attention from his hands. He worked up my thigh and then took my foot in his hand and bent my leg at the knee, pushing my knee up into my stomach.

"How does that feel?" Knight asked.

"Good," I managed. He pulled my leg straight and put it back on the floor, reaching for the other one. A massage of my other thigh followed, and although I didn't want to admit it to myself, I was getting incredibly turned on.

"We've been noticing these sudden comas popping up for over two months," he said. Hmm, hence his repeated calls to me over the last couple of months. He didn't say it but it was there in his eyes. I felt a little bit guilty, but quickly banished the feeling. If Knight had really needed to get in touch with me, he would have invaded my happy little jog months earlier.

"So, I guess you want me to review the files?" I asked, thinking I could use some consultant work. My savings account had been dwindling recently, but I just hadn't been able to bring myself to call Knight for work—it wasn't that I was avoiding jobs, I was avoiding Knight.

"If you feel so inclined," he answered with a grin and brought my foot back to the ground, offering his hands. I took them, and he pulled me up.

"Any ideas on what could be causing all the comas?" I asked.

He made his way back to the couch and sunk into it, stretching his arms above his head and clasped them behind his neck. I was convinced he liked showing off his chest and huge biceps. "Healthy victim one day, comatose the next."

"*Toad Wallow*?" *Toad Wallow* was a potion—one drop and you'd be dead to the world for a week at the most, then you'd wake up with one raging headache, but at least you'd wake up. Course, it didn't seem the same could be said for these victims.

Knight shook his head. "None of the patients have reflexes, and their EKGs come back inactive."

"*Somnogobelinus*," I whispered. "A sleep goblin, a *Dreamstalker*."

Knight nodded. "All roads lead to Rome, or a *Dreamstalker* in this case."

I shook my head. "There are only two registered *Dreamstalkers* in the ANC files: one has been locked away in a Netherworld prison for centuries and..."

"The second was locked away five years ago," Knight finished for me, with an approving smile.

"Ah, so you have done your homework." Apprehending Druiva, the *Dreamstalker* in question, had been one of the most difficult cases Splendor ANC had ever seen. I'd been a junior Regulator at the time and hadn't really been involved, but it was one of those legendary cases that was still discussed, even now.

"I have."

"And are they still locked away?" I demanded, thinking we'd found our solution if the answer was "no."

"Yes, as of yesterday, they are both doing time in Banshee Prison from here until eternity, both under extra security."

"How can this be then?" I asked, and slunk back into the computer chair, suddenly irritated by the fact that I'd let Knight touch me. I was like mush in his hands—if I was going to keep my distance, I needed to avoid him. Damn it all, I'd been doing a pretty good job before he'd just waltzed back into my life as pretty as he pleased.

Knight shook his head and dropped his arms, thank Hades. A chest that broad should have been illegal. "We're baffled, which is why I wanted to bring you into the case." He stood up and approached me, causing me to shrink back into my chair. "Will you help me, Dulce?"

I just nodded before the vision of his lips against my neck slapped me back into reality. Knight needed to know this arrangement would be purely professional, purely business. "Yes, on a few conditions."

Knight sighed and started pacing my living room. "Name them."

"One, you have to be professional."

He faced me, his mouth open in mock offense. "I'm always..."

"No flirting, no accidental touches, no running your fingers down my neck, no lips on my shoulders..."

He chuckled. "You enjoyed that; don't deny it."

I had enjoyed it and couldn't deny it, so I merely ignored him. "No double-entendres, no gifts..."

"Okay, I get it," he said none too happily. "Is that all?"

"No sex jokes, no invading my personal space, no comments on my appearance, no lustful glances and absolutely no winking."

Knight threw himself back into the couch and faced me with a perturbed expression. "I should have found someone else to help with the case."

I laughed. "Don't be a spoil sport. You know I'm the best."

He offered me a boyish grin. "Yes, you are."

Inwardly, I breathed a sigh of relief. Maybe this would be easier than I'd assumed. As long as Knight kept his distance, I could keep my guard up. "Good, now that we've reached an understanding, let's meet up again tomorrow night. Bring the files with you."

"What about tonight?"

"Tonight's not good; I have plans." And plans I wasn't thrilled about. I had a date with a vampire. Well, I didn't exactly think of it as a date—more like two people accompanying one another to a party.

"Plans?" Knight asked, warily.

"Yes," I started before interrupting myself. "Add that to the list of rules: no being nosy and definitely no being jealous."

He dropped his pinched lip expression and exchanged it for one of detached indifference. "I'm not jealous."

"No use in lying," I said with a broad smile. "I know you are—call it my instincts, one hundred percent pure Dulcie O'Neil."

With a chuckle, Knight stood and approached the door, the sunlight of morning just peeking through my windows, basking him in a yellow glow until he looked like an angel. Ha, Knight was no angel.

"Until tomorrow night then," he said and reached for the doorknob.

"Yes."

He smiled. "It's a date." Then he opened the door, winked and walked into the daylight.

Men.

#

As I mentioned earlier, Bram was a vampire and it just happened to be his three hundredth birthday. Every hundred year birthday found a vampire stronger, quicker, more powerful and in Bram's case, he'd even gotten better looking. His day old stubble was still in full effect but that wasn't something he'd ever be able to do anything about, seeing as how he'd had it when he'd been turned. But, there was something about him that was just more attractive—maybe it wasn't so much his features that had improved but more his control over what other people thought of him.

"Ah, Sweet, you are ravishing," Bram said in his lofty English accent and kissed my hand as his eyes devoured every inch of me.

I smiled my thanks and accepted his arm as he escorted me down my front walkway and into the leather plushness of a black stretch Hummer. Our driver, a were, doffed his head politely as I pulled myself into the stretch limo. Bram was just behind me and once he'd taken his seat across from mine, eyed me with undisguised admiration.

"Dulcie, these many months of separation have been difficult on my memory. I do not recall you appearing quite so beautiful."

I sighed and tried to smile. I was just not good at accepting compliments. Was Bram sincere? Yeah, I thought so. Did he want to get into my pants? Yeppers and always had. But, regardless of Bram's intentions, I had to admit I did feel...pretty.

I'd worn a knee-length, strapless black evening gown in a diaphanous material that graced my skin like a whisper. Even though the gossamer material hinted at the curves of my body, it was just that—a hint. My lace thong panties were my only undergarments, the dress not lending itself to a bra. Not exactly comfortable exposing so much skin, I'd covered the dress with a fitted black leather jacket. And to finish off my evening attire, I'd worn the highest heels I owned—four inch Jimmy Choos with so many straps, they would have pleased any dominatrix. I wore my hair down which wasn't a surprise since I wasn't exactly thrilled with showing off my ears. As a fairy, my ears came to points at the top and they were my least favorite of my physical attributes. I'd considered getting an ear reduction but threw the idea out because it was just too risky. Fairies didn't do well with human sedatives. That and my old boss, Quillan, had said I didn't need it, that I was beautiful just as I was.

A sadness descended on me at the thought of Quillan, so I brushed it aside and focused on my handsome vampire date. Over six four, he had the physique of a swimmer—broad shoulders tapering to a trim waist with a pair of legs that seemed to be as long as I was tall (not that I was tall). His black hair was on the longish side, just curling over his ears. His licentious smile was...sexy. But, like my relationship with Knight or lack thereof, I wanted to keep things strictly platonic with Bram. Although I had started dating more recently, I still wasn't completely comfortable with it and rather than running for cover with my tail between my legs, I just decided to take it one step at a time. The fact that I was even out tonight was a step in and of itself.

"Thanks for the compliment," I said with a small smile.

He returned the smile and appeared to be studying me. Feeling entirely too uncomfortable under his libidinous stare, I fought to find something to say. "So, are you feeling any different on your birthday?"

He nodded but didn't expound.

I cocked my head and considered him. "And? What's different?"

"I'm faster."

"Faster?" I started but Bram had suddenly....disappeared. Just dissolved into the air as if he'd never been, as if I'd been imagining him all along. As a vamp, he'd always been fast—moving like a blur from point A to point B but as a blur, that's exactly what you'd been able to see. This was different.

"Bram?" I repeated, shifting my gaze from one end of the limo to the other. Just like that, I felt an icy cold penetrating my back. I whipped around to find Bram sitting beside me, smiling smugly. "What was that?" I demanded, shock straining my voice. "You can disappear now?"

He shook his head. "No."

"But..."

"I merely moved too quickly for you to follow with your naked eye."

"Bullshit," I bit out, wondering if he was going to backpedal and try to talk his way out of it. It would do no good. I knew what I'd seen...or hadn't seen in this case.

He laughed. "Your mind tricked you, Dulce. I have been sitting here all along but you were relying on the incorrect sense."

"Incorrect sense?" I asked dubiously and crossed my arms against my chest as I regarded him coolly.

He leaned into me until his icy breath fanned across my naked collarbone and brought goose bumps to my skin. But, I held my ground and didn't move away.

"Close your eyes," he whispered.

"You'd better not try anything," I started, eyeing him suspiciously.

"I know you too well, Sweet, to attempt anything. You would have me flat on my back with a stake over my heart before I could blink."

He did know me well. I closed my eyes and then I heard him. It was the tiniest, most insignificant disturbance in the otherwise still air. I opened my eyes and glanced to my right and there he was.

"You see?" he asked.

I nodded and watched him disappear as if the air had swallowed him—right there in front of me. I didn't have enough time to think to rely on my other senses rather than my eyesight and suddenly felt myself falling, pushed backward by unseen hands. The leather of the seat met the back of my head, and I inhaled sharply as adrenaline pounded through my veins. My dress slinked up my thighs but I wasn't concerned with propriety at the moment. What I was concerned with was the fact that Bram had materialized and was now on top of me.

"Back the hell off me," I hissed and pushed against his chest, suddenly angry with myself that I'd ever agreed to be his date in the first place. I could never truly trust Bram. Sure, he'd helped me with certain cases when I'd been a Regulator but he definitely wasn't a lawfully abiding citizen. If he had one hand in the morally upstanding cookie jar, the other hand was in the process of stealing all the cookies.

His fangs descended, and he was panting. His eyes, though, were far more scary. There was a depth to them I'd never seen before, something wiser and older. If I hadn't been a fairy with my level of magical ability, I'd now be under the vampire's spell, allowing him to do whatever he wanted to with me. As it was, I was finding it difficult to fight. "Bram, I'm giving you three seconds to back the fuck off me."

Bram suddenly sat up and adjusted the tie at his neck while his fangs retracted. "Apologies."

I pushed myself aside and pulled my dress down, throwing him an angry glare. "What the hell is wrong with you? Are you trying to make me hate you?"

"I was curious to learn if my increased age could make you submit to me," he answered tersely, casually, as if he hadn't just attacked me. But, somewhere in his comment was disappointment. He'd been hoping I was weak enough to submit to him. But, to what end?

"You're lucky I didn't taser you, bastard!" I retorted although it was an empty threat. I hadn't brought a taser with me. But Bram didn't need to know that.

"I would not have injured you, Sweet," Bram said and pasted an artificial smile on his handsome face. "It was merely a test."

"Well, I don't like tests so don't do it again," I snapped, feeling the pounding of my heartbeat start to slow. Maybe it *had* merely been a test and not something more sinister. "If we're going to be friends..."

"I do so enjoy our friendship," he interrupted.

"Then don't screw it up." My eyes narrowed as I reconsidered his earlier statement. "If your powers of persuasion had worked, what would you have done?"

"Kissed you, Sweet, as I am still dying to do." He leaned forward like he thought he'd give it a try.

"Keep away from me," I said angrily. To reinforce the comment, I quickly moved to the seat across from him. I crossed my arms against my chest and wondered how I'd get through the evening.

"I apologize for offending you. I seem to lose my wits where you are concerned."

I was spared the need to respond as the limo came to a halt and moments later, our driver opened the door. I hopped down and glanced up at the restaurant before us, The Chateaus. It was the same place Bram had taken me when I'd agreed to a first "date" with him. I had half a mind to leave him at the curb and walk inside without him but forced myself not to. This was Bram's big night, and I didn't want to embarrass him. Granted, he'd just tried to molest me but hopefully he'd learned his lesson. And I'd learned my lesson to pack heat no matter where I was going or who I was seeing—you never knew when some jackass vampire was going to try to nibble your goodies.

The jackass vampire in question was beside me momentarily and offered his arm as he leaned down and whispered. "I apologize, Sweet, I will never impose myself on you again. Do you accept my apology?"

"Yes," I grumbled and took his arm as we started up the marble walkway of the grand restaurant. A doorman greeted Bram by name and pulled open the ornate ten foot high mahogany door, revealing the crowd within. That was when I realized we must have been pretty late. Not that it was a surprise—Bram definitely labored under the misguided notion of his own self-importance. Of course he'd be late to his own party.

As we entered the overcrowded room, I felt like I was on exhibit—"Bram's date, who can she be?" going through everyone's minds. I dropped my attention to the click of my heels against the black marble floors. When I could still feel the flush of anxiety on my cheeks, I forced myself to take in the dark red of the walls, the open ceiling, warehouse like with its rows of exposed metal piping. Candelabras topped with slender red candles stood proudly at the center of each table, throwing a yellow glow against the plates, soup bowls and the silver of utensils that decorated each table. My eyes fell to one table, dead center in the room, separated from the other tables by a girth of about two to three feet all the way around. And, guess whose table that was? I swallowed down my anxiety and allowed Bram to lead me to the small table currently playing the part of island. There were only two chairs. Holy Hades...

As soon as we reached the table, Bram's posse descended on us, smiling and offering congratulations. Many of his female acquaintances embraced him, there were even some kisses, from which he quickly pulled away and eyed me speculatively. I just shook my head and took a seat at the table, pretending extreme interest in the cutlery.

"Looks like you've got the best seat in the house."

I glanced up into Knight's smiling face and felt my stomach drop.

TWO

I was about to accuse Knight of stalking me when I noticed his arm intertwined with a woman's—Angela, the bartender from Bram's nightclub. She smiled at me but I wasn't sure I returned the greeting, my stomach was still in the process of reeling from the fact that Knight was here and worse, that he and Angela appeared to be... together? Were they dating? Maybe already an item? If so, Knight was a bigger asshole than I'd previously imagined considering the way he'd been flirting with me this morning.

"Hi, Dulcie," Angela said sweetly and I hoped I wasn't still scowling at her, at them. I'd always liked Angela but just then I could have clawed her eyes out. I had to swallow the primitive reaction and stood up, forcing a smile.

"Hi Angela and, uh, Knight, I didn't know you...both were coming." Okay, so far so good. My voice had sounded pretty steady and my brain had been able to phrase a sentence together even though my stomach was threatening to make a spectacle of itself all over the shiny floors.

"Well, of course Angela would be invited," Knight said. My stomach dropped further. "She *does* work for Bram."

"Yes, I'm aware of that," I answered tightly and internally told myself to cool it. No use in blowing my cover of an uninterested and definitely not jealous Dulcie. Not that I was interested or jealous. I was just...surprised. Yeah, I'd go with that.

"And I'm Angela's date," Knight finished, turning his attention on me again, an innocent smile on his face. A smile that said all his flirting earlier had been just a game, a whim. A smile that said he knew I was jealous and was enjoying my jealousy. Well, touché, Knight and your stupid perfect smile.

"Apologies," I said to Angela and clarified the response with "for having to be Knight's date."

She laughed and pushed her orange bangs behind her ear. Her hair wasn't naturally orange—she just had an addiction where hair color was concerned. After all the bleach involved, I was surprised she even had any hair left. Course, maybe that was why it was so short—as in boy short. So, about Angela, much though I really didn't want to admit it, she was an attractive woman—she was decently tall and stick thin with a nice set of fake boobs. The nice set of fake boobs were currently residing in a black halterneck top with ribbons lacing down the front, criss-crossing against a backdrop of naked skin. Two ribbons covered her nipples but there wasn't enough of the halterneck top to cover the underside of her breasts or the swell of the top. The "dress" continued in the same manner with ribbons lacing up the sides of her hips and thighs but thank Hades there was some sort of material in the front—it looked like rubber. All in all, with the missing fabric it looked like a were had made fast work of her dress. But, it wasn't like I was going to say anything.

"Bram was excited you agreed to be his date, Dulcie," Angela started and sidled closer to Knight until you couldn't tell where he began and she ended.

I mumbled something that was so quiet I couldn't even understand it while Knight laughed. "Was this another favor you owed him, Dulce?" he asked.

I narrowed my eyes. Knight was here on a date...willingly. That was a fact. And I was jealous; that was also a fact. So, even though some people might have accused me of being childish, I did what I had to do. "No, not a favor," I snapped at Knight before turning a sweet smile on Angela. "I've also been looking forward to Bram's and my...date." Knight snickered but I forced myself to hold Angela's gaze. "And has Bram gotten amazingly fast or what?" My eyebrow arched in what I hoped was a sexy expression—one of those femme fatale sort of "I know something you don't know" looks.

"Did he show off for you?" Angela asked, shaking her head.

I nodded, watching from the corner of my eye as Knight's smile vanished. Ha, served him right, the cocky bastard. Angela then turned to Knight and dropped her hand from his as she explained she had to visit the ladies' room. Knight watched her depart, before planting his gaze back on me.

"What the hell are you doing here?" I demanded, pleased I could finally speak my mind.

"What does it look like? I was invited."

"You can't stand Bram," I said, eyeing the throng of admirers who still circled Bram like he was the great messiah. What was it with cocksure men? And why in hell did I have to be surrounded by them? I shook my head at the injustice of it all and returned my gaze to Bram who threw his head back and laughed heartily at some compliment a bottle blond offered him. She leaned into him and whispered something in his ear, making his fangs descend. Apparently remembering he had a date, he scanned the room for me and offered an apologetic smile that said he was still at the mercy of his...fans. Better them than me.

"Bram didn't invite me," Knight responded and smiled at the unspoken statement—that Angela had. He took the vacant seat next to me, but I refused to look at him, pretending extreme interest in the flirtations between Bram and his female guests.

"So, what, you both are an item now?" I asked, trying to wrestle the words down even as they left my tongue.

He shrugged—I caught it with my peripheral vision. "Are you and the vampire an item?"

"No," I said quickly, facing him again. He was wearing a black suit with a crisp white shirt underneath, unbuttoned down to his clavicle. The black of his suit was the same shade of velvet darkness as his hair. And with his strong jaw, piercing blue eyes and Roman nose, most women would have imagined him God's gift to the female sex. Or, in Knight's case, Hades' gift. I, myself, couldn't say I was grateful to Hades in the least.

"Ah, so it was a favor then?" he continued, and his smirk was enough to ignite my anger.

"New subject," I interrupted, tired of playing word games with the *Loki*. "Why did you ask me if we could meet up tonight to work on the *Dreamstalker* case when you knew you'd be here?"

He leaned back into his chair and regarded me coolly. "I asked what your plans were; you didn't inquire after mine."

I narrowed my eyes. "You wanted me to say I was free so you could let me know you had a date with Angela, didn't you? Really adult of you, Knight."

He shrugged and raised his brows. "Why would you care if I had a date with Angela?"

Although I was pissed, I tried to appear indifferent. "I don't." I'm not sure I succeeded.

He leaned forward, and there was something in his eyes—irritation? "Then what does it matter?"

Not wanting to back down, I leaned closer to him, until only about four inches separated us. His spicy male scent hit me like a punch. "It matters because I don't like games. Mean what you say and say what you mean." I wanted to pat myself on the back for such an awesome answer. "I neither have the time nor the interest to play tag with you, Knight."

Knight didn't respond right away and neither of us pulled back. Instead, we just sat there, staring at one another. It had become a challenge—who would back down first? Who would pull away and allow the buffer of a few more inches of personal space?

It wouldn't be me.

Knight smirked and leaned back into his seat, eyeing the room around him with ennui. "So the vampire is stronger and faster now?" he asked noncommittally, apparently ill at ease with the fact that I'd just called him out and let him know he was full of crap. So, he wouldn't let me soak up the afterglow of a conversation won. Hmm, was someone a sore loser?

I nodded, focusing on Bram as he continued to laugh and flirt, reminding me of that black Bird of Paradise as it pranced around doing a mating dance. But unlike the pitiable bird that ended its display of passion with only a bored hen as its reward, Bram's hens were anything but disinterested. They continued to rub against him like cats in heat, and the vampire was eating it up. Apparently feeling my eyes on him, Bram turned his attention to me and winced as if he wasn't enjoying all the attention. Ha, as if. I held up my hand to say "take your time; I'm enjoying myself" even though I couldn't say I was enjoying myself. Jealousy was still in the process of eating a big hole in my stomach and if nothing else, I wanted to go home and drown my sorrows in a vat of Ben and Jerry's cookie dough ice cream. And that was really saying something because I didn't even like sweets.

"Is he trustworthy?" Knight continued.

"What?" I asked, completely at a loss. "What are you talking about?"

"Maybe if you'd stop staring at the vampire, you'd know." His voice was stilted, angry.

"I wasn't staring at him," I muttered, realizing I'd been doing exactly that.

"Is Bram trustworthy?" Knight repeated. "Since he's so much stronger and faster now, is that going to cause trouble for the ANC or trouble for you?"

I frowned and shrugged at the same time. "He's as trustworthy as the next vampire."

"That isn't saying much."

"It's saying I don't know what the answer to your question is. Do I trust Bram? Most the time yes. Do I think he's going to get more cocky and take more risks due to his increased strength and power? Probably so. Do I think he's a risk to the ANC? No, probably not." I took a deep breath—I needed it since that had been a mouthful.

"If he's so much stronger, it will be harder for you to defend yourself against him, if the need ever arose."

Based on Bram's little example of his increased speed in the limo, I also wondered if I'd be able to defend myself against him, not that I thought I'd ever need to... "Bram and I go way back."

Knight's lips were still tight—maybe even angry. And there was a rigidness to his body. "So what? He's vampire."

I smiled as warmly as I could. "You're *Loki*, and I hardly know you."

He nodded and cocked his head to the side, studying me like he was a great artist and I was a muse to be reckoned with. "I would never hurt you."

I swallowed hard, not wanting to admit how his words had created warmth in me, a feeling of, dare I say it, endearment. "Neither would Bram." At Knight's dubious expression, I continued. "He's harmless, Knight. Bram just wants to have sex with me and then he'd be completely over this...crush."

At the word "sex," Knight shifted uncomfortably, focusing his attention on Bram. His expression wasn't a pretty one. When he faced me again, there was heat in his eyes, a certain glow I'd never seen before.

"What was that?" I demanded, sort of weirded out.

"What?"

"Your eyes just started...glowing."

I was pretty sure I didn't imagine the reddish blush that stained his cheeks. "It's something *Lokis* do—we have no control over it."

I narrowed my eyes—would his *Loki* traits ever stop revealing themselves? "And what is 'it' that you have no control over?"

He exhaled deeply. "Not something I really want to—"

He never had the chance to finish the statement as Angela was suddenly beside him. I was so irritated, I had half a mind to open the floor and have it swallow her whole, but restrained myself. I'd find out what this glowing eye bit really meant soon enough. The fact that Knight was clearly uncomfortable with it and didn't want to discuss it was all the more reason to find out why. Anything I could wield over his head held a lot of value.

"Well, I think we'd best find our table, Knight," Angela started as her eyes followed Bram, who was en route to our table.

Knight hoisted himself to his feet, offered me a crooked smile and off they went to their table, arm in arm. My stomach flopped at the sight of them and I had to talk myself out of the fact that I was...jealous. I wasn't jealous...I was surprised, remember?

"Sweet," Bram greeted me as he took his seat. "I apologize for leaving you unattended."

"It's okay, Angela and Knight kept me company."

"Very good," the vampire said although I could tell he was less than happy hearing Knight's name on my tongue.

I was about to respond but was spared the need when servers began pouring into the room from one of three doorways. They were dressed in black, each with a small red apron wrapped around his middle. They carried silver soup tureens to every table, laid them down and began ladling what looked like cream of potato or maybe leek soup into each bowl, skipping a few patrons here and there, those patrons either being vamps or people opposed to soup.

I brought my attention back to Bram and found he'd been staring at me the whole time. "What?" I insisted.

He shook his head, a slight laugh escaping his lips. "I am pleased to be with you tonight, my sweet Dulce."

"Well, thanks for inviting me," I grumbled, not exactly able to return the sentiment. So far this evening, I'd done a three-sixty from uncomfortable to angry to jealous back to uncomfortable again.

The soup tureen made its way to our table and once the server had ladled and departed, Bram watched contentedly as I stirred it around my bowl, making no motion to sample it. My mind teamed with images of Knight and Angela, while images of Bram jumping me in the limo fought to the surface of my overwhelmed brain. A visual of Quillan interrupted the tempest of my thoughts, and I suddenly felt an almost indescribable ease wash over me, followed by melancholy as I realized how much I missed him, how I wished we were still friends so we could laugh about the fact that I'd gone on a date with Bram.

"You do not appear well," Bram said and his expression revealed concern.

"I have a lot on my mind," I answered, and it was one hundred percent the truth.

"Well, let us speak of friendlier subjects. Have you an update on your book?"

I nodded, pleased with the distraction from the tailspin of thoughts colliding in my head. Yes, my book was a great subject, a neutral, easy subject. Bram only wanted to discuss it because he happened to be the muse for my main character, also a vampire. Only I'd named my vampire Raven. Aside from the name change, the book was pretty much solely about Bram—his life, how he'd become a vamp and his experiences over the last three hundred years.

"Well, as you know, I finished it a few months ago."

"Yes, I do recall."

I continued to stir my soup, feeling like a witch tending to her cauldron. "I think I told you I'd been attempting to get an agent?" Bram just nodded, so I continued. "I sent out my queries, and one agent requested the entire book."

Bram smiled widely. "I did not doubt you, Sweet. I am very pleased."

"Yeah, I'm pretty stoked, myself."

"And what will happen now?" Bram continued and accidentally or not, brushed his foot against my leg underneath the table. Instantly I shifted my leg and pretended not to notice.

"Now I'll just wait to see if they want to offer me representation."

"Well, do ensure this is the best possible agent, Sweet. We want the best for our book."

I didn't find his reference to the book as "ours" at all offensive. In fact, I was proud, happy that Bram claimed ownership to something that meant a lot to me. The more I thought about it, the more I realized it was as much his book as mine because it was his life, so he probably had just as much invested in it as I did. "The agency is well respected," I finished.

"Very good," Bram said and eyed my untouched soup. "Are you not hungry?"

I let go of the spoon, realizing how rude it was to play with one's food without ever trying it or intending to.

Bram laughed. "No wonder you are of such slight figure. If I did not know better I would think you must be vampire as I do not believe I have ever seen you eat."

"You saw me eat the last time we were here, remember? On our first...date."

Bram relaxed into his chair and eyed me with an expression that was difficult to categorize—a studious gaze, as piercing as it was appreciative. "And now we are on our second date." He was quiet for a moment. "Does this mean we are...dating?"

I was quick to answer "no."

He didn't lose that bizarre expression. If anything it was now deeper, more exacting. "Then what would you call this, Sweet?"

"I would call it what it is—you want to get into my pants, and I won't let you so you figure the more dates we go on, the more I'll drop my defenses and eventually, my panties."

Bram was silent for exactly two seconds and then threw his head back and exploded into a raucous chuckle. "Do you think so little of me?"

"I don't know that I think little of you," I started. "I just know you for who and what you are."

Bram nodded, a smile still highlighting his full and sensual lips. "Perhaps we should give this theory of yours a try?"

I returned the smile and before he got too excited, shook my head. "Thanks but no thanks. I prefer our friendship."

He didn't look disappointed. "I will not give up, you do realize that, Sweet?"

"Bram, I would never accuse you of being anything other than...persistent."

"Ah, you do know me well."

"I like to think I do." I paused, and he leaned back into his chair, his arms crossed over his chest. "So, as long as you don't jump me like you did earlier," I continued. "We can continue our friendship."

"I did already apologize for that, Sweet."

"You did but I'm not convinced it was sincere."

Bram held up two fingers like he thought he was a boy scout or something. "I do honestly and truthfully regret it," he pledged, then dropped his hand. "I should have known I could not force my will upon you and furthermore, had I succeeded, I would not have enjoyed the conquest. I prefer you in your natural cantankerous state."

I laughed. That had been a pretty good one.

#

After Bram and his limo dropped me off later that evening, and Bram attempted to steal a kiss which I rebutted, I entered my apartment, greeted Blue and threw my purse against the couch with a heartfelt sigh. My sigh spoke volumes as my mind swam with images of Knight and Angela that I couldn't dispel. Why was I so concerned? Why was I so bothered by it, by them? I was completely and totally un-okay with the possibility that maybe I was developing feelings for Knight, maybe I'd already developed them. And, furthermore, maybe they'd been developing all along—ever since I'd first met Knight outside my apartment building when I'd tried to take him down with magic and he'd just laughed at me. Knight and I had been through a lot together—hunting down a *Kragengen* shifter who'd been eating some of our less than law abiding citizens. Knight had also been there when I'd discovered Quillan was not whom I'd supposed him to be and had been lying to me for Hades only knew how long. And then there was the time when Knight had actually saved my life...

The piercing ring of the phone interrupted my soliloquy, and I answered it, noting my best friend's name and number on the caller ID.

"Hi, Sam," I said and collapsed into my sofa as Blue jumped up beside me, nudging his big head into my lap.

"How was your date?" Sam asked with a laugh. She'd known I wasn't exactly looking forward to this evening.

"It sucked," I began. "Hey, did you know Knight was going to be there?"

"How would I have known that?"

I shrugged and then remembered she couldn't see me. "Just thought he might have brought it up at work." Sam was not only my best friend, but she was also a gifted witch and just happened to be working for Knight.

"Nope. So, what was he doing there? He and Bram aren't exactly BFFs."

I laughed. "Nope, they aren't. He was there with...Angela." My whole body seemed to deflate on itself at the mention of Angela. How bad did I have it?

Sam was quiet for a second or two. "And by the sound of it, you weren't happy to see them together?"

I sighed, long and hard. "Sam, I'm afraid I'm...into Knight."

More silence on the other end and if that wasn't telling, I didn't know what was. "Hmm," she started and was quiet again. "I don't know that that's a good idea. I mean, I like Knight but there's just something about him. I can't put my finger on it."

Okay if Sam didn't think crushing on Knight was a good idea, then it really wasn't because Sam was about as smart as they came. "I know it's not a good idea and I'm not happy about it."

"What about Bram?" Sam quickly asked and there was a note of veiled curiosity to her voice. "Were you able to keep your mind off Knight with Bram?"

I was quiet as I considered the facts before me. Sam and Bram had had a fling about a year ago and Sam had been pretty hot for Bram but he hadn't exactly returned the interest. Sam had said she'd gotten over it and while I believed her, it seemed maybe there was something residual still there? "Um, no...Bram and I are just friends, you know that."

"You keep saying that but you know he wants more from you."

"It's easy to keep him at arm's length." I was quiet for a few seconds. "Sam, do you still have the hots for him?"

It was her turn to sigh. "No."

"Are you sure?"

"There will always be a part of me that will be attracted to him but I would never date him again, not after I know what he's like. And I'm not looking for another one night stand."

A flush of relief washed through me. If Sam was worried about my attraction to Knight, I'd definitely be worried if she was still hot for Bram. As far as I was concerned, neither one was a good choice. "Okay, good."

"So, back to you and Knight."

"There's nothing to say about Knight and me. He and Angela are probably enjoying themselves together as we speak, and that's what I need to focus on.

I've already had about the crappiest breakup ever with Jack, I really don't want to go through that again."

"I actually agree with you, Dulce," Sam said with a sadness to her voice. "I really wanted you to get out there and date and get over Jack but I have a feeling Knight might mess you up even worse than Jack did. None of us really knows him."

"And what we do know of him just screams player."

"I can see that too."

Somehow this conversation made me feel better. It cemented the fact that Knight wasn't a good choice, not that I'd been going full steam ahead previously but it still helped strengthen my will not to get involved.

"Are you going to be okay?" Sam asked.

Yes, I'd be fine. It was merely a small and inconsequential crush that had sort of come out of nowhere. Maybe it was just the fact that I hadn't seen Knight in such a long time and then he'd dropped back into my life like a bomb. I hadn't been able to prepare myself, to talk myself out of the fact that he was incredibly hot and the fact that even though his sexy, flirty and playful nature drove me nuts, it was also pretty...attractive. "Yep, I'm steadfast when it comes to these things—if I have to get over something, I will."

"That's one of the things I really admire about you, Dulce, you're strong."

I laughed as I considered it. I was strong. I'd always been strong. And it was one of my character traits I loved the most. "You and I make a pretty good team, don't we?"

She returned the laugh. "We sure do."

After I hung up, I started for my bedroom to change out of my clothes when the phone rang again. Thinking Sam must have forgotten to tell me something, I grabbed it without checking caller ID.

"Hello?"

"Dulce." It was Knight. My stomach dropped for the nth time this evening.

"What?"

"Just wanted to make sure you made it home okay."

I was taken aback and didn't know how to respond. Was Angela still with him? If so, was she pissed he was calling me? Was I pissed he was calling me? I didn't feel angry or annoyed. "I'm fine...thanks."

He was quiet for a few seconds. "I was thinking about what you said."

"I've said a lot of things to you."

He laughed. "About meaning what I say and saying what I mean. I think it's good advice."

I couldn't help my surprise. He'd actually listened to me? It hadn't gone in one ear and out the other? "Good, you can pay me whatever it's worth to you."

He chuckled heartily, a sexy sound if I had to judge. "Can I come by tomorrow afternoon to go over the details of the *Dreamstalker* case with you?"

"Yeah, sure," I started, pleased we could focus on the case. *That* I could handle. "Okay, well goodnight."

"Goodnight, Dulce. Until tomorrow."

I hung up the phone and didn't know what to think so I didn't think anything at all.

THREE

When the doorbell rang at seven pm the following evening, I didn't even need to look through the peephole to know it was Knight. But, I did, anyway—you can never be too careful. Course, Blue was like an alarm system in his own right—howling and pawing at the door as if determined to take down whoever happened to be on the other side. I eyed Knight through the peephole for a second or two as he leaned against the wall and watched a car drive by.

I closed my eyes and forced myself to kill every last one of the butterflies in my stomach—to smash them into oblivion, shredding their gossamer wings while discouraging my feelings for Knight. Just as he was about to knock again, I opened the door and offered him a quick smile in greeting, grabbing Blue's collar as he attempted to break free. I pushed Blue back into the house and shut the door behind us with my foot. Glancing at Knight, I noticed his hands were full with what looked like a foil-covered casserole dish topped with three manila folders.

"Dulce," he said upon entering my humble abode. He headed for the kitchen, placing the manila folders on the kitchen table before he uncovered whatever was beneath the foil.

"What is that?" I asked, sounding less than thrilled.

"Lasagna," he answered without facing me. Instead, he opened the oven door and plopped the concoction into the oven, slapping his hands together with satisfaction and faced me. "I made it."

I raised a brow in skepticism. "*You* made it?"

"Yep, I'm a good cook." He sounded...proud.

The idea of Knight as a chef seemed totally alien to me for some reason—like it was too casual an occurrence, too everyday in its simplicity. But, unsettling or not, it had to mean he'd found a long-term place to live in Splendor. He'd been looking for somewhere more permanent than the Marriott Hotel due to the fact that he'd be continuing his stint as head of the ANC division here in Splendor until the Netherworld found his replacement.

"So, you found an apartment then?" I asked.

Knight nodded and pulled out one of my kitchen chairs, straddling it backwards and leaned his big arms over the chair back. "I did."

"And?"

"It's nice. Over on Shamrock Street."

Shamrock Street was the Beverly Hills of Splendor. "Well, good to see they pay you well," I grumbled, thinking about the fact that I was about to be late on my rent.

"I'm worth it, Dulce," he said with a smile, a smile that said his comment wasn't just limited to his position as head of the ANC. Before I had the chance to respond, Blue casually trotted over to Knight and sniffed his feet curiously.

The visual of what happened next will forever live in my head in infamy. Blue simply jumped up onto Knight's leg and with unbridled abandon, began humping his knee, thrusting back and forth with the expression of extreme concentration on his canine face.

"Blue!" I squealed and lurched for him.

Knight's laugh was deep as he pushed the dog away. "Really, Dog, we only met yesterday."

Blue apparently had it bad for Knight and resumed his straddled position, bracing Knight's knee between his paws as my mouth dropped open again. As if doubly determined to let Knight's knee know just how much affection he held for it, Blue started gyrating again.

"You get down right now, bad boy!" I yelled and yanked on his collar but he didn't budge. He just tightened his grip on Knight's leg and glanced back at me with an expression that said "mind your own business. This is between me and the *Loki*'s knee."

Finally able to separate my dog from Knight's pant leg, I forced him outside and tried to keep the flush from my cheeks, still in disbelief that my dog had just mounted him. "I'm sorry," I mumbled.

"Don't be," Knight said with a grin. "That's the most action I've gotten in months."

I settled my attention on the three manila folders, trying not to think about Knight getting action at all and searched for a change of subject. "You want to review those now or after dinner?"

"Now is good," he said, eyeing my flustered face all the while as he handed me the first folder.

Opening it, I immediately noted two pictures paper-clipped to the interior of the folder, one of a smiling brunette with round, twinkling eyes. She looked to be about my age, in her mid-twenties. The other picture was of a woman asleep in a hospital bed, probably in a coma given the context. The still figure on the hospital cot was nothing like the happy woman in the other photo. Her hair had lost its luster and her skin was pale—as if the *Dreamstalker* had blanched away the color in her cheeks as easily as he'd taken control of her life.

"Her name is Anna Murphy," Knight said. "The next folder under hers is a woman named Heather Green."

Anna Murphy...I rolled her name around on my tongue, thinking it sounded strangely familiar, though I wasn't sure why. Course, it was a pretty common name so maybe it wasn't anything at all. Heather Green didn't ring any déjà-vu bells. "And the third person?"

"Jennifer Garrity...but she went by Jenny."

Jennifer Garrity. A bolt of realization jolted through me. I did know that name. I knew that name well because Jenny Garrity had been my nanny when I was a child. I almost dropped Anna's file onto the floor. "I knew...I know her," I said in a small voice, my hands shaking.

"How?" Knight demanded, eyeing me with extreme interest.

"She was my nanny from the time I was born until I went to Kindergarten." She'd been loving and wonderful.

Knight nodded and opened the third file, Jenny Garrity's I presumed, and jotted down a note. "And Anna Murphy or Heather Green?" he asked.

"Anna Murphy sounds familiar but not Heather Green."

"Well, they both should sound familiar," he said and observing my dumbfounded expression, continued. "They were in your second grade class."

I swallowed hard and felt like I needed to sit down. So, I did. I took the chair next to Knight and grabbed the file on top, opening it to see Heather's name. What I presumed was her senior year photo smiled out at me, revealing a woman with platinum blond hair and full lips. There was no hospital photo. I gulped.

"Did she die?" I asked in a strained voice.

"Yes," Knight responded.

I closed the file and reached for the third one, for Jenny's. Relief washed through me when I deduced that Jenny was still alive. According to Knight, there had only been one death. I opened the folder and saw the same Jenny I remembered from my childhood, only she was older now—a few crow's feet defined her eyes, and some laugh lines etched her mouth.

"What do you suppose this means?" I asked, glancing up at Knight who just stared at me. "Is it a coincidence that I know all three of them?" I wanted nothing more than him to agree, and say, "Yes, it's definitely coincidence"—that there was nothing to the fact that all three of them were somehow linked to me.

He shrugged. "Could mean something or could mean nothing at all."

I frowned. "Thanks, that was incredibly insightful."

He chuckled. “It could merely be coincidence, Dulcie. Don’t you know most of the people in Splendor?”

Yes, I did. I felt relief course through me as I thought about it. How many times had a crime been perpetrated against someone with whom I was personally acquainted? Well, it hadn’t been everyday, but it had definitely happened. Splendor was a small town. “Were all three in Splendor?” I asked.

It was his turn to nod. “Yep. That’s why I wasn’t jumping to any conclusions.”

“So, that means you’d already made the connection between them and me?”

“Of course,” he said as he stood up and headed to the oven, where he opened the door and pulled out his lasagna. Hmm, it actually looked good. “Fork?” he asked, over his shoulder.

“Top drawer on the right.”

He retrieved the fork, tested his lasagna and apparently not satisfied, pushed it back in the oven. Then he turned around to face me, leaning his incredibly shapely ass against the oven as he crossed his arms against his expansive chest. He was wearing dark jeans and a navy blue tee-shirt that made his blue eyes pop. “Did you doubt I’d do my homework regarding the victims?”

I shook my head. “No, just thought I’d double check.”

He cleared his throat and dropped his attention to the ground before bringing it back up to me. “There were two other victims, one in Estuary and one in Moon.”

“Names?” I asked, suddenly feeling a weight in my stomach again.

“Travis Decker from Estuary and...”

And the weight in my stomach suddenly made sense. Now it couldn’t really be described as a “weight” but more a boulder that had settled right in my gut. “Wait just a minute, Travis?”

Knight’s eyes narrowed. “You know him?”

“Yeah, I dated him,” I said and felt the air escape my lungs. I glanced back at Knight. “So much for coincidence?”

He shrugged. “I’m still not convinced though starting to warm up to it.”

“And the fifth victim?”

“An elderly woman, Shirley Mickelson.”

Shirley Mickelson—I tried the name on for size and couldn’t say I recognized it. “Doesn’t sound familiar. Background on her?” I glanced at the file folders, noticing two were missing and faced him with annoyance. “Why didn’t you bring all the folders?”

"Travis and Shirley just happened, and Elsie didn't have time to put the folders together." Elsie was the receptionist at the ANC. Nice to know that Knight wasn't able to do anything himself...

"What do you mean by just happened?"

"Travis was last night and Shirley was this morning."

I couldn't help the guilt that suffused me as I thought about the fact that while I'd been not exactly enjoying myself at Bram's party, poor Travis Decker, the sweet boy I'd dated for all of a month during my junior year in high school, had succumbed to a *Dreamstalker*. "What do you know about this Shirley person?"

He shrugged. "Not much. She was a librarian at Rio High School in Moon."

Hmm, I definitely knew nothing about Rio High, and my dealings with anything in Moon had always been limited because it was two hours from Splendor. "I still think it's weird that two girls who were in second grade with me, my nanny and old boyfriend were all victims."

Knight sighed, long and deep. "I think it's weird too."

I faced him in annoyance. "But not weird enough that it extends out of the circumference of coincidence."

"Could be coincidence but could be something more threatening." He paused for a moment before bringing his eyes back to mine. "I want you to stay with me."

"What?!" I retorted, laughing in disbelief. "Are you kidding?"

"You'll be safer if I can keep an eye on you."

The sudden memory of Knight invading my dreams silenced an acid response that was perched on my tongue. My first introduction to Knight hadn't truly been an introduction at all. He'd tried to reach me when I'd been dreaming about Quillan who had just happened to be dressed up as a pirate. As if the dream weren't embarrassing enough, the fact that Knight had witnessed it had been enough to forever humiliate me. But, what concerned me most at the moment was the fact that Knight had been able to influence my dreams—maybe he could protect against a *Dreamstalker*?

"You first contacted me when I was asleep," I started. "Does that mean you can..."

Knight shook his head with a heartfelt sigh. "Unfortunately not. I'm able to interrupt someone's slumber to communicate with them but I don't have the ability to protect them. But, that doesn't change the fact that you'd be safer with me."

So, as to living with him—there was no point. Besides, I wasn't a stranger to living with Knight. During our first and most recent case together, we'd been shacked up in my little apartment for over a week, and it hadn't been pretty. Knight was demanding, difficult, self-centered....ah, the list went on. "No way in hell."

"If there is more to this situation than coincidence..."

"What part of 'no way in hell' don't you get?" I demanded. "It was bad enough that I had to deal with you in my own apartment."

He didn't seem offended, maybe more amused. "I quite enjoyed myself."

"I bet you did," I said, when a bolt of jealousy ricocheted through me as I considered the fact that Angela wouldn't exactly like it if I were living under Knight's roof. "And what would you tell Angela?"

He shrugged, and a look of surprise pasted itself on his handsome face. "Why would Angela need to know?"

"You're impossible." I shook my head as anger wound its way up my throat, bypassing the boulder that was still resident in my gut. "I like Angela and if you play her and hurt her..."

"Who said I was playing her or going to hurt her?" He looked amused, entirely too amused.

I stood up and wasn't sure why. It was like my body went into auto pilot and wanted to get as far away from him as possible. But, I didn't retreat, I wouldn't allow myself. "Remember when I said 'mean what you say and say what you mean'?"

He nodded as I continued. "You aren't doing a good job."

Knight lumbered toward me, a smile on his mouth. He reached out to grasp my shoulders. "Your jealousy is very...becoming."

I narrowed my eyes. "I'm not jealous. I'm merely concerned for...Angela."

"Angela's a big girl."

"What's that supposed to mean?"

"It means she can make her own decisions. She knows I'm not in the market for a relationship."

I snaked out of his hold and backed away. "You are a pig."

He chuckled but his laugh was laced with derision. "Why? Because I'm honest?"

"Because you want your cake and eat it too. Haven't you considered that people have feelings, Knight? That you can't just play a woman and expect her to accept it submissively?"

He studied me for a moment. "Where is this coming from, and why are you so upset?"

I felt a fiery flow of anger bubble up within me. Knight represented everything I disliked and distrusted about the opposite sex. He was another Jack, a clone of the asshole I'd dated two years ago, who had cheated on me and basically destroyed my drive to ever get involved with a man again. Someone who was only out for himself, for whatever he deemed his prize and then he was on to the next kill as pretty as he pleased. "I detest men like you."

Knight's eyes went wide, as if he hadn't been expecting such rancor from me. He grabbed my arm, and I shrugged out of his hold. "Whoa, Dulcie, if you're going to detest me, I at least deserve to know why."

"I don't like players."

"Who said I'm a player?" His asked and he clutched my arm as if to say he wouldn't release me until I'd given him a damn good reason as to why I detested him. Well, he was about to get it.

"The way you flirt with Angela and me and well, really, every woman alive, and pretend to be totally interested but then say you aren't looking for a relationship..." I tried to pull out of his grip but he wouldn't release me. His fingers were beginning to hurt.

He chuckled harder this time and grabbed both my arms. When I attempted to wiggle away from him, he clamped down...hard. "Allow me to defend myself. I am not what you term a 'player'. I've never lied to Angela. On our first date..."

"Oh, there was a first date?" I snapped and suddenly felt a spire of embarrassment course through me. I hadn't wanted to sound so freaking concerned.

"Yes," he hissed. "I told her exactly what my intentions were."

"And what were they?"

"That I'm not planning on sticking around Splendor for a long time, and I'm not looking for a relationship."

I swallowed my pride. Hot Hades, why did I give such a damn about this hulking man? What was it about him that just set me off? He made me feel things I hadn't felt in years. And what did it say about me that I had to fight feelings for someone who was such an...

"And Angela just blindly agreed to your stipulations?" I demanded, anger in every crevice of my voice. "Agreed to just have sex with you? Yeah, I really believe that." And if she had agreed, Angela went way down in my estimation.

"Sex? Whoever said anything about sex?" Knight insisted, and his grip on my arms tightened, as if just the word sex had released the latent animal within him. I wondered if his eyes would start glowing again. Before they had the chance, he looked away for maybe two seconds before glancing back at me, apparently now more in control of himself. His strangle hold on my arms softened.

"Angela and I are friends," he said softly.

I tried to break free of his grasp again and was surprised when he released me. I rubbed the soreness out of my arms and glared up at him again. "How stupid do you think I am?"

"I don't think you're stupid at all, Dulcie," he said firmly. "But, you won't let me defend myself."

I wouldn't allow him to defend himself because there was nothing to defend. His alibi wasn't exactly water tight. "So, if you and Angela are just friends as you claim, why was she all over you at Bram's party?"

He shrugged. "She'd had a lot to drink."

"And why were you all over her?" That wasn't a fair question—he hadn't exactly been all over her. In fact, any initiation of closeness had really been on her part. But, the words were out so no use in taking them back.

"I don't recall that I was." He was silent a moment before a smile captured his lips. "And any...attentions I might have paid Angela were merely to make a certain beautiful fairy jealous."

I swallowed hard and if I'd had a baseball bat, I would have beaten down the ray of pleasure that visited me at his words. "You wanted to make me jealous?" I asked dubiously. "Why?"

Knight's lips were tight and his jaw even tighter. He took a step closer to me, and I took one back. "Because in case you haven't been paying attention," he paused. "I like you."

"But you aren't looking for a relationship," I spat back in his face.

"With Angela."

I had to beat down another feeling of happiness. Was I really buying this crap? Was I, Dulcie O'Neil, known for being tough as nails, really succumbing to this trite shit? What the hell was wrong with me? "Oh, so you aren't looking for a relationship in general, but you want one with me?" Good, my voice had sounded angry and laced with sarcasm.

He shrugged casually before offering me the sexiest smile I'd ever seen. "I wouldn't be opposed to it."

I dropped my eyes, trying to wipe away the visual of his smile and how it lit his entire face. "This whole conversation is stupid."

"You brought it up," he started, and there was something in his tone—something reserved and angry. "I was just defending myself against your accusation of me being a player. Regardless of what you think, I'm honest and I always have been."

"This is becoming way too personal for me. Let's shelve it and move on."

Knight's jaw was tight. "Let's not. How about you tell me why you were with Bram last night?"

If his jaw was tight, mine was suddenly tighter. Who the hell did he think he was, questioning me? Granted I'd just questioned him but...so what? "That's none of your business."

"You made it your business to snoop into my affairs with Angela so I'm making it my business."

I took two steps closer to him until we were nose to nose. I was fuming, irate. "You chose to answer my questions. That doesn't mean I have to answer yours."

"It doesn't work that way, Dulcie." He eradicated any distance between us until we were so close, I could feel his breath against my neck. A tremor started deep down in my belly and worked its way up into my gut.

"What is Bram to you?" Knight whispered, and I could feel hardness emanating between his legs and brushing against my thigh.

I didn't drop my gaze but glared at him full bore. "He's my lover," I lied.

Knight laughed but it was an ugly sound. He grabbed the back of my neck, holding me immobile and returned my glare. "Liar."

I narrowed my eyes. "Let go of me."

"Tell me Bram is not your lover."

"Why, are you jealous?" I asked.

"Yes," he growled, and his eyes warned me not to play with him, not to incite him when he was this close to the edge. I was quiet as I watched him, watched that bizarre glow overtake his eyes and this time he didn't avert his gaze to hide it. No, he wanted me to see what I was doing to him, that there was something in him he couldn't control. I'd never been so turned on in my life.

"Bram isn't my lover," I said in a soft voice and nearly fell over when Knight released me. He grabbed my arm to stabilize me and immediately let go as if I'd burned him. Suddenly the smell of cheese was thick in my nose. "Smells like your lasagna is burning."

#

I knew I was sleeping but my dreams had never been quite so lucid, images so vibrant and crisp, I felt as if I could reach out and touch them. I sat up and rubbed my eyes, finding the velvet blackness of night was still in full effect. There was something I needed to do, something that was on the brink of happening. Something bad. It was one of those gut feelings.

I stood up and was seized by a pain reverberating through my head. It felt as if my brain was being torn apart, all my memories and thoughts being dissected by a sharp blade. I fell to my knees and grabbed my throbbing head, willing the pain to go away.

And, just like that, it did. I was suddenly free of pain but I was somewhere I couldn't comprehend—somewhere unknown to me. It was like I'd been plucked from my bedroom and deposited on a street I didn't recognize. A cold wind whipped around my shoulders, and I glanced down at my white lace singlet and baby blue pajama shorts. I wrapped my arms around myself, trying to ward off the cold and glanced up at the front of a townhouse—a modern structure that glared down at me in an array of hard angles and bleak whiteness. The numbers 3467 delineated the corner of the door, and somehow I knew those numbers were important, that I had to remember them.

Before I had the chance to think, something flashed by me. I couldn't see it but I could feel the death imprint it carried—something powerful, something evil. In an amorphous blur of darkness, it vaporized into the door before me, and I had no choice but to follow. It wanted me to follow—I could feel the distinct urge to continue after it, as if it were beckoning me. I reached for the doorknob, and my hand went through it. Shrugging, I took a hesitant step forward and found myself merging with the door, entering the room beyond it.

The sounds of crashing and fighting snapped me out of my initial trepidation and I forced myself forward, following the noises down a dark hallway and into a bedroom where my eyes settled on the shadows of two men. One was in a huge bed that dominated the room and the other was atop him, pummeling him with fists full of hatred. The man in the bed didn't resist his attacker. He merely lay there in quiet repose while the entity pounded him repeatedly. I had the sudden desire, the sheer need to protect the man in the bed.

I started forward and suddenly came up against an invisible barrier, something stopping me from reaching the bed. I shook my hand, waiting for the telltale sign of fairy dust to emerge in my palm so I could blow the dust toward the barrier and simply eliminate it but my fairy dust never materialized.

The man in the bed continued to lie there, immobile, amidst his blood-stained sheets. The thing atop him shifted to the side, pulling itself away from the bed and allowed me to gaze at the man. My heart about stopped.

"Knight!" I screamed and beat my ineffectual palms against the invisible wall. My voice just bounced off the unseen barrier and died in the air.

Knight's attacker was no longer an amorphous shadow. He'd taken an outline of a man and was now facing me. I couldn't make out his features, I couldn't even see his face. He was just etched in darkness, outlined by night. But I didn't have to see his face to realize what and who he was. I knew it deep down in my gut because he wanted me to know it. The Dreamstalker. I felt a smile radiating outward from him. A smile coming from that dark shade of his face.

He leaned over Knight while I held my breath.

I woke with a start, my heart pounding.

I couldn't shake the nightmare from my mind. And the main reason was that I was convinced it hadn't been a nightmare at all but an omen from my own subconscious. It had been a warning. A warning from the *Dreamstalker*.

I leapt out of my bed and glanced at the clock. It was two a.m. Reaching for the phone on my side table, I speed dialed Knight. It just rang.

I dialed again. It just rang.

I dialed again.

It just rang.

FOUR

I wasted no time in throwing on a pair of panties, jeans, a bra and an oversized sweatshirt. I grabbed the Op 6 (a gun most similar to a 9mm Glock but loaded with dragon blood bullets instead of lead —dragon's blood being toxic to any Netherworld creatures) from underneath my mattress and slid it into the waist of the back of my pants, the way I'd seen Knight do so many times. Slipping on my Reef thongs, I grabbed my keys and headed for my Wrangler which was luckily parked just outside my apartment.

I beeped the car unlocked with my remote, hoisted myself into the driver's seat and tore out of my spot, headed for Shamrock Street. I could see the numbers 3467 in my head as if the imprint of Knight's door was forever burned into my subconscious. I could only hope it was the right address and not some trick of my mind. I wouldn't allow myself to ponder whether I'd just had a meaningless nightmare. Assumptions led to dead people and I wasn't about to include Knight in that thought. Better to be too careful.

There was no one on the road at this hour which was just as well since I was driving like a demon on *Bayn*, the Netherworld's version of speed. Unfortunately, Shamrock Street was on the opposite end of Splendor so I'd just have to drive that much faster to get there before Knight succumbed to whatever the *Dreamstalker* was doing to him.

Images of Knight being pummeled into a bloody mess continued to plague me, reinventing themselves into a myriad of bloody possibilities until I wanted to scream. Hoping to find a distraction, I turned on the radio and tried to focus on the inane chatter of the DJ. I took a turn a little too sharply and the tires squealed in protest. No matter, I was almost to Shamrock.

When I turned on Shamrock, it was like I was in slow motion—like I'd just entered my nightmare. Everything was as I'd seen it—a wide street with various cars interrupting the concrete line of the curb. Dark oak trees dominated either side of the street, growing out of the ground like gnarled and deformed hands. I didn't need to look at the house numbers to know which was Knight's—it was at the end of the street, on the right with the numbers 3467 vertically embossed on the door.

I stepped on the gas and turned the headlights off, not wanting to draw attention to myself. It was tough to see, especially since any moonlight was prohibited from helping me because the oak trees created an umbra of darkness above me. I peered out at the row of houses and recognizing Knight's townhouse, pulled over. No lights illuminated the windows—it was quiet, deathly in its serenity.

Even though there was an open spot directly in front of Knight's house, I parked the Wrangler at the end of the street, not wanting to alert the *Dreamstalker* to the fact that I was outside. I killed the engine and opened the door, hopping down on the concrete. I kicked off my thongs and checked my waistband for the Op 6. Feeling the coldness of steel reassured me, and I gulped as I started for the townhouse barefoot. I didn't lock the Wrangler's doors—in case we needed to make a quick escape.

I tip toed to the door and fisted my hand, shaking it until a mound of fairy dust emerged from my palm. It felt like clutching glitter, and some lustrous flakes escaped my palm, twinkling in the shards of moonlight as they danced through the night air and landed on the ground. I opened my palm and leaned down until I was eye level with the doorknob. Then I closed my eyes, imagining the door unlocking and opening with a soundproof shield so as not to enlighten anyone as to what I was up to. I blew the particles and opened my eyes, watching them sail through the still air and penetrate the keyhole. The knob turned to the left and didn't make a sound. The door opened as if a ghost were bidding me entrance.

Pulling the Op 6 from my waistband, I held it up against my face and continued forward, the cold of the concrete assaulting my feet and wending its way up my legs like a rash. I entered Knight's house and blinked against the intense darkness. Even though it had been dark outside, the few glints of moonlight forcing themselves through the tree branches had seemed like the sun compared to the velvet blackness of Knight's house. I could have whipped up some fairy dust and magicked myself night vision but I was too afraid of losing my focus—situations like these didn't allow for a lack of focus.

Instead, I sidled along the wall, my Op 6 clutched in my hands as my heart hammered through my ears, the sound as deafening as a roaring wave. That was when I realized the only noise I could hear was my heart—there were no sounds of struggling, no sounds of escaping, no sounds of anything. I had to swallow the sudden nausea that overcame me—silence could mean Knight was dead, that I was too late. But, I wouldn't think of that, I couldn't allow myself to even consider it. I forced myself down the hallway, knowing where his bedroom was, where I might be confronted with a scene that would forever burn itself in my memory.

His bedroom door was closed. I took a deep breath, gripped the gun even tighter and pivoted on my left foot until I was directly in front of the door. Then

I silently counted to three, turned the doorknob and dropped to my knees (so someone shooting at the door wouldn't take my head off), aiming the gun into the darkness. Nothing.

I stood up and with my gun held arm's length in front of me, I checked the perimeter of the room, noticing a bathroom just beyond the bed. The bed…Knight wasn't in it and from what I could tell in the sliver of moonlight eclipsing the narrow slit of the curtains, there wasn't any blood staining the sheets. Yes, the blankets were rumpled but…no Knight. I started for the bathroom when I heard the sounds of something big, and that something big was moving fast. Before I had the chance to respond, it bowled into me and knocked me clear across the room. I let out a scream as my Op 6 flew out of my hand and skidded across the floor, coming to a stop underneath the bed. Dammit!

I braced myself for my attacker and felt him atop me as soon as I turned onto my back. Remembering my training, I went for his eyes.

"Dulcie, for fuck's sake!" Knight screamed as he avoided my fingers.

"Knight!" I gasped and pulled away from him, relieved my fingers had just missed his eyes. Instead, I'd landed a pretty good scratch to the side of his face. "You aren't dead?" I whispered.

"Dead?" he repeated, shaking his head. "No, but I came close to joining ranks with Stevie Wonder and Ray Charles." He paused for a minute and then glanced at me again. "What the hell are you doing breaking in here and then pulling a Three Stooges on me?"

"Going for the eyes is the first thing you learn in self-defense training," I started and then remembering the fact that the *Dreamstalker* might still be in our proximity, I immediately lunged for my gun which was still underneath the bed. After grabbing it, I lurched to my feet. "Where the hell is the *Dreamstalker*?"

"Calm down, Curly, I'm alone."

I faced him but didn't drop my gun. "No one attacked you tonight?"

Knight was silent a moment before a smile appeared on his lips. "Just you."

I gulped and felt the heat of complete and total mortification flood my cheeks. It *had* been a nightmare, just a meaningless, innocuous fabrication of my mind. A fabrication that had led me to breaking and entering and in the process, I'd nearly blinded Knight. "Shit," I began.

"Shit?" Knight repeated and turned on the light. I blinked against the sudden attack on my retinas and squinted up at him, noticing a trail of blood coursing down his temple where I'd clawed him.

"I thought you were being attacked," I said in a small voice and turned for the bathroom, where I noticed a hand towel on the towel rack. I grabbed it and didn't miss my reflection in the mirror. I was completely white, any trace of color in my face drained. A sheen of sweat highlighted my forehead, and I had to catch my breath to force the adrenalin that was currently pumping through me to dissipate. I sighed a deep breath and remembering Knight and his bleeding wound, approached him with an embarrassed smile. He leaned down, and I held the towel up to the contusion, applying pressure to get the blood to ebb.

"Those towels were expensive," he said.

"Well, luckily for you, blood comes out in cold water."

"You've got a lot of explaining to do," he said but his voice wasn't angry.

I nodded. "That's fair enough."

He took the towel from me, apparently uncomfortable with bending down to accept my ministrations. "Let's get some coffee and start from the beginning." He started for the hallway with me on his tail. Turning on another light in the hall, he led me into the kitchen, where I took a seat at the bar.

For the first time that evening, I had enough of my wits to take in Knight's house. It was completely and totally modern, just like I'd imagined it would be. A black leather sofa dominated the living room and the black and white New York skyline wall art behind it merely added to the starkness. A white sheepskin rug and a glass coffee table were the only other items to share the room. Oh, and the enormous flat screen TV.

I turned my attention back to Knight and watched him starting a pot of coffee. That was when I realized he was dressed only in a pair of navy blue boxer shorts. His naked chest with its incredible proportions and the scar running across one of his pecs met me like an old friend. I remembered first seeing it when we'd been en route to Dagan's S&M club, Payne. Knight had told me a were had been at fault but I'd never really gotten the gory details. There had been something in his body language that hinted to the fact that it wasn't a pleasant memory.

Knight's deep chuckle pulled me from my reverie, and I realized I'd been zoning out, staring at his midsection. I glanced up at him and frowned. He was just temptation rolled into one luscious package.

"Can't you put on some clothes?" I grumbled.

"Sorry, Lady, you chose to break into my house—this is how I sleep."

"I didn't break into your house," I snapped and then caught myself. "Well, I did, but it was only to defend you from the *Dreamstalker*."

Knight nodded and folded his arms across his chest, hiding my view of his scar. His eyes were smiling, as if he was amused with the whole situation; as if he'd chosen to spend his evening defending himself from a home intrusion.

"This is where it would be good to start from the beginning," he said.

So, I did. I described my nightmare in vivid detail, down to the fact that I could see the numbers of his house in my mind. And that was the part of my story that struck me the hardest. How could I have known where Knight lived? "It wasn't like you ever told me what the numbers were," I continued. "You just told me you lived on Shamrock Street."

Knight shrugged, acting as though there was nothing unusual at all. "Maybe you had my full address stored in your subconscious—you could have seen a letter with the address, or maybe Sam told you."

I shook my head, anger suddenly overtaking me. "How would I have gotten my hands on your mail?" I didn't wait for him to respond. "And I hate to break your self-centered bubble, Knight, but Sam and I don't waste our time talking about you." Okay, that was a lie if ever I'd said one but I had some face to save. And the guy was cocky as all get out so he deserved it.

Seemingly disregarding the direction of our conversation, he opened his cupboard and pulled out two white mugs before glancing at me. "How do you take your coffee?"

"Milk and sugar."

We both were silent as he poured milk into my cup of coffee, followed by two spoonfuls of sugar before stirring it. He handed me the cup and watched me for a second or two before turning to tend to his own. "So, back to the *Dreamstalker*...you thought I was being murdered?"

I nodded but didn't say anything. Instead, I cradled the coffee cup in my hands, allowing the heat to warm me.

Knight glanced at me over his shoulder while he poured himself a cup of black coffee, not pausing to add sugar or milk. "So, you drove over here and took your life into your hands?"

I was quiet as I considered it. "Yeah, I guess I did."

He faced me and took a sip of his coffee, not waiting for it to cool. But, I wasn't surprised—the fact that heat didn't bother him was a trait of his that was already in the *Loki* list of abilities I kept on him. I think it was around number five or so.

"It didn't occur to you to call the ANC?"

Hmm, I hadn't even considered calling the ANC. The next thought that ram-rodded my mind was whether or not he was judging me. Did he think I'd made a mistake in not reporting it to the ANC? If he did, he had an argument coming. "I didn't have a lot of time to think, Knight," I blurted out.

He appeared unfazed. "So, it looks like I'm indebted to you for saving my life yet again?"

He was referring to the time I'd had to make a decision between letting Quillan escape or acting as backup for Knight. I'd let Quill go and I'd never forgiven myself for it. "I don't want to get into that subject," I began, suddenly feeling exhausted.

"I know you don't, Dulce, so we won't. But, I do want to say thanks...again." His gaze was so intense, it was like he was looking through me. Finally he smiled. "You definitely have my back."

I cocked my head and took a sip of the coffee. "I guess you could say that."

He leaned against the counter, directly in front of me. He held his coffee but made no motion to sip it and instead just watched me. "You are braver than most men I've worked with, Dulcie."

"Brave or stupid?" I laughed but the laugh was wiped clean off my face when I brought my eyes back to his.

"Brave," he said in a very deep voice, almost gravelly.

"Don't look at me like that," I started and dropped my attention to my shaking hands. I wasn't sure if I was shaking from left-over adrenalin or due to the fact that Knight was staring at me so blatantly. I could feel myself shrinking underneath his gaze and didn't like the feeling so I forced myself to meet his stare.

"Why?" he insisted, finally taking a sip of his coffee. His eyes never left mine.

"Because it makes me uncomfortable."

"Why?"

Ergh, the "fun" was about to start. "Can't you just accept the fact that I forced myself out of bed at two a.m. to come and save your ass? Nothing is ever easy with you."

"Can't you accept the fact that I want nothing more than to feel you writhing underneath me?" Knight asked with a wicked smile, and I felt my stomach disintegrate. "Nothing is ever easy with you."

"Touché," I said and stood up, starting for the door. I had the sudden urge to escape, to withdraw into the safety of my car and get the hell home. "Well, seeing as how you're fine, I guess I can be going."

"Nope." He was incredibly fast and was in front of me before I could even take another step.

"What the hell was that?" I demanded, shocked. He'd moved almost as fast as Bram had in the limo—well, not quite that fast but fast enough to be concerned.

"Add it to your list of my *Loki* abilities," Knight said in a dismissive tone. "You aren't going anywhere. Not at this hour and not when you're still shaken up."

"I'm fine," I said although I wasn't sure I was. I felt like I needed a long soak in a hot bath and afterwards an even longer nap.

"I'm not taking any chances with you out there alone."

"So follow me home."

"It's too cold outside."

"It's sixty degrees. Any more excuses?"

He laughed. "I'm fresh out. But, that doesn't change the fact that you aren't leaving."

I didn't say anything more but started past him. He just sidestepped me and grabbed hold of my upper arms. "Don't make me hold you kicking and screaming."

I pulled out of his grip and faced him with my hands on my hips and said nothing for a second or two as I battled with what to say. "I'm not going to have sex with you, Knight, so if that's the reason you're forcing me to stay, you might as well let me go."

His jaw was tight. "You think that's the reason I won't let you leave?"

I shrugged. "Eight ball's sources say yes."

He chuckled. "Dulcie, we both know I want nothing more than to have wild, raw sex with you, but that has nothing to do with my decision. It's obvious you're still freaked out over your nightmare—you're shaking so bad you look like you have palsy. You need company tonight."

I attempted to push him aside but it was like pushing a wall. "I'm fine."

He grabbed hold of my arms again and turned me to face him. "Do you trust me?"

Hmm, trust was a tough subject. I'd trusted Jack and look where that had led me. Moreover, trust was anything but black and white—there were levels of trust. And, based on the fact that Knight and I were partners, I guess I had to trust him to an extent. "I guess so."

His eyes were caring, opened wide in their blue depths. He took my hand and squeezed it. "I just want to make sure you're okay."

Feeling myself cornered with no way out, I exhaled. Well, the truth of the matter was it was late, and I was tired and didn't want to drive all the way back to my house. And, yes, I was still afraid I'd have another nightmare. "Do you have a guest room?" I asked in a tired, defeated voice.

"I do but there isn't any furniture in it." He smiled.

"Of course there isn't."

"Do you trust me or don't you?"

I sighed. "I trust you."

"Then sleep in my bed. You have my word that I won't try a thing. But, all the adrenaline I wasted when you attacked me is taking its toll and I'm tired." He stepped aside and motioned to the hallway. "After you."

Shaking my head, I started down the hallway and turned toward his bedroom. The thought of sleeping next to him was a strange one. I mean, on the one hand I was afraid—afraid of the burgeoning feelings I had for Knight—especially when I didn't think it was a good idea to feel anything for him. And on the other hand, I wanted nothing more than to feel his large hands all over my body—he was awakening sexual desires within me that I'd been repressing for years, ever since Jack had done his damage.

"Get in my bed and take your clothes off," Knight's voice was a whisper behind me.

"I thought I told you..."

"Trust, Dulcie, trust."

I set the Op 6 down on his dresser and considered my options. He had a point—I couldn't exactly sleep in jeans—well, more pointedly, it wouldn't be comfortable. But, just because I was going to strip down didn't mean he had to witness the whole thing. "Can I have some privacy please?"

"Of course," he said with a secretive smile and rather than exiting the room, merely turned to face the wall.

I wasn't in the mood to argue and, instead, just approached the bed, tearing off my sweatshirt and jeans. I checked behind my shoulder to make sure Knight was still facing the wall and then hurled myself under the covers in record time, just in case he turned around early.

"Alright, I'm decent," I said.

He turned to face me with a smile that sent shivers racing up my spine. I was in Knight's bed and we were both half naked. Granted, I didn't think anything would happen, but the thought was enough to cause a flurry of anxiety in my stomach. Knight didn't say anything but headed for the bed, his eyes on mine the entire time. He pulled the covers aside and slid in next to me, his body as scorching hot as the desert in the middle of summer. Even so, I couldn't seem to stop shaking. I turned on my side, away from him.

"Keep your boxers on," I said.

"Wasn't planning on removing them." He rolled over until he was facing me—I could tell by the fact that his breath was fanning across my cheek and shoulder and giving me goosebumps.

"So, tell me more about the *Dreamstalker*. Do you think the dream was a warning?"

I snuggled into the covers and closed my eyes, suddenly feeling extremely tired, aided no doubt by the warmth radiating from him. He was like a heater. "I thought you said you were tired?"

He chuckled. "It passed. Just humor me, will you?"

"I think it was just a nightmare."

I gulped at the feel of his hands on my back. "You have knots in your back...tension knots."

I didn't say anything but rolled onto my stomach, thinking nothing would feel better than a backrub ala Knight. Remembering how great Knight's hands had been on my calf cramp, I reminded myself that a massage didn't have to be sexual. People got massages all the time, right? How was this any different? Not wanting to face the lie in that statement, I merely closed my eyes and tried to focus on sleeping.

I felt Knight pull the covers away, and the cold air fiercely assaulted my backside. Knight straddled me above my thighs, and I couldn't say I felt the cold anymore. All I could feel was heat on my face considering my butt was basically bare—just clad in a white thong. I started to shift uneasily until I felt Knight's hand against my back.

"Dulcie, I won't do anything."

I swallowed and nodded, closing my eyes as he started rubbing the tops of my shoulders, manipulating the stress out of my muscles.

"Although I will say you have one hell of a great ass," Knight added with a chuckle. "That's a visual I'll commit to memory."

"Knight," I started.

"Just playing with you," he whispered and set to massaging my entire back, kneading my sore muscles until I could feel myself beginning to relax little by little. "Thanks for what you did tonight, Dulce."

I didn't open my eyes and was dangerously close to falling asleep. "Welcome."

"You probably don't believe it but it means a lot to me."

I was so tired I didn't even complain when I felt his hands on my butt. The funny part was that I did trust him. Even though I was almost naked in his bed and he was rubbing my butt, I trusted him, and I knew he wouldn't try anything. It just wasn't in him to—Knight was the type of man who would want a woman to come to him one hundred percent of her own accord.

"I believe you," I whispered.

"I will always keep you safe, Dulce. You're the best thing that's happened to me in a long time."

I wasn't sure if he really said it or if I dreamt he had.

FIVE

Sam was in a coma.

Now I was taking things personally.

I glanced down at the unmoving body of my best friend and felt a sob choke my throat. Sam's face was pale—almost as pale as the unnatural white of the pillow beneath her head, the same stark, bleached non-color that characterized the entirety of the hospital room. There was an unattended chair beside Sam's cot but I didn't take it. Instead, I stood staring down at her, cringing at the sound of a beeping monitor, endless in its monotony.

Knight had delivered the news this morning—almost immediately after I'd snuck out, leaving him sleeping in his bed and driven to my house, completely confused as to where things stood with him. But, I had no time to come to a realization because the second I stepped through my door, I was accosted by the shrill ring of the phone.

I'd come as quickly as I could.

Apparently, Sam had succumbed to the *Dreamstalker* the previous evening...when I'd been at Knight's. Guilt had been my constant companion since I'd learned the news this morning. I kept replaying the "what ifs" through my mind, over and over again. What if I'd stayed home and hadn't gone to Knight's—would Sam still be in a coma? Had Sam tried to call me while I was at Knight's? I'd checked my machine and I didn't have any messages or missed calls. Even so, I couldn't shake the guilt. And more than the guilt, anger and humiliation coursed through me. The *Dreamstalker* had set me up—and I'd fallen for his bait like a dumbass. The bastard had to be laughing now—at the fact that he'd orchestrated his plan so well—he'd duped me with the nightmare about Knight and knowing I'd rush to Knight's side, Sam was his for the taking. He'd easily influenced her dreams and landed her in the hospital. Piece of cake.

Another sob strangled me, and I reached for Sam's hand. It felt cold and lifeless in mine. Even with the incessant beeping of the life support machine that had now wedged itself into my head like a pulsating electric wire, I checked the monitor above her head to ensure her heartbeat was still strong. White lines traveled across the black display in perfect uniformity which meant Sam was still holding on.

"I'm so sorry, Sam," I whispered. "If you can hear me, I want you to know I'm going to get you out of this, I promise."

"Hey, Dulce."

My breath caught in my throat even as I realized it wasn't Sam's voice. I glanced up at the intruder, feeling my hand instinctively covering my heart, trying to calm the sporadic beating. I was met with the concerned person of Trey, my old coworker.

I smiled but didn't feel it. "Hi, Trey, I didn't hear you come in."

He took a few hesitant steps, forcing his hands into his pants pockets as he skulked forward. Trey and I had a long history of working together, and he used to be the perpetual thorn in my side. After our last case, though, he'd really proven himself to be a useful member of our team, and I guess I had to admit I liked him.

"How are you doing?" he asked and from his swollen eyes, I could see he hadn't taken Sam's dire predicament well. He ran a grubby hand across his forehead and pushed a piece of oily hair back into place. Trey was not a good looking person—he was overweight, short, and for all intents and purposes, resembled a tree stump.

"I'm doing," I answered in a small voice and turned my face so he wouldn't see the tears trailing down my cheeks.

"Knight called and said he's on his way down," he replied while handing me a wadded up piece of tissue from his pants pocket. It felt warm and wet but I accepted it anyway, hoping to Hades it was wet with tears and not something more...gross.

I wiped my eyes. "Thanks."

"How long have you been here?"

I glanced at the clock. "Maybe forty minutes." It felt incredibly longer, like I'd been staring down at my unmoving friend for an eternity.

He nodded. "And you think it's the *Dreamstalker*?"

At the mention of the vile creature's name, my jaw tightened. "I don't think, Trey—I'm sure it is."

Trey nodded again and I wasn't sure what was going through his mind. He, himself, was a goblin though not of the same family as a *somnogobelinus*, or sleep goblin. Trey was a hobgoblin. Many hobgoblins possessed the ability to see glimpses of the future and the past and in Trey's case, his ability was profound which is why he'd made it into the ANC. His gift was definitely an asset for law enforcement.

The sound of heavy footsteps reverberated down the hall, and I turned my attention to the doorway just as Knight's large body filled it. I couldn't keep my heartbeat from skipping and returned my attention to Sam. A pang of guilt stabbed my gut, guilt over being at Knight's, yes, but also guilt over the fact that I'd bailed on him this morning without so much as a goodbye.

"How's she doing?" Knight asked in his deep baritone and strode up until he was right beside me, the warmth of his breath fanning the back of my neck. I glanced up at him, and he smiled in greeting, but it was sad and once his attention found Sam again, he dropped his eyes and sighed.

I shrugged. "Last time I saw the nurse, she said Sam was stable...that she was basically just asleep—a deep sleep."

He nodded, and his smell wafted around me—something spicy and entirely male. I decided to breathe through my mouth.

"I requested ANC staff to tend to Sam. Was that seen to?" Knight asked, in a stern voice. By ANC staff, he meant creatures of the Netherworld as opposed to humans. As otherworldly creatures, we'd been out of the proverbial closet for over fifty years, and in that time we'd managed to assimilate with humans. While this was good for everyday purposes such as voting rights, marriage rights and non-segregated schools, it wasn't great when it came to life and death situations, such as emergency room visits. Supposing you were a fairy or a warlock who ended up in a human-run emergency room? Yeah, you might as well be dead. Luckily for Sam, she had us looking after her.

"Yes, the last nurse to visit was a Hydra," I answered.

Hydras were water serpents and they were known for their foul tempers, as well as their multiple heads. Luckily, this nurse just had one—I'd never been comfortable making conversation with more than one head—I never knew which one to focus on. And Hydras with two or more heads—they could argue with themselves for hours. Trying to interview one about a case wasn't easy, much less, fun.

"Good, good," Knight mumbled as his eyes settled on mine. The room was dead silent for a second or two, aside from the infernal beeping of the monitor.

I cleared my throat. "So, I think it's fair to say I'm now considering this case a personal one." My voice was sharp, as if daring Knight to argue with me. "The *Dreamstalker* is doing this to toy with me, to let me know I'm next."

He was quiet for a second or two and then nodded, as if in agreement. "I think that's safe to assume."

"So, what are we going to do?" Trey demanded and took a step closer to me, anger flexing his voice. "We can't let the freakazoid get anywhere near Dulcie, Knight."

"Astute," Knight answered him with the façade of a smile.

"I'm not gonna wait around and watch my friends get picked off one by one," Trey finished, and I patted him on the back as if to say I wasn't about to be picked off—that this *Dreamstalker* was going to have one hell of a fight on his hands.

"I've arranged a visit to Moon," Knight started and cracked his knuckles. "We need to find out what the Regulators there know about this business." One more crack of his knuckles and then he glanced at me. "Didn't you say there was one victim's name you didn't recognize?"

"Yeah, the old woman."

"Mrs. Mickelson," Trey finished.

"Shirley, wasn't it?" I asked.

"Yes," Knight finished. "She lives in Moon so it's only fair that we contact Moon's ANC force and get them involved."

I smiled. "I didn't know teamwork was part of your vocab."

Knight returned the smile. "Then I guess I'm full of surprises, aren't I?"

"Oh, barf!" Trey interrupted, shaking his head. "You both are going to make me spew up my lunch. There should be a new rule for Regulators—no flirting."

I didn't correct him by saying I wasn't really considered a Regulator anymore. No, I was too mortified that I'd been caught flirting with Knight. Flirting—it wasn't even a word that should have been part of my vocab. Ergh.

#

It took us two and a half hours to reach Moon, thanks to the unrelenting traffic. Knight drove us in his souped-up BMW and after Trey's comment about us flirting, I'd willingly offered him the front seat to which Knight had arched his brow but said nothing. There was definitely an elephant in the room where Knight and I were concerned, but we had bigger fish to fry so the elephant would remain.

The ANC headquarters in Moon wasn't quite as large as our ANC headquarters but the building seemed to be newer and in much better condition. Rather than being stark white with only two windows looming out of the whiteness like a pair of angry eyes, Moon's ANC was built entirely of bricks, warm brown in color. There were multiple windows and nothing that reminded me of the Amityville House—something that always came to mind whenever I visited our Headquarters.

Knight approached the front desk attendant while Trey and I took a seat in the waiting room—a large space with green and blue carpeting, matching upholstered chairs and an Ikea looking coffee table, overflowing with a cornucopia of magazines. Trey hobbled up to the table and inspected each magazine as if he were a pulp connoisseur. He reached out a pudgy hand, selecting his reading material and upon further inspection, I had to swallow the laugh in my throat.

"Glamour? Trey, really?"

"Don't hate, Dulce, there are some hot ass women in these mags." He didn't wait for my response but opened the magazine and started shaking his head in silent appreciation, pursing his lips like he was about to whistle.

"Dulce, Trey," Knight called to us and tilted his head toward the hallway, giving us the charade of "follow me." I stood up, and Trey trailed me, rolling the magazine and tucking it into the back of his pants. I just shook my head and followed Knight down a long corridor, which ended in an office. I couldn't see past Knight's broad shoulders so I stood behind him, waiting for introductions.

"Well, hello to you, tall, dark and handsome..."

Knight laughed, and I felt like kicking him right in the ass. Or maybe I should have delivered the kicking blow to the woman. Course, she had no idea how big Knight's ego already was...

"Today isn't my birthday so what can I do for you?" she continued.

Knight entered the woman's office and offered his hand. "I'm Knight Vander, acting chief of the ANC Headquarters in Splendor. Thanks for agreeing to meet with us."

"Ah, I thought you looked important," the woman answered with a bell-like laugh. "And I do like important men."

Knight stepped aside and allowed Trey and me to enter. The woman turned her attention to us and looked a little surprised; probably not having realized Knight had brought his entourage. She sat behind a large oak desk, the brilliant red of her blouse in contrast with the rich caramel of the wood.

"Dia Robinson, I presume?" Knight asked with a flirtatious smile.

"Honey, I'll answer to anything as long as it's coming from you," she gushed at him prettily with the slightest inkling of a southern drawl. She motioned to the seat directly opposite her desk, and Knight took it, nodding his head in thanks.

The woman faced me next, and I took a step forward, offering my hand. "I'm Dulcie O'Neil."

She shook my hand, and I was immediately taken by the feeling of energy coming off her. It was as if an army of ants was charging its way down her hand and into my arm, forcing their way into my chest. I swore my heart sped up a beat or two. It was all I could do not to pull my hand away because at that moment, I realized what type of creature Dia was. She was a goblin. Of the sleep variety, a *somnogobelinus*.

After a few seconds, I yanked my hand away and eyed her warily, but she didn't seem to notice. Instead, she looked me up and down, a warm smile on her kind and pretty face before she turned back to Knight.

"Well, you two look like the dream team," she said, facing me again. "I'm Dia but my friends call me Diva." She paused a second or two, eyeing me as if she were studying a bug she was about to dissect. "And seeing as how you're a fairy, you must have deduced what type of creature I am." There was nothing accusatory or defensive in her tone.

"Yes," I answered between stiff lips. Even as I answered her, I knew it was wrong to judge her merely by the fact that she happened to be a sleep goblin. All that meant was that she could influence people through their dreams. It didn't mean she had anything in common with the *Dreamstalker,* and it also didn't mean there was anything at all sinister about her. Plus, in working for the ANC, I had to imagine she was on our side.

"And what type of creature would that be, Dulce?" Knight asked curiously, as if he were a teacher quizzing me.

"A *somnogobelinus*," I answered in a constricted tone.

"Shit balls," Trey whispered, shaking his head like he definitely hadn't seen that one coming.

Knight frowned, glancing at Trey, then me and his expression wasn't encouraging. He shook his head, pasting on a smile as he turned to regard Dia again. "You'll have to excuse my partners. We're working on a *somnogobelinus* case at the moment and it's becoming a bit personal for Dulcie."

I wanted to snort at his understatement. "A bit personal" didn't even begin to sum it up.

Dia didn't take her eyes off mine and smiled warmly. "Ah, the *Dreamstalker* case."

I glanced up at her, surprised. I'm not sure why it hadn't crossed my mind that Moon Regulators might have reached the same conclusion about the nature of their perpetrator but it was a surprise all the same.

"We're working on that one ourselves," Dia finished, tapping her manicured nails against the top of her desk.

"Are you?" I asked.

"Yes, and it just so happens that I can offer a great deal of help to you, being of the same species. I know how they act, think, talk." She paused a moment and pulled out a nail file, polishing her nails as she continued. "Are you aware, Ms. O'Neil, how a perfectly law abiding sleep goblin even becomes a *Dreamstalker* in the first place?"

I shook my head. I couldn't say I was.

She continued buffing her nails, taking her sweet ass time to respond. "On the eve of our twentieth birthday, the *somnogobelinus* goes through what we refer to as *Transcendence*. This is basically our entry into adulthood. The *somnogobelinus* is, by nature, a strong creature—we are headstrong as well as soul strong and for most, this *Transcendence* is not a big deal. But, for some, it is a big deal. For those *somnogobelinae* who are missing something in their genetic makeup, the *Transcendence* poses a huge risk—some have died and others have become mentally unstable."

"The *Dreamstalkers* are those who couldn't fully stomach the *Transcendence*?" Knight asked.

Dia nodded and buffed her index finger nail for three seconds. "Exactly."

"So, this new *Dreamstalker* could have been a sleep goblin who couldn't handle the change?" I asked.

Dia stopped buffing and glanced at me, then she shook her head. "We would have felt it. All *somnogobelinae* are linked deep down in their DNA. We can sense one another, feel one another, and when one of us turns into something dark, we all know it."

"How many of you are there?" Knight asked.

Dia shrugged. "Not many. Twenty two across the United States."

"And in the Netherworld?" I prodded.

"Even fewer," Dia answered.

"So, how is that possible then?" I asked. "I mean, if it looks like a *Dreamstalker*, sounds like a *Dreamstalker*."

"It's not a *Dreamstalker*," Dia finished, looking up at me as if to further emphasize her point.

"So, what is it?" I insisted.

"I don't know," she answered, and there was fear in the dark depths of her eyes. "What I can tell you, though, is that this particular creature, we'll call him the *Dreamstalker* for lack of a better title, has really ticked me off."

"Why's that?" Knight demanded.

Dia dropped the nail file back into her top desk drawer and glanced up at him. There was no emotion on her face. "Bastard's responsible for putting sweet ol' Mrs. Mickelson into a coma."

"So we've heard," Knight finished and glanced at me, why I wasn't sure.

Dia turned to face Trey with confusion in her eyes. "So, Mr. Tall, Dark and Handsome is Knight, and the fairy with the personal vendetta is Dulcie. The only words I've heard you say are "shit balls" and I hope that isn't your name?"

Trey shook his head, a laugh rippling through his stomach like an earthquake. "No, Ma'am," he started.

"This is Trey, a Regulator from ANC Splendor," Knight said, offering Trey an apologetic smile for omitting his introduction.

Dia faced Trey and extended her hand. "Nice to meet you." She motioned to the empty seats in the corner of the room, and Trey and I sat down.

I didn't know what it was but there was something about Dia that made me relax and feel comfortable around her, something intangible but likeable all the same. She was maybe five foot six and her skin was the color of midnight. With her curly, short haircut, you couldn't help but focus on her dancing eyes and laughing mouth. She was probably in her mid to late twenties if I had to guess and was one of those people who attracted others like magnets—they had this certain *je ne sais quoi* about them—something that appealed to others. Yep, Dia Robinson had that *je ne sais quoi* by the boatloads.

"So, what can I help y'all with?" Dia asked like she was getting down to business.

I nodded. "Just tell us everything you know about your *Dreamstalker*."

Dia picked up a pencil lying atop her desk and tapped it against her mouth. "When you said this case was personal?"

"I meant I think the *Dreamstalker* is targeting me personally. I've been somehow linked to all the victims so far with the exception of the librarian, Shirley Mickelson."

"That you know of," Knight added. "There could be a connection of which you aren't aware."

"Yeah, there could be," I said and then faced Dia again. "Now he's targeted my best friend and I've had enough. We need to crack this case and nail this guy's ass today."

Dia laughed—it was a high pitched and pretty sound. "I appreciate your zest, Honey, but it's not as easy as you think."

I frowned. "I don't care about easy. My best friend's in a coma, and time is a luxury I can't afford."

She turned to a bookshelf behind her that was filled with binders. She trailed her index finger along the binding of three then, apparently finding what she was looking for, pulled out one of the binders and opened it. The room was silent as Dia continued perusing whatever was in the binder. Finally, she glanced up at me. "There are only two known *Dreamstalkers*..."

"Druiva and Trafu are locked up in Banshee prison," I finished for her. "You didn't need your binder—I could have told you that."

Dia smiled and leaned back into her seat. "Can you tell me if there are any junior *Dreamstalkers*?"

I guessed she meant had either of the *somnogobelinae* in Banshee Prison spawned offspring. "No, neither has any children—we were pretty thorough with the investigation when Druiva was locked up the first time."

And it wasn't like either *Dreamstalker* was getting any funny business at Banshee—conjugal visits were prohibited.

"So, that's a dead end?" Dia asked. "Scary thing, then."

"Why do you say that?" Knight asked.

"It means we're dealing with something that's either imitating a *Dreamstalker,* or there's more to this story than meets the eye."

"Imitating a *Dreamstalker*?" I started, "how would that even be possible?"

Dia shrugged. "Maybe someone is purposely misleading us. How do you know it's a *Dreamstalker* we're dealing with? How rigorously did you test your victims?"

"It can't be an imitation," Knight said. "We ran blood tests, brain scans, the whole she-bang. There were no narcotics in the victims' bloodstreams that might point to this being anything other than a *Dreamstalker*."

"Well, then we should continue forward with the assumption that we're dealing with a *Dreamstalker*," Dia said but she clearly wasn't convinced.

After an impending silence, Knight leaned forward. "What can you tell us, Dia?"

She leaned back into her chair and rocked back and forth a few times. "I can tell you we're going to need to work together on this case—four heads are better than one. And because of the fact that one of the victims was a citizen of Moon, I need to be involved."

"We never said we didn't want your help," Knight answered.

"Just wanted to make it crystal clear," Dia said in a serious tone. "Sometimes ANC people come here and ask their questions and try to take over. That won't fly on my watch."

"Understood," I said. "We'll share freely with you if you do the same with us, and hopefully we can crack this case that much faster."

Dia faced Knight with a smile. "I like the way she thinks."

#

It was two a.m. and I'd been awake for twenty four hours now, hyped up on caffeine in fear of going to sleep and possibly witnessing another nightmare concocted by the *Dreamstalker*. Instead, I planted myself at my desk and forced myself to type the notes on the case so far.

Victims:

Anna Murphy: in my second grade class, located in Splendor

Heather Green: in my second grade class, located in Splendor

Jenny Garrity: my nanny as a child, located in Splendor

Travis Decker: my high school boyfriend, located in Estuary

Shirley Mickelson: librarian, Rio Mesa High School in Moon, is there a connection to me? (Note to self—ask Trey to find out everything there is to know about Shirley Mickelson)

My heart grew heavy as I typed the last name.

Samantha White, witch, employee of the ANC, located in Splendor

I heaved a sigh and glanced at the cursor blinking at me. There was so much going through my head—images of Sam on the hospital cot fought with images of Knight's still body, beaten to a pulp in his bed. At least that last vision hadn't been real, I reminded myself—it was just a decoy, a ploy. Knight was safe...at least for now. I walked my empty coffee mug back to the kitchen and refilled it, the beginnings of a caffeine headache already pounding through my temples.

I felt another sob choke my throat and had to swallow it down. Sam was my closest friend. As I'd mentioned earlier, I wasn't a social person—I didn't have a legion of friends. I really only had two people I considered at all close to me—Sam and Quillan, my old boss. And due to recent events, I'd had to scratch Quillan off my friend list. The pain was still there and sometimes late at night, I found myself repeatedly wondering how Quillan had become one of the bad guys. How had he deceived everyone, and why had he done it? I couldn't help but take the betrayal personally—I'd let Quillan get close to me, and the only thing that had encouraged was disappointment and pain.

I took a sip of the coffee but never tasted it. My thoughts were wholly encompassed by the fact that every time I allowed a man to get close to me, somehow I got screwed. And Jack, my ex-boyfriend, had really done a bang up job of it—he was the poster asshole for cheaters. And then Quill...I couldn't finish the thought. An image of Knight blossomed in my mind's eye, and I sighed. I had to build up my defensive wall until it was impossibly high and thick, impenetrable in its dimensions. I wouldn't allow myself to be disappointed again by a man—I couldn't allow myself to hurt again, to succumb to that weakness.

I marched back over to my computer and glanced at the word document: my list of victims' information. I downscreened it, needing another outlet, something else to occupy my thoughts for a moment. I opened up my Yahoo inbox and sorted through the spam emails. The mention of my book, *A Vampire and A Gentleman,* in one of the subject lines grasped my attention, and I opened the email. It was from Barbara Mandley, a literary agent with Great Fiction Agency—the same agency that had recently asked to review my book.

I read through the email without any emotion and couldn't even bring myself to get excited by the fact that Barbara said she hadn't been able to put my book down. She finished the email by stating that she thought my book was "amazing" and she'd be in touch shortly. I closed out of my Yahoo inbox, pondering the fact that I hadn't written a word since this whole *Dreamstalker* business had started. I definitely wasn't going to make my self-imposed deadline of one month or less. But, I couldn't bring myself to think about it; couldn't focus on anything but the details of the *somnogobelinus* case.

I pulled my notes back up on screen and started a new paragraph, trying to recall not only what I already knew about *Dreamstalkers*, but also what Dia Robinson had told us about the habits and characteristics of the *somnogobelinus.*

Dia Robinson, Somnogobelinus but not a Dreamstalker, Chief of ANC Headquarters, Moon

Is there a third Dreamstalker? If we know there were no offspring from both Dreamstalkers locked away in Banshee Prison, how are these events even possible? Could another somnogobelinus have taken a dark detour into Dreamstalker territory? Dia insists that it isn't possible, but is it?

Dreamstalkers are:

1. *Driven to feed off the dreams of both humans and Netherworld creatures alike. This is why both Dreamstalkers at Banshee Prison were separated from all other creatures. They were held in solitary confinement, isolated in their cells, the cell walls fortified with four inches of solid steel. Steel prohibits psychic communication and, therefore, could ensure the safety of the other inmates.*
2. *Dreamstalkers must be within one hundred feet of the creature whose dreams they are attacking. Therefore, the night the Dreamstalker targeted me with scenes of Knight being attacked, it had to have been nearby. Which means it knows where I live. And it revealed Knight's*

address to me in sleep which means it also knows where Knight lives. (Dilemma—what to do? Hotel for a while?)

3. *Dreamstalkers will return for their victims. They're like Komodo Dragons who bite their prey and then track them as they die, returning days later to claim their feast. A Dreamstalker really isn't that different. They strike, sending their victims into comas and days or weeks later, they return to finish the victims off.*

    a. *Our plan: Sit and wait it out. Dia can sense a Dreamstalker but she has to be within one hundred feet of one. Knight, Trey and I will park ourselves next to the victims, looking for any sign of foul play. At the merest indication that something might not be right, we'll notify Dia and she'll scout the location, using her somnogobelinus radar to apprehend the offender.*

4. *Dreamstalkers' victims appear to be in comas, but they are actually stuck between life and death—trying to defeat the Dreamstalker in their mind. If the Dreamstalker kills them in sleep, they die in life. Heather Green was the first to die—meaning she couldn't defeat the Dreamstalker in her imagination. The only way to free all of the victims is to kill the Dreamstalker or get it locked up in a steel enforced cell where it can't control the minds of its victims. (Note to self: my vote is to kill the bastard).*

SIX

It had been three days that I'd been awake and I'd lost count of how many cups of coffee I'd downed. Even though I'd managed not to fall asleep, I was in a haze—events and days just blending into one lump of time that felt nebulous and indescribable. I stared out the window of my kitchen, not focusing on anything but the black of the night and the way the moonlight danced between the tree branches, rays of light breaking the homogeneity of night.

Sometime during the past three days, I'd managed to visit Sam but each visit yielded the same return—she was still in a coma, hanging onto life and the constant beeping of the monitors still played with my sanity. It had been earlier today that I'd made my customary rounds to Sam's bedside but the constant hum of life support had acted like the droning of Morpheus, the God of Sleep. I'd nearly collapsed into slumber right on top of Sam and that was when I knew I needed to get out of there, and better still, I needed more coffee, lots more.

I'd also asked Dia to make inquiries to the other *somnogobelinae* with whom she was familiar, just to ensure her "*Dreamstalker* radar" wasn't on the mend. After Dia agreed, albeit none too happily, she announced that her radar was in top performing condition because all her sleep goblin cohorts said they hadn't been alerted to the creation of any new *Dreamstalkers* which basically left me right where I'd started.

Knight had been keeping Trey and the other ANC Splendor staff busy with in-depth research into the lives of Druiva and Trafu, the *Dreamstalkers* in custody at Banshee Prison. They were searching all records, looking for any clues as to relationships that could have yielded progeny. And we'd come up with gaping holes there too—Trafu had been in Netherworld custody for hundreds of years. And I'd learned a little tidbit that hadn't been pretty—apparently when Netherworld creatures didn't exercise their libidos, their genitalia did shrivel up and fall off. And, yes, Knight had had a field day with that one—telling me if I truly valued him as a friend and partner, I'd ensure the safety of his male equipment. I'd just told him there were plenty of women who'd be up for the job.

So, Trafu was basically a eunuch and had been for over one hundred years which left Druiva... After much investigation into his roots, we did learn that Druiva had entertained many lovers during his time as a free *somnogobelinus* but what we hadn't been counting on was the fact that all of those lovers had been male, obliterating any chance for Druiva juniors.

Yep, I was back to square one. I'd had three days of no sleep and nothing to show for it. The clock had been ticking and urgency had been boiling up within me until it was now overflowing into a broth of panic.

I grabbed the handle of Mr. Coffee and poured myself my nth cup, turning to refill it and start another brew. I brought the mug to my lips and had to force down the sudden overwhelming desire to throw up. My body needed sleep badly—it was as obvious as the fact that I had to force the coffee down my throat, in my feeble effort to compel my body into submission. Gagging, I swallowed four mouthfuls and walked to my desk, needing something to occupy my mind.

I opened the email from Barbara Mandley of Great Fiction Agency and read it again, trying to drum up some excitement about the fact that someone actually liked my book and, from the way it sounded, maybe was going to offer me representation. But, excitement had abandoned me at least two days ago. Now I was like a car coasting on empty, with only a few whiffs of gasoline to keep my engine from dying.

I opened the word document I'd saved as "Book Two Titles" and read through the list of four titles I was proposing for my second book in the Bram "Vampire and a Gentleman" series.

1. Speak vamp to me
2. A Bloodsucker named Raven
3. Vampires don't leave hickies
4. Don't invite a vampire in

It was like I was reading the work of someone else. I couldn't even remember coming up with the titles. And I had to just shake my head in total bewilderment at "Vampires don't leave hickies." Hello? What in the hell had I been thinking with that one?

I stared at the blinking cursor and wracked my mind, trying to drum up new titles but each time I attempted to get the creative juices flowing, all I could think about was more coffee and then the feelings of nausea weren't far behind. After a few more minutes of strenuous thinking and even more strenuous gagging, I figured it was fair to admit that nothing creative was going to happen tonight...today...whatever.

The little black cursor continued to blink, as if announcing it wasn't going to give up, that there was a creative bone in my body somewhere—that my blood hadn't turned to coffee within my veins. I continued staring at it until it appeared to be getting larger and the blinking more pronounced, more anxious. I could feel myself moving closer to it. My elbows touched the top of the desk and before I knew it, my head was resting on my forearm. The need to close my eyes was pounding through my body—a command coming from Hades only knew where. The desire to see the velvety black of my eyelids was overwhelming, almost as strong as the constant stinging sensation that had been plaguing my eyes for the last two days...and nights. If I just closed my eyes and rested them for a second or two, I'd feel better. I'd still be in control of myself...

#

I opened my eyes and lifted my head off the desk. I'd fallen asleep—who knew for how long. I was suddenly frightened and angry with myself. I'd been incredibly lucky that the *Dreamstalker* hadn't realized I was immobilized by sleep and his for the taking. Stupid, I'd been so stupid. I stood up, angst pounding through me and walked my cold cup of coffee to the sink, promptly pouring myself another. I threw my head back and emptied the lukewarm liquid into my mouth, squelching the urge to gag. I wiped my mouth with my sleeve.

The sudden compulsion to go check on Sam almost blindsided me and before I could even register what I was doing, I had my keys in my hand and I was headed down to the Wrangler which was parked just outside. I glanced up at the dark night sky and even though the thought crossed my mind that visitor's hours were well over, my feet didn't slow down.

Before I knew it, I'd unlocked the door and was seated behind the wheel, my hand already turning the keys in the ignition. I put the car into drive and started down the street. The streetlights reflected through my windows and I shielded my eyes against the glare. The momentary thought that I hadn't buckled up crossed my mind but I couldn't focus on it. I arrived at the stop sign at the end of the street and had no memory of getting there. All I knew was that the hospital was to the right but for some reason, I turned to the left.

I couldn't even really grasp the fact that before setting foot into the car, I'd planned to visit Sam at the hospital yet now I was headed for the highway leading out of Splendor and into the BFE district of Charity which was home to a herd of cows and endless miles of lush farmland.

I attempted to turn the Wrangler around, even issued the command to my arms, but the wheel appeared to be stuck or maybe somewhere in my subconscious I really wanted to visit Charity because my body seemed to be in complete opposition to my mind. I continued along Highway Five toward mile after mile of white fences and rolling hills, farther and farther from the hospital.

The radio suddenly flickered on and my heartbeat increased tenfold as I wondered how in the hell that was even possible. There was static for a moment and I watched the screen as it rolled through FM station after FM station. Finally it settled on something that sounded like fifties music. I wanted to turn the sound down but my hands were plastered to the steering wheel so the music continued to pour out of the speakers. I could practically see Patsy Cline in her poodle skirt and saddle shoes as she wailed into the microphone, "I Go Out Walking After Midnight."

My brain began to protest the fact that my body had a mind of its own and was now holding me hostage. I glanced out at the night sky, realizing it was getting darker, the street lights no longer lighting my way as I entered the border of Charity. Sure enough, dark outlines of cows on the hillsides pointed to the fact that I'd just arrived in no man's land.

Lights from behind me suddenly filled the Wrangler and I depressed the accelerator, hoping the person would pass me. I didn't even have the chance to marvel at the fact that my body had carried out my mind's wishes because it was suddenly apparent that the person behind me wasn't going to pass. Instead, the car pulled up right behind me, close—as in bumpers kissing close. The headlights of the car illuminated the inside of the Wrangler and made it exceedingly difficult to see the road before me. I yanked the wheel to the right, pulling over to the side of the road and hoped the person would get the clue that I didn't appreciate being tailed.

The car veered to the left of the Wrangler and just when I thought it was going to pass, it pulled alongside me until we were neck and neck. I couldn't help the feeling of panic wending its way up my throat until I felt like I was going to throw up again. I glanced over and could see nothing but darkness emanating from within the car. It was so dark, I couldn't even tell if there was a person in it. I shook my head at the absurdity of that thought—of course there was someone in it—it couldn't just drive itself.

The fifties music continued to pour out of my speakers and the melody acted like a fire burning away at my sanity. The car beside me suddenly lunged to a stop and pulled up behind me again, flooding my car with its headlights. I wanted nothing more than to stop but my body seemed to have taken on a mind of its own again and I'd pulled back into the street and pressed the accelerator down until I was going ten miles over the speed limit. The car behind me revved its engine and kept pace.

I watched as my foot pressed the accelerator harder and the speedometer began to climb from forty five to fifty five to sixty five. I passed a white sign proclaiming the speed limit to be thirty five and somewhere deep inside me concern blossomed—this was a country road, windy and dangerous for extreme speeds. I glanced back at the speed gauge and watched in horror as it hit seventy five.

The car behind me pulled alongside me again and then suddenly sped up, passing me instantly. It veered into the lane ahead of me and before I could respond, the red of its brake lights suddenly interrupted my vision. The sound of the Wrangler crashing into the car shattered my thoughts, the melody of the fifties music still in the background. I suddenly felt myself flying forward and the explosion of glass was thick in my ears as I felt my chest smash into the steering wheel. Then before I could even gasp, the Wrangler was airborne.

I glanced down at my clenched palm and realized I'd shaken a mound of fairy dust somewhere along the way. I tossed it in the air, imagining a thick, insulating bubble surrounding me. The feel of rubber was thick against my cheek as I crashed through the passenger window and felt myself smash against the pavement.

#

"Girl, you really did a number on yourself."

I tried to open my eyes. It was that damned beeping monitor again—thick in my ears. "Can someone turn that fucking thing off?" I demanded and my voice was so gravelly, I barely recognized it as my own.

"Ah, Dulcie is back." It was Trey. There was relief in his voice.

I opened my eyes and the first thing I saw was a ceiling with individual white squares and fluorescent lights glaring down at me. I turned my neck and saw Dia and Trey gazing over me, both smiling. My neck hurt. I turned the other way and found Knight right beside me.

"Where the hell am I?" I insisted, even though it was becoming pretty crystal clear based on the crappy ceiling and the constant beeping.

"You're in the hospital," Knight answered with eyes that were smiling, relieved and happy. He grinned down at me and for as crappy as I'm sure I looked, he looked beautiful. I shook my head against the injustice of it all. Knight was like temptation wrapped in a pretty red bow and dropped on my doorstep from Hades, the King of all assholes.

"You were in a car accident," Trey said, his voice thick with tears. "But, they say you're going to be ok."

I closed my eyes, realizing what this meant. "I let him get to me, didn't I?" I asked, glancing at Knight again. He didn't answer but squeezed my hand as if to say none of that mattered now, what did matter was that I survived. But, while it might not have mattered to him, it mattered a hell of a lot to me. The *Dreamstalker* had won again. Dammit! I'd sworn to take him down but all it had taken was three days of no sleep and I'd failed. Again.

"Yep, you sure as heck did let him get to you," Dia said and I glanced at her, surprised. "You were lucky to survive, girl."

"If this is lucky, I'd hate to see unlucky," I grumbled.

"Do you remember what happened, Dulce?" Knight asked, rubbing my hand in his. He sat down on the doctor's swivel stool until he was eye level with me and smiled warmly. I sighed, trying to summon up the energy to recall what had happened.

"I just wanted to rest my eyes," I began, recreating the visual of the moments before I'd fallen asleep. "Then next thing I knew, I was in the Wrangler and headed for Charity." I stopped for a second, remembering my cheery yellow car always parked outside my apartment. If it was possible to love inanimate objects, I loved that car. And realizing what had happened to me, I could only imagine what had happened to it.

"My car?" I squeaked.

"May it rest in peace," Trey said and looked like he was going to start crying again. He'd always liked the Wrangler too.

I shook my head. "Dammit."

Knight chuckled. "We'll get you another one, Dulce, don't even waste your time thinking about it." His jaw was tight. "You just focus on healing."

I nodded, not really wanting to contemplate the fact that Knight was being so caring—he was making it harder and harder not to want him, not to allow him to get closer to me. I shook off the feelings—I had more important things to focus on at the moment. Instead, I tried to remember the events that had led to this point. "I remember seeing a car behind me." The memory of the other vehicle with the garish headlights came crashing in on me and I felt myself wince. "The car pulled in front of me and then it just stopped. I...I must have hit it." I paused for a minute or two, blinking back tears. I hadn't realized I was emotionally traumatized until I'd remembered the events, replayed them in gory detail, relived the feelings of helplessness and fear all over again. I dropped my head to the side, hoping to hide my tears. "That's all I really remember."

Everyone was quiet for a second or two, probably drumming up their own visuals of my story.

"It was all a dream, Dulcie," Knight started and at my expression of confusion and disbelief, continued. "They only recovered one car at the scene, yours. It appears you ran into a tree."

I couldn't even respond. A dream? And I'd run into a tree?

"You should have been killed, Dulcie," Knight said. "You weren't wearing your seat belt and the Wrangler rolled. You were thrown out of the side window and it should have killed you."

"Like I said before, I'm hard to kill," I said with an insincere laugh, feeling pain in every joint of my body.

"Dulcie, that's not my point," Knight said and leaned closer to me. "You used magic...you were able to protect yourself."

I suddenly remembered the fairy dust in my palm, throwing it and thinking of a protective buttress against the pavement. "Yeah, I did."

Knight glanced up at Dia and she inhaled deeply. "I knew it," she said in a tight voice. "Magic won't work against a *Dreamstalker*," she continued. "The dream world is their turf, not ours. *Dreamstalkers* control the dreamer."

"Maybe you were right, Dia," Trey said, biting his lower lip. "Maybe it's not a *Dreamstalker*."

"I told you it wasn't," she said and shook her head. "If this isn't proof enough for y'all, I don't know what is."

I couldn't say I was really paying attention to their conversation. My mind hadn't quite progressed past the point of realizing that I'd been able to use my magic while under the power of the *Dreamstalker*. And that was the key to defeating him—it had to be. "Knight, if we can manipulate the dream, we can defeat him."

Knight glanced at me, his brow furrowed. "That is a dangerous thought."

Dia scoffed. "Dangerous isn't even the word for it. Suicidal is more like it. Didn't you hear me when I said the dream world is their turf? If this thing even is a *Dreamstalker*, we'd be idiots to think of defeating it on its playground."

Knight nodded. "She has a point."

"So, what, we're just going to sit here and let it claim its victims?" I insisted. "I, for one, sure as hell am not going to let that happen."

Dia shook her head. "We stick to the plan. If it's a *Dreamstalker*, I can track it and if it's pretending to be a *Dreamstalker*, it will still follow the same pattern. Either way, it will be coming for its victims and when it does, we'll be here to stop it."

Apparently it was two against one—Trey was silent so he didn't count. I sat up and everyone came nearer, concern drawing their faces like they thought I was about to break into acrobatics ala Cirque Du Soleil. "I need to get out of here," I started.

"You can't leave, Dulce," Knight said sternly and stood up. "You haven't been released yet."

I shook my head. "This sucks, Knight. I have too much to do to be stuck in this damn place all day." I glanced down at myself, taking in the white hospital robe, complete with mini pink rosebuds repeated across the white surface. Couldn't they make hospital attire a little less grandma-like? I leaned forward but Knight pushed me back into the downy pillows.

"Take it easy, Dulce. There's no rush," he insisted.

"There is a rush," I argued, suddenly remembering the fact that Sam was in this same hospital, still fighting the *Dreamstalker*. There was an absolute rush. Rush wasn't even the word for it. "Is Sam okay?"

Knight nodded. "She's fine. She's in the next room over." He grabbed my hands again, as if to say he'd ensure I was immobilized if need be. "You just need to relax and let yourself heal. Even though you don't have broken bones, your muscles are bruised."

"I don't have time to rest," I said, even though I could already see the writing on the wall. If the hospital wasn't ready to release me, I'd stay. Knight would see to it. He was definitely the most annoyingly bossy person I'd ever met. If he thought I needed to stay and heal, I'd stay and heal. Dammit. "I have to get this guy."

"Nope, not happening," Knight said and his jaw was set with that stubborn defiance I'd only otherwise seen in myself.

I frowned and sighed, realizing I'd been bested. "So, what's wrong with me?"

Knight arched a brow, apparently surprised by the fact that I wasn't still arguing. "Nothing, as far as they can tell."

"So if nothing is wrong with me, why can't I leave?"

He shook his head and chuckled. "They want to keep you here for a day or so to make sure everything is okay—they're still running tests to ensure you didn't suffer internal injuries."

"Great," I said with as much irritation as I could muster.

"You need to just sleep and heal," Knight continued.

I glanced up at him, anger suddenly overtaking me. "Sleep?" I demanded. "Are you insane? Look what sleeping did to me!"

He ran his finger down my cheek and I attempted to push it away but the IV in my arm punished me with a smart, stinging pinch.

"You'll have Dia here with you. She's volunteered to stay," he finished.

I glanced at Dia and she smiled at me like she was some great gift. "No offense to Dia but how the hell is she going to help me when I'm sound asleep and the *Dreamstalker* decides to take me for another joy ride?"

Dia laughed. "Girl, have you not listened to a word I've been saying since we met?"

I glanced at her and frowned so she continued. "I'm a sleep goblin."

So sue me if I wasn't following but I hadn't slept for three days and I'd just been in a major accident. "So what?"

She shook her head like I was a slow kid. "So, I can chaperone your slumber to make sure nothing interferes."

"You can protect me in my sleep?" I asked, my tone sounding like she also had a bridge to sell me.

She nodded proudly, like she was the shit. Well, if she could protect me while I was asleep, she was more than the shit in my books. And, hell, I'd even buy any bridges she was selling.

"I told you I'd come in handy," she said.

"So, why can't you protect my dreams all the time?" I demanded, suddenly angry again. "You mean, I could have been sleeping all this time? Why couldn't you have saved me from totaling my car?" I didn't mean for my voice to sound so shrill but I really couldn't help it.

"It takes a huge amount of concentration to maintain the psychic protective walls around you," Dia started defensively. "I can do it for maybe an hour at the most and afterwards, I'm exhausted for days. It's not something that's easy to do."

I nodded, relinquishing my anger. "Sorry, my nerves are just a little bit shot."

"No need to apologize, Dulce, I gotcha," Dia said and winked.

The sound of splashing interrupted our conversation and I craned my neck to the right, glancing at the perpetrator—a Hyacinth Water Pixie sitting on a fist-sized rock in a glass bowl, surrounded by water and lotus blooms. Anger coursed through me—I detested pixies. "What the hell is that and why is it in my room?"

The pixie looked at me with distaste and began pouring water over her back, taking a bath and ignoring my outburst, like she was the bigger person. Ha. That was one reason I despised pixies—they were so damn patronizing. And more so, the pixie I used to work with at the ANC was constantly digging me about this and that—mainly because she'd been in love with Quillan and he and I had been...tight.

"It's a Hyacinth Water Healer," Trey said, his tone repeating the "duh" sentiment that must have been going through his head.

"I know what it is," I spat out. "I don't want it in here."

Hyacinth Water Pixies were known for their healing powers and Netherworld creatures sent them to each other to help promote healing. They were like a better version of "get well soon" flowers. Only I hated pixies so it wasn't doing much of anything for me, other than pissing me off.

Dia laughed and seized the fish tank, the pixie nearly falling off the rock as she grabbed the sides of the tank to stable herself. "Can't stand these darn things, myself," she said and headed for the hallway, her laugh trailing after her.

I faced Knight again. "Nice joke."

He shrugged. "It wasn't my doing."

Trey suddenly looked especially guilty and pretended extreme interest in his shoes. Realizing I was acting more than bitchy, I reached for his hand and smiled. "You're awesome, Trey."

He grinned from ear to ear and hopefully the pixie was forgotten. I glanced at Knight again. "Since I obviously can't leave this bed, I need you to do me a favor."

He leaned forward and eyed me speculatively. "I think I could be persuaded into doing you a favor."

"Go to the library and get me every book you can on dreaming," I started and watched his expression fall. No doubt he'd thought I was flirting with him. Sigh.

"Dulcie, I thought we were sticking with the plan?" Knight said grumpily.

"We are," I ground out. "But, since I'm going to be stuck here with nothing to do and all day and night to do it in, I need some reading material."

"Trey, are you taking notes?" Knight asked and turned to Trey.

"Of course, I'm the grunt," he muttered.

Knight didn't respond and I just shook my head. "Thank you, Trey."

"Yeah, yeah, Ms. I'm so smart, I read books."

"Smart and beautiful," Knight said and threw me a boyish smile.

Trey shook his head and started for the door. "You two just need to do it and get it over with."

Knight was right behind him. "I couldn't agree with you more."

I watched them walk into the hallway and then they were gone. Minutes after Trey and Knight left, Dia entered, minus the Hyacinth Water Pixie, thank Hades.

"You ready to get some sleep, Girl?" Dia asked with a smile as she strode up to my bedside.

I nodded. "Thank you, I really appreciate it."

She seemed to hesitate for a second or two, her lips clenched. "Can I offer some unsolicited advice?" Dia began and I glanced up at her in surprise.

"Shoot."

She took another few seconds to collect her thoughts. "I used to have a cockatiel named Tweety, and I loved that bird. He was bright yellow with orange spots on his head and he used to whistle every time I came home." She had this far away sort of expression on her face, like she was living a totally different time.

"Um, that's a nice story, Dia, but what does that have to do with anything?" I asked, not meaning to sound so brusque.

She didn't seem to hear me or if she did, she didn't care but just continued her story. "This bird would sing constantly and I used to love to listen to him. I had him for thirteen years which is a really long time for a cockatiel to live, you know?"

I didn't but anyway...

"Then one day he passed away from a heart attack and it just broke my heart." She glanced at me and it looked like she was waiting for me to respond but the problem was, I wasn't sure what to say.

"I'm sorry?" I asked, frowning.

"Even though I miss that bird now, I had thirteen years of love, Dulcie, and even though it hurts to think of him now, if I had it to do over again, I wouldn't change anything because it was better to have loved him and lost him than never to have had him at all."

I nodded, sort of figuring where she was going with all of this. But, I didn't say anything.

"I don't know what your background is and I don't know why you wear that shield up wherever you go," she said and her gaze was so piercing, I felt like she was seeing through me. "But, I do know you're a good person and deserve to love someone like I loved Tweety."

"Thanks," I started but she held up her hand as if to say she wasn't yet finished.

"And I also don't know much about Mr. Vander other than the fact that he is just gorgeous on a stick but I know he cares about you—I can see it in his eyes. And you'd be making a big mistake if you didn't take a chance with that one."

"You definitely don't know Knight," I said, a myriad of reasons why he wasn't a good idea bubbling through my mind.

"I know enough to know when you're trying to talk yourself out of something, Girl, and you just want to make sure you aren't missing out on a Tweety."

The truth of it was that I wasn't sure Tennyson was right when he'd said it was better to have loved and lost than never to have loved at all. I'd loved and lost and I could honestly say it was better to let the assholes go and break some other dumbass's heart than risk mine again.

Tweety be damned.

SEVEN

So, I'd spent the rest of the day and night in the hospital and it had been a major bitch. At least Knight had been true to his word and rather than Trey showing up with a stack of library books, Knight had come by later in the afternoon with an iPad, complete with Nook and Kindle apps. I hadn't wanted to accept such an expensive gift but it was necessary to learn more about the *Dreamstalker* so we could fight him on level ground. So, I swallowed my pride and became an ereader owner.

And I'd spent my time in the hospital researching the dream state and what I'd learned was encouraging. In order to maintain control of my dreams, I'd have to enter what was termed the "lucid dream" state which meant my sleeping mind would be aware that it was, in fact, sleeping. If I could inform my body that it was dreaming, I could manipulate the dream in my favor, aka I could control my sleeping mind. And I had to imagine this control would be pivotal in defeating the *Dreamstalker*. The only part that was less than ideal was the fact that lucid dreaming took practice and unfortunately for me, I was SOL where practice was concerned because I wouldn't allow myself to sleep. But, I had to admit things were looking up—I had an option and options were important things to have.

While I'd been recuperating and learning all there was to know about lucid dreaming, Knight, Trey and Dia had been scouting the hospital, checking on Anna, Jenny, Sam and me while also searching for any sign of the *Dreamstalker*. Of course, there hadn't been so much as a peep from our enemy.

I'd managed to sleep for an hour and a half, courtesy of Dia and even though it wasn't much, I felt incredibly refreshed. Moreover, I wasn't sure if I'd actually slept while the *Dreamstalker* had attacked me but based on the fact that I basically sleepwalked myself into an accident, I had to imagine the answer was a resounding no.

The hospital had discharged me the following morning and Knight had been there to pick me up and take me home. He'd tried incredibly hard to make a case for me living with him for the time being but I'd flatly declined, saying as long as I stayed awake, I'd be fine. Besides, I had lots of things to do—the first thing on my list being a new set of wheels. I couldn't afford to be without a vehicle.

Even though my savings account had now become embarrassing, I shelled out six thousand dollars for a used bright red Suzuki DL 650 motorcycle with only five thousand miles on it. It probably sounds crazy that I'd buy a street bike after barely surviving the car accident with the Wrangler but what it came down to was the fact that I didn't have much money and I had even less time. My neighbor had sold me the bike with the promise that he'd fix it if anything broke. It was a deal good enough and easy enough for me so I took it. Besides, motorcycles were faster escape-vehicles than cars...so there.

While I was happy to be out of the hospital and though I felt slightly rested thanks to Dia and finally had a mode of transportation again, I wasn't exactly happy with what I had to do next. While I'd been immobile in the hospital bed, I'd wracked my brain over and over again trying to come up with an alternative—trying to think of any option other than the one I was seriously considering. But, I was fresh out of options and time was ticking by, leaking minutes and seconds. And I couldn't afford to lose even a split second.

Anna Murphy had died. Knight had informed me on the way to my house after I'd been discharged from the hospital. And it hadn't mattered that Dia had been scouting the perimeter of the hospital, she'd never detected the *Dreamstalker*. Knight said it looked as if Anna's death might have been due to complications with her heart, and that he wasn't sure the *Dreamstalker* had come for her but I wasn't convinced.

Heather had been the first to go and now Anna was the second. I could only imagine a pattern was emerging here and Jenny Garrity, my favorite childhood nanny would be next. After her, it would be Travis and Mrs. Mickelson and then...Sam.

Judging from the time when Heather and Anna became comatose to the point at which they died, we figured that Jenny Garrity had a matter of days to live, Travis and Mrs. Mickelson had maybe four or five days and Sam had about a week.

Sam was dying.

That was the realization that had hit me like the breath of a *Kraken*. I'd visited her after I'd been discharged and to say she hadn't looked good was an understatement. Her breathing was shallow and dark circles hung from her eyes, pointing to the fact that although she appeared to be happily slumbering away, she wasn't. She was fighting the hold of the *Dreamstalker* and by her appearance, I would have bet he was winning. That told me I was running out of time. I had to get this guy and I had to get him now.

The one problem interfering with my mission was the fact that I was exhausted. Granted I'd had a little over an hour of rich and glorious sleep but it wasn't enough. I could already feel exhaustion seeping into my bones, making my response times slower, my brain power slower...me slower.

And a slow response time wouldn't help me—not when Sam only had a week left to live. That meant I had to hunt this asshole down and kill him before he killed her. And the kicker of the whole equation was that I wasn't going to be able to defeat a *Dreamstalker* if I were a sleep zombie. I had to be alert and level headed.

Luckily for me, there was a solution to my problem. Unluckily for me, that solution happened to be *Gargoyle's Mandrake* potion—a narcotic that had gained extreme popularity with college kids due to the fact that it meant a human or Netherworld creature could live for weeks on end without sleeping. And the user wouldn't suffer any of the fatigue of not sleeping—they operated as if on a high—energetic and vibrant. The appeal to the college students was pretty obvious—more partying and more time for studying. What users hadn't counted on, though, was the fact that *Gargoyle's Mandrake* was incredibly addictive and those with weak temperaments could end up addicted to it forever. I'd seen kids in homes who were going through withdrawals and it hadn't been pretty—some of them never fully recovered. Needless-to-say, *Gargoyle's Mandrake* was illegal. The ANC had seen to that over two years ago.

Yes, I'd refuted the idea as soon as it had birthed itself in my head—yes, I'd searched for every other possibility and no, I hadn't found one. Much though I hated the very idea, what it came down to was the fact that Sam's life was at stake. And in cases of life and death, we did things we otherwise wouldn't, things we'd otherwise detest.

I had come to terms with the fact that I was going to inhale *Gargoyle's Mandrake* as soon as I could get my hands on some. Was I afraid that I'd succumb the way others had? No. I would take it for a few days at the most and then I'd lock myself away and deal with the withdrawals, if I even experienced any. I didn't possess an addictive personality so I wasn't one of those people who would be in the exceptional risk category. I'd do what I had to do and then I'd be done with it. And Sam, Jenny, Travis and Shirley would all be the better for it. End of story.

Now that my mind was made up, I had to figure out where to procure the illegal narcotic. There were times in my life when I realized just how helpful it was to have a hand in the ANC and this was one of those times. As a Regulator, I'd had to run investigations into the various dealers in our district and although

I'd been out of practice for a while now, I knew where to go and who to ask for more information...Bram.

As I mentioned before, Bram wasn't quite one of the bad guys but he definitely wasn't one of the good guys—he dwelt somewhere in the nether regions in between. But, one thing he'd always been good for were useful leads...he'd scratch my back and I'd scratch his. And now I definitely had a big itch that had to be scratched—I needed Bram to tell me where I could find Quillan.

#

No Regrets was always packed. It was a night club, bar none—if you wanted to see and be seen, you went to No Regrets. And luckily for Bram, he owned it.

I pulled into the lot and found a small space just beside the front door where I left the Suzuki. I took off my helmet and wedged it beneath my arm as I started for the door, waving to Nick, the bouncer who also happened to be an ogre. He waved back and gave me the go ahead to bypass everyone else in line. It was good to have friends in high places and even better to have friends who owned those high places.

Once inside, it took my eyes a second to adjust to the darkness of the club, a periodic strobe light highlighting the patrons. The sounds of Timbaland's "The Way I Are" pounded through my ears and I actually felt myself relaxing. I mean, who didn't love that song?

I pushed through a throng of dancers, my fairy ability of creature detection like a Jack Russell in a room full of rats. Weres, vamps and demons partied alongside humans which was an absolute recipe for disaster; but one thing I could say for Bram, he didn't tolerate fights. When I'd worked the ANC, I'd never had any issues with No Regrets.

I wound my way through the crowd, searching for Bram's tall person but not finding him, I plopped my helmet on the bar and waved to Angela. Seeing her didn't hit me the way I thought it might. No, now that I knew Knight wasn't truly interested in her, I actually felt sorry for her more than anything else. Of course, Angela was a strong woman so she probably knew what was up, especially if Knight had spelled it out for her as clearly as he claimed he had.

"Dulcie! What can I do for you?" she asked with a wide smile. Her hair was purple tonight and with her black bra and tight black leather miniskirt, she looked like a Goth princess.

"Hi Angela," I started and glanced around for Bram again. "Do you know where Bram is?"

Angela nodded. "He's in the back." She seemed somehow nervous and eyed the growing crowd at her bar warily before turning to the back of the club again. "I'll just go let him know you're here."

I got her gist.

I held up my hand dismissively and started toward the rear of No Regrets. "Don't worry about it, Angela. If he's with a woman, I really don't care."

She laughed and it was a laugh that said she appreciated the fact that I was a woman who wouldn't be played. I hoped I could say the same for her.

"He'll care though," she said and stepped around the bar, offering me a knowing smile. "You know how he is where you're concerned."

I just shook my head and allowed her to warn Bram that I was about to interrupt whatever the hell he'd been doing. I leaned against the bar and felt myself swaying to Kesha's "Tik Tok." Well, one thing I could say for Bram was he had awesome taste in music.

"Holy shit."

I glanced up at a were who was regarding me with hunger in his eyes. He was maybe six feet tall and thick across the chest and thighs, like most weres were. His hair was long and on the scruffy side and it looked as if he hadn't shaved in a few days. He was okay looking, I guessed, but definitely not my type...a little too unkempt.

"Where the hell have you been all my life?" he demanded, eating me up with his eyes from head to toe.

I didn't bother responding, since I wanted nothing to do with the dumbass. Guys like him were the ones that gave men a bad name—just jerks who thought they could walk up to any woman and she'd drop her panties without so much as a hello.

I glanced behind me, wondering what the hell was taking Bram so long. There wasn't any motion in the hallway so I turned back around to find the were had been joined by his buddy, another were.

"Look what I found," Were One said to Were Two and pointed at me like he'd just located his missing backpack.

Were One took a step closer to me and I gave him an icy stare, daring him to come any closer. "Back off," I hissed.

"She's got attitude," Were Two said in disgust but Were One smiled, apparently taking my less than thrilled greeting as a challenge. He took another step closer to me.

"I like to train 'em," he said and snickered at me. "Teach her who's boss." He reached out and grazed the side of my face with his finger. There was dirt underneath his fingernail.

I was fast—faster than I thought I would have been considering I was operating on an hour and half of sleep. Before the bastard could say "uncle", I had his arm behind his back...painfully.

"You ask me before you touch me, got it?" I seethed.

Were Two started laughing while Were One whined for me to release him. He was all bark and no bite.

"You boys causing problems?" Angela asked from behind me. "You chose the wrong chick to mess with, I'll tell you that much."

I released Were One and he backed away as if I'd turned into a ghoul and tried to bite him. Were Two was still laughing and harassed his friend as they strode back into the crowd of dancers. I watched them disappear into the throbbing multitude before turning to Angela with a sigh.

"It's early and I'm already off to a bad start," I said, shaking my head.

"They deserved it and then some," Angela laughed. "Bastards." She glanced out into the crowd, as if searching for a sign of them but they'd been swallowed by the sea of people.

She faced me again. "Bram is ready for you."

"Thanks," I said and grabbed my helmet, starting for the short corridor that led to Bram's office.

The door was closed even though Bram knew I was coming. He was such a sucker for pretense. I knocked on the door and there was no answer so I knocked again, irritated that I had to play his game.

"Enter."

His voice came from the other side of the door and with a shake of my head, I opened the door and took a few steps into the plush carpet of his office. There was even less light in Bram's office and I had to make out the outline of the door behind me in order to close it. Inside, the music was muted and the smell of burning incense was thick in the air. I dropped my helmet into a nearby chair, my eyes still growing accustomed to the low light.

"Hi, Bram," I said, once I noticed him sitting behind a desk, outlined by the glow of a candle just behind him. The desk was a new addition to his office but the black lacquer fit perfectly against the red, white and black motif of his office.

He glanced up as if he hadn't expected me, as if he'd been poring over the papers in his hand, without any clue that he had a visitor. His fangs immediately descended as soon as he glanced at me, the papers falling from his hand, scattering across his desk.

"Are you okay?" I asked, wondering what the hell had gotten into him.

He shook his head in what appeared to be bewilderment and stood up. He took the five steps separating us and stretched a long, slender finger toward me, running it down the leather of my bike jacket, just above my left breast. I was reminded of what had happened the last time a man had touched me without asking permission but figured Bram wouldn't take it well if I attacked him...or maybe he would. Either way, I wasn't going to try it, not while I needed a favor.

He opened his mouth and inhaled, like a cat smelling the air. When his eyes found mine again, there was something in their depths—something I couldn't put my finger on. Ever since Bram had turned three hundred, I wasn't quite sure what to expect from him, it was as if his power had increased twofold, and his aura emanated it. And it wasn't something I liked. An unpredictable vampire was not an easily managed vampire.

"You exist merely to plague me." His voice was rough, like diamonds cutting glass.

"What the hell are you talking about?" I demanded. I didn't have the time nor the energy for this crap. I had to get in and get out—find out where Quillan was and move on. The night might have been young but Sam's battle wasn't.

"You...your outfit," he started, giving me the once over again. "You try my will power not to take you right where you stand."

I glanced down at myself, taking in the black leather riding pants and boots I'd magicked for myself. I was wearing a tight black turtleneck underneath the black leather jacket. My outfit was utilitarian—meant to protect from road rash, should I take a fall off the bike. Granted my pants were snug but Bram's reaction was a bit much.

"Keep your distance, Bram," I muttered and seated myself in one of his chairs. My hair had caught in the neck of my jacket so I pulled it free and allowed it to cascade around me in a flow of gold. Hmm, I was having a good hair night—maybe that was why Bram's panties were all in a bunch.

Bram leaned over me, resting his hands on either chair arm, still staring at me as if I were a walking, talking vat of blood.

"The beauty of you, Dulcie Sweet, is that you have no notion, no knowledge of what you do to me. If you were any other woman, I would have had you by now...repeatedly."

"Humble much?" I asked with a frown. I wanted to take my jacket off because it was hot in Bram's club, but after that little display, I doubted if it would be a wise decision.

He laughed and as if to continue his completely bizarre actions, dropped to one knee before me, wedging himself between my legs. I immediately sat up straight, on complete alert, and reached into my waistband, fingering the Op 6...just in case. I watched Bram grasp my wrist and I was suddenly aware of how much larger he was than I was. My small wrist was nearly swallowed by his hand. He pushed the leather sleeve up, bringing my wrist to his face.

"If you bite me, I'll kill you," I whispered and I meant it. I'd never been bitten by a vampire and I'd sworn I never would be. Playing dinner entree was not my idea of a good time.

"I want to bite you, Sweet." His voice was low and his fangs tickled the sensitive skin of my wrist as he ran them back and forth.

As if death was of no consequence to him, he closed his eyes and inhaled just above the area where my veins were closest to the surface. I closed my fingers over the Op 6, wondering if I'd need to pull it free. I really didn't want to shoot Bram...

He opened his eyes and focused them on me. "One day, my Sweet, you will beg me to bite you. And I will bite you and swallow your blood as I push into you and listen to you cry out in pleasure."

I laughed. I couldn't help it. "Okay, Barbara Cartland, can we stop the sex talk and, instead, talk about why I'm here please?"

He dropped my wrist but didn't move out from between my thighs and I'm not sure why, but I allowed him to stay there. Maybe because I knew I was asking for information I shouldn't have been.

"Please enlighten me," he said although his tone was anything but interested.

I sighed, long and hard. It brought his attention to my face and when he realized I was less than thrilled with what was about to come out of my mouth, he was rapt, his attention mine.

"I need to know where I can find Quillan," I said in a small voice.

Bram narrowed his eyes and stared at me for a long time. I stared back. He leaned into me until we were nose to nose.

"Are you asking this as a Regulator?"

I was asking for my own personal reasons, because I had to get my hands on some *Gargoyle's Mandrake*. But, Bram didn't need to know that. I swallowed. "No."

He licked his top lip and smiled. I swallowed harder. "It would not look good for me to be offering location tips about those involved in street potions to a Regulator."

I leaned closer to him and turned my head as I whispered in his ear. "I'm no longer a Regulator and I would never do anything to damage our...relationship. You can trust me, Bram."

His hands found my upper thighs and he squeezed them suggestively. "*Can* I trust you, Sweet?"

"You once said my word was good," I started and grabbed his hands before he got any other ideas.

He pulled away and stood up, a deep chuckle echoing through him. When he faced me again, his eyes were wild. "It does bother me, Dulcie."

"What does?"

"The fact that I covet you so. You pose a challenge, yes, but on the flip side, this constant hungering for you takes its toll. Sometimes I do wonder if it would be better if you did not exist."

"Are you threatening me?" I demanded, wondering if Bram was going to join my throng of enemies. I sincerely hoped he wouldn't. Granted, I liked the fact that he was a bridge to the less than noble members of Splendor but beyond that, I actually did like Bram. He was....amusing.

He laughed again. "Me? No." He shook his head. "I would never harm you but your death by another's hand, hmm....I do not know what I should think of it. Perhaps it would be a bit of a relief."

I stood up and frowned, figuring this errand had been a waste of time. It appeared Bram wasn't in a forthcoming mood. I had to wonder if I'd interrupted his dinner. "Thanks for the vote of confidence."

He walked to his desk and sat down, as if needing to put a buffer between us. I started for the door and just as I grasped the doorknob, his voice stopped me.

"Why do you seek Quillan?"

I didn't turn around right away. "I need to ask him a question," I said finally.

He nodded and rocked back and forth. "I imagine it was quite a blow to learn your partner was deceiving you all these years?"

I didn't release the doorknob but turned to regard him, ignoring the pain that coursed through me at the mention of Quillan's deceit. "Yes, it was."

"Some people thought perhaps you were in on the operation all along." He didn't stop rocking.

I dropped my hold on the doorknob and faced him fully. "And what do you think, Bram? Do you think I was in on it?"

He shrugged. "I do not care."

"Then why bring it up?"

He stopped rocking and stood up, taking a few steps closer to me. "You were going to leave and I wanted to prohibit you."

I shook my head. "Bram, I really don't have time to play games with you. People's lives depend on you giving me the information I need."

"I thought you said this was not involving the ANC?"

I gulped. "It's not."

He materialized directly in front of me, so close I could feel the cold steel of his belt buckle against my stomach. I couldn't help my gasp. I took a step back until the door pre-empted me from further escape. My heartbeat was pounding. "I hate it when you do that," I whispered.

He grabbed my jacket and slid it off my shoulders.

"What are you doing?" I insisted, growing more and more unnerved.

He smiled down at me and it was the smile of a shark. "There is too much heat radiating off you, Sweet. You must be suffocating under all that leather."

I had been. Between the anxiety pounding through me and the temperature in Bram's office, the heat had been squelching. He pulled the jacket off me and carefully laid it on the chair. I glanced down at myself and realized the material of my turtleneck was slightly see-through. I could see the outline of my black bra. I glanced up at Bram and found his gaze fastened on my breasts.

"I'm up here," I snorted.

He didn't look up from my breasts. "I do appreciate a woman with an ample bust line."

"Are you going to help me or aren't you?"

"Help can come in many forms, Sweet," he said, finally returning his eyes to mine.

"Tell me where I can find Quillan."

"Why must you speak with Quillan, Sweet?"

"It's personal."

Bram regarded me curiously. "Tell me, Dulcie, has Quillan ever sampled your body? Does he know what your face looks like when in complete bliss?"

I pushed away from him. I'd been hanging on his every word, hoping he was going to help me, hoping this little act would be short lived. Apparently I'd been stupid. "Holy Hades, Bram, what the hell is wrong with you? Do you need to feed or what?"

"Answer the question," he ordered. "Does Quillan know what it means to taste you?"

I counted to three in my head. No, I didn't have time to play cat and mouse games but it was easier to attract flies with honey than vinegar and in this case, it was easier to get Bram to give me the information I wanted if I played his sex games.

"No, he doesn't."

Bram grinned, his fangs cresting his lower lip. "But you were attracted to him, no?"

I gulped down an acid response. "Yes."

"And have you imagined what it would feel like to take him into your body?"

I forced myself to hold his gaze, and not to look away. "Yes."

He chuckled without mirth. "I do enjoy playing with you, Dulcie. Your one flaw is your inability to tell anything other than the truth."

"Those are your words, not mine."

"Tell me, have you imagined what my lips would feel like against your skin? Have you imagined making love to me, Dulcie?"

It was my turn to laugh. "Game's up, Bram. You've exhausted your interrogation for the night. Now it's my turn."

He sighed and backed away from me, returning to his desk. "I have heard your Quillan has been spending time with a...rough crowd. I would not advise you to seek him out alone."

"So, what, you'd be willing to go with me?"

He was quiet for a moment before nodding. "I would."

"Thanks but you'd spoil my cover."

"It is too dangerous for you to go alone," Bram said, his former playfulness now absent from his voice.

"Weren't you just saying you wanted me dead?"

He shook his head. "You always turn my words against me, Sweet."

"Where can I find Quillan, Bram?" I demanded.

"Sanctity. The Devil's Harlot."

"What the hell is that?"

Bram smiled and revealed the fact that his canines were still in full effect. "A strip club, Sweet."

I shook my head. "Figures."

"You will be taking your life into your hands," Bram continued. "There are wards reinforcing the building. You will not be able to use magic to change your appearance and I daresay most there would recognize you as an ANC Regulator."

I nodded; I'd figured such would be the case. I picked up my long blond locks and sighed as I thought of dying them. "Guess I'll have to change my appearance the old fashioned way then."

"I would still escort you. Perhaps my being there would attract attention away from you."

"If anything, you'd attract more attention. I can do this alone." I paused for a second or two as I thought of riding the Suzuki clad only in some slutty getup. "But, I could use a lift."

Bram threw his head back and laughed heartily. "Of course you could, Sweet, of course."

"Is that a yes?" I asked, feeling exhaustion in the very depths of my soul.

"Yes, I will gladly drive you." He eyed me for a few seconds, a smile still gracing his handsome face. "When we arrive, do not enter through the front door. If you walk around to the back of the establishment, you will see a small door off to the side. Knock twice and when the bouncer opens it, tell him you are there as a gift for Quillan. Tell him I sent you."

I eyed him for a second or two while I tried to make sense of the statement. "So, I'm going as a whore then?"

Bram smiled and his eyes twinkled. "When you play with the big boys, you must play big boy games, Dulcie Sweet."

"Wonderful," I grumbled. "Anything else?"

"It is the only way you will make it into the club. And do be careful not to blow your cover; I do not want this to come back and bite me in the ass."

"I'll do my best." I turned the doorknob and opened the door before glancing back at him. "Can you pick me up in about two hours?"

He steepled his fingers and regarded me with amusement. "I will be there with bells on."

Then I walked out and closed the door behind me.

EIGHT

After leaving Bram's, I visited the local drug store and purchased several boxes of hair dye and the wildest makeup I could get my hands on. It had been painful but I dyed my naturally honey golden hair licorice black. I dyed it three times before the color actually took and didn't look purple. I also cut off four inches and curled it into tight sausage curls until I looked like a dark-haired version of *Sideshow Bob.*

As to my makeup...sigh. I definitely looked like a skank with my bright red lips, caked on liquid foundation and lively pink blush. I loaded my eyes with glitter, black eyeliner, silver eye shadow and more glitter. Then, just for the hell of it, I gave myself a mole above my lip with my brown eyeliner pencil. I glanced at the mirror and didn't know what to think. I was definitely not me but was it enough to throw everyone else off? My springy hair pretty much obscured my face so hopefully that would be enough.

I raided my closet until I located the shortest skirt I owned but it wasn't short enough so I attacked it with scissors until it just kissed my upper thighs. Remembering Angela's getup from No Regrets, I decided to stick with a black bra. Unfortunately, there was no room for my Op 6 but knowing the scumbags I'd soon be interacting with, they'd search me anyway. And finding a weapon would definitely blow my cover.

A knock on the door heralded Bram's arrival and Blue's barking eclipsed the otherwise quiet evening.

"Shhh, Blue, be quiet!" I yelled as I pushed my feet into my knee-high black boots and gave myself another once over before I headed for the door. I grabbed the dog's collar and pulled open the door, excited to see Bram's reaction to the new me.

He didn't say anything but stared at me for a few seconds. And during those few seconds, Blue growled and barked at him as if daring Bram to enter his house.

"Well?" I demanded, wondering if his silence was good or bad.

Bram brought his hand to his mouth and tapped his fingers against his plump lips while he continued to ponder me as if I defied earthly laws. "You are you but you are not you," he said finally.

"Astute," I retorted, suddenly realizing I was quoting Knight. Speaking of the devil, I had to make this little errand quick because I was due at the hospital in a few hours to play victim-sitter to Jenny and Sam.

"I do not know what to make of your appearance, Sweet." Bram reached out and grasped a tendril of my hair, rubbing it between his fingers and Blue lunged for him, nearly yanking my arms out of their sockets. I finally settled the dog down and brought my attention back to Bram who regarded the dog dismissively before returning his attention to me. "I do miss your golden locks."

"Who cares about my hair, Bram?" I started. "Is my getup good enough?" I suddenly felt like a sheep with a cheap lion costume who was about to enter the lion's den. "Would you know I was me?"

Bram stepped inside and I closed the door behind him, struggling to drag Blue to the backyard, where I forced him to stay. When I returned, Bram grabbed my arm, and rotated me like a ballerina. "Perhaps I am the wrong person to ask since I have every line of your face, every angle of your body permanently etched in my memory."

I shook my head. Bram was getting good but I wasn't that impressed. I'd bet if I closed my eyes and asked him what color they were, he wouldn't have a clue. "What are you, a poet now?" I asked facetiously.

"I do not know that your disguise is strong enough, Dulcie," he said warily, apparently ignoring my slight. "And if it is not, I will be sending you to your death."

"Which would be a relief to you," I finished for him with a smile and pushed him toward the front door. He cleared his throat, apparently not appreciating being pushed around and stepped onto the concrete path outside. I pulled the door closed behind me and started for his black Porsche Carrera.

"I should never have mentioned those words to you, Sweet. I do take them back," he said and opened the passenger door for me. I seated myself, noticing my skirt was doing a very poor job of covering my thighs fully so I parked my hands in my lap.

"You can't take them back," I said and watched him walk to the drivers' side. Bram was a big guy and the Porsche seemed entirely too small for him.

He slipped into his seat, closed the door and turned the car on; the Carrera literally purred. I'd never been in a Porsche before and was lapping it up. I didn't consider myself a car person (other than my love for the Wrangler) but I couldn't help but respect the beautiful machine I was sitting in.

"Nice wheels," I said appreciatively, glancing around the plush, black leather interior and shiny dashboard.

"Thank you, Sweet."

It took us thirty minutes to reach Sanctity and Bram was surprisingly and uncharacteristically quiet the entire way. When we pulled into a shabby looking parking lot, complete with weeds sprouting up through the broken concrete, he guided the Carrera into a spot as far as was possible from the decrepit building standing in the middle of the lot. He turned the car off and faced me.

"Do you recall what I told you?" he asked.

I nodded, feeling like a little girl on her first day of school. Course, in my case, this was stripper school. "Yeah, go to the back entrance and tell Bubba the Bouncer that I'm a gift for Quill from you." Bram laughed at "Bubba the Bouncer."

"Anything else?" I finished.

He eyed me as if still trying to decide whether I could pull off my stunt and dupe a room full of thugs who would probably kill me if they knew who I truly was.

"I will give you thirty minutes. If you are not out before then, I will come in for you."

"Bram, do you really think you could take on a room full of Netherworld creatures?"

He was strong but not that strong.

"My three hundred years have increased my stamina and strength, Sweet. Do not argue with me. Thirty minutes."

I reached for the door handle, suddenly remembering my house keys in my lap. I handed them to Bram. "Keep these in a safe place, will you?"

He nodded and I could feel his eyes on me as I closed the car door and approached the back end of the building. Nerves short-circuited through me, making my heart pound so fast I was afraid it might stop. I took a deep, steadying breath and told myself I'd be fine, that I'd get through this and in thirty minutes, Bram and I would be en route to my apartment, easy peasy.

If I'd thought the parking lot looked like it had seen better days, the building was in even worse repair. It was a one story hovel of a place that looked as if one good breath of wind would knock it to Kingdom Come. The click of my heels against the pavement was the only sound in the dark night and I forced myself to the rear of the shack, searching for the door.

I found it hidden behind an overgrown bush and pushed the branches aside, knocking twice. There was no answer. Thinking maybe I should knock again, I held my hand up at the same moment as the door opened a fraction of an inch and I could just make out the crooked nose and yellow teeth of the man I presumed to be the bouncer.

"I'm here as a gift for Quillan, from Bram," I said, my voice two octaves higher than it normally was. And it wasn't from nerves—I'd planned that one. "Is Quillan here?"

"Gift from Bram, you said?" the man repeated and I could feel his gaze as it followed my body from chest to toe. "Gimme a minute."

He should have asked for five minutes because that's how long his absence felt. Finally he returned and opened the door. He was a huge guy—over six feet two and...as wide as he was tall. He was maybe in his late thirties and had the look of someone who had worked the boat docks for too long. I didn't recognize him which was a good thing. I stepped inside and gasped when he pushed me against the wall.

"Gotta check ya for weapons," he grunted and the smile on his face said he'd enjoy it.

I clenched my teeth but didn't say anything, just held my hands up as he copped a feel left and right. After he patted me down once, his hands returned to my bust and I pushed him away. "No weapons there, asshole," I whispered, hoping he'd think I was just a call girl with attitude.

He snickered. "I gotta tell Bram ta send me a gift. He picks the good ones."

I arched a brow to show I wasn't pleased and waited for him to lead me to Quillan. He looked me up and down again and then started down the dank hallway. I followed him, the smell of mildew thick in my nose. There was a door at the end of the hallway and he pulled out a set of keys. As soon as he unlocked and opened the door, the raucous sound of laughter and Finger Eleven's "Paralyzer" was thick in my ears. The acrid scent of cigarette smoke billowed into the hallway like nicotine ghosts and was enough to gag me. Bubba ushered me into the room and I felt my heart drop at the sound of the key in the doorknob behind me, locking us in.

I glanced up and noticed four girls on an impromptu dance floor, each one gyrating around a pole connecting the floor to the ceiling. They were humans and only had on shoes. I tried to remember not to appear prudish and pumped my hair, trying to appear like any other call girl concerned with her appearance. The truth of the matter was that I wanted to hide my face as best I could—there were men, (well, vamps and demons mostly) in the room, sitting in booths in the far corners. Luckily for me, it was dark enough that they couldn't see me and I couldn't see them. That suited me just fine.

"Follow me," Bubba grunted and I was quick behind him. He led me through the strippers and I could feel the hungry eyes of the males in the room—I was fresh meat and to some of them, that was probably exactly what I was—a new tasty morsel.

Bubba stopped before another door and knocked. The door opened and he and whoever was on the other side had an exchange I couldn't make out. Not that it really mattered—I imagined Bubba was explaining that I was the gift Quillan was waiting for. Quillan...just the idea that I was going to see him again was settling in my stomach like a hive full of bees. I was excited, yes and I'd missed him so much but at the same time, he was leading a life now that was so foreign. The fact that he was even in a dump like this was an eye opener. He didn't belong here—he wasn't this caliber of person.

The doorman stepped aside and allowed us both entrance. Inside, the room was nicer than the stripper room. There were a few weres playing cards and others sat around the perimeter of the room with women on their laps. I glanced around for Quillan but couldn't find him. I did, however, recognize many faces and dropped my own, worried they might recognize me.

"He's up here," Bubba announced and started up a ramp into a section of the room that sat higher than the rest of it. It was completely dark aside from the glow of a few candles. A large round table dominated the area and there were four people seated around it. From the looks of it, they were playing Poker... I glanced at a bra looped over one of the chairs...hmm, Strip Poker.

"For you," Bubba announced and gave me a firm shove forward.

I glanced down at the figure of a man seated at the table. He leaned against his elbow languidly and looked up at us indifferently.

Quillan.

"All of you out," Quillan said and everyone around the table scattered. Bubba was quick behind them.

Quillan glanced at me and smiled warmly. "So, why would Bram send me a gift when I have no relationship with him?"

I couldn't respond right away. I was still in shock to find Quillan hanging out in this craphole, surrounded by naked women. I wasn't sure if it was jealousy that was reverberating through me but whatever the feeling, I didn't like it.

"Don't you speak?" he demanded and reminded me of the fact that he'd said his first statement a little too loudly. A new feeling of angst pounded through me. The last thing I needed was a roomful of thugs wondering who the hell I was.

I approached his chair and dropped to my knees, hoping he'd recognize me, hoping I wouldn't have to say anything. He continued staring at me like I was dumb. Dammit, he wasn't getting it. I pulled my hair back and put my face right up into his, pretending like I was going to kiss him. He didn't pull away, so I turned my face until my mouth was right beside his ear, my breasts up close and personal with his face.

"It's me, Dulcie," I whispered.

He grabbed my arms and pushed me away from him, as if he thought I was lying and wanted to get a better look. When he did, realization dawned in his eyes. "Ah, Bram sent me a good one," he said, apparently now on to my ruse. "I wonder if you taste as good as you look?"

Before I knew it, his lips were on mine, demanding and hungry. I closed my eyes, I couldn't help it. I'd imagined kissing Quillan so many times and once a long time ago, we actually had. Now the feel of his lips brought that memory pouring back into me—how much I once cared about Quillan, how he'd been one of my closest friends, how he'd betrayed me...

I pulled away and he stood up, grabbing my hand. He started down the ramp and drew me close behind him. We reached the entryway again and Quillan yanked aside a curtain to his left that had been obscuring another door. He glanced at the doorman and the doorman unlocked it.

"I don't want to be disturbed," Quillan warned him. I had to wonder how high Quillan ranked in the underground hierarchy. Based on the way people treated him here, it seemed pretty high.

The doorman glanced at me and nodded, saying nothing. Quillan turned to face me and held the door wide. "After you."

I entered the room and was suddenly aware of the fact that Quillan truly was one of the bad guys. If I hadn't thought it before, I definitely thought it now. He was up to his neck in a lifestyle that was so alien from mine, and so completely foreign from what his used to be. Maybe I wasn't welcome here—maybe he'd turn me over to the dogs of this establishment and was just biding his time? Maybe it had been incredibly stupid of me to come, trusting that he still cared for me.

"Dulcie, what the hell were you thinking coming here?" he demanded once he'd locked the door behind him. He flipped on the light which bathed him and the room in an eerie red. It was the first chance I'd had to really get a good look at him. He seemed somehow broader, stronger. His face was the same old Quillan I knew so well—clean shaven, angular and universally handsome.

I glanced around, wondering if it was safe to talk, wondering if people on the other side of the door could hear us. Would they even be listening? I felt unbelievably uncomfortable but based on the fact that Quillan was acting as if everything was okay, I calmed down.

"I didn't have anyone else to come to," I started. "I'm in trouble."

He was beside me momentarily, engulfing me in his big arms. His scent was thick in my nostrils—Tommy Bahama aftershave I'd missed so much. I rested my head against his chest and wrapped my arms around him, I couldn't help it.

"What's wrong?" he insisted and I was suddenly overcome by the fact that I wasn't angry with him anymore. The last time I'd seen him, when I'd attempted to apprehend him, I'd been hurt and furiously angry. I'd had to talk myself out of shooting him. And now? Now I only felt empty.

"There's too much to tell you now, Quill."

He smiled at the old nickname and pulled away from me, glancing down at me. "I thought maybe you'd come to take me into custody." But, by the sound of his voice, I knew he was kidding.

"No, I'm here to break the law," I said and shook my head at the absurdity of the whole thing. "I can't talk long, Bram is waiting for me in the parking lot and he said if I didn't come out in thirty minutes, he'd come in. If I had to guess, I probably have twenty minutes left."

"How can I help you, Dulce?" he whispered before running his hand through my hair. "What did you do to yourself?"

"I could hardly come waltzing in here without some sort of getup, could I?"

He laughed. "No, hardly." He was quiet again as he pushed a lock of hair behind my ear as tenderly as a lover. "You look just as beautiful as I remember," he said and the tone of his voice matched the same sense of sorrow that was coursing through me. He knew as well as I did that things would never be the same between us. Maybe in another life, another time, we could have been something great together. But, not now.

"I've missed you," he continued.

I couldn't bring myself to admit that I'd missed him too. There was just so far my hurt ego would reach. And I wouldn't let it go there. I stepped away from him and focused on the reason I was here. "There's a *Dreamstalker* after me, Quill, and it nearly took me down a few nights ago. I'm lucky to be alive."

He leaned against the wall and folded his arms across his chest and in the red light coming from the corner of the room, I could see shock and anger in his gaze. He looked like he was going to say something but I beat him to it.

"I need *Gargoyle's Mandrake* and I need enough to last me the rest of this week." I was quiet after the words left my mouth, allowing them to sink in. He said nothing and the silence of the room was deafening. "Can you get it for me?"

"Yes, easily," he said but his voice was troubled.

I dropped my gaze from his, feeling suddenly guilty that I was asking for an illegal narcotic—me, a previous Regulator. I couldn't even allow myself to consider what Knight would think. Instead, I pushed the thoughts out of my mind and tried to make small talk. "It seems like you're pretty high up on the totem pole?" I asked. "How are you even hanging out with these guys, Quill? This isn't you."

He faced me angrily. "Yes, I'm at the top of the totem pole but I hope you didn't come to lecture me."

I approached him and grabbed his hand. "I didn't mean to offend you. I just...just hate seeing you like this. You don't belong here."

He pulled his hand away and ran it through his wavy blond hair. "This is my life now, Dulce. You can't save me. This is who I am and I'm okay with it."

I sighed, hating the words even as he said them. But, this wasn't my fight—he was what he was and someday we'd butt heads in a major way—of that I was sure. But that day wasn't now. Now I needed his help. Maybe someday he'd come to me and I could offer the same.

"So, you can get it for me?" I demanded.

He didn't say anything right away and I wondered if this trip had been a huge waste of my time. After another few seconds, he nodded and a huge sigh of relief traveled through me.

"You know how addictive it is?"

"I don't care," I answered, dropping my attention to the stained carpet beneath my feet. "I've wracked my mind, Quill, I've tried to find any other solution but I can't. It's come down to life and death. I can't fall asleep or the *Dreamstalker* will kill me." I paused for a moment, not sure how to tell him there was more and that it was terrible. "Quill, Sam's in a coma."

He brought his gaze from his shoes to my face and there was worry and pain in his eyes. "How long?"

"She has maybe a week left," I didn't even recognize my voice—it was so full of pain. If Sam died...no, I would not allow myself to consider the thought. Quill shook his head but I didn't let him comment. "I want to know all the details of the time you apprehended Druiva. I need to know what I'm up against. And I need the *Mandrake*."

"It's not the same case."

"Well, obviously. Druiva is locked up," I started, but he interrupted me.

"There's a new form of criminal out there, Dulce."

I narrowed my eyes. "What do you mean?"

He sighed, deep and hard. "There's blood being sold on the black market. Blood taken from Netherworld creatures and sold to other creatures so they can become that much stronger."

I felt my heart actually stop. My mouth dropped open and I thought I might throw up. This was bad, very bad. But, suddenly it all made sense—the fact that Dia hadn't been able to feel the dark power of a *somnogobelinus* going through the *Transcendence*, the fact that my magic had worked the night of the accident. The scary part was now I had no clue what I was up against. What I was sure of, though, was the fact that whatever it was, it wasn't a true *Dreamstalker*, it was just ingesting the blood of one.

Then something ugly dawned on me and I brought my gaze to his. "Are you dealing this blood, Quill? Is that how you know about it?"

"No, of course not," he answered like I should never have asked. "I know about it because I've seen it—I've seen creatures here who demonstrated powers they never should have. I kept my ears and eyes open—I have to in my position."

I nodded, but my heart was low in my chest as I realized how deeply imbued he was in this lifestyle. He grabbed my hand and squeezed it.

"Dulcie, please be careful," he said and his compassion was enough to paralyze me. It was the same comment he'd made so many times when we'd worked side by side at the ANC.

"Please don't say that," I said, pulling my hand away as I felt my voice crack. "This is hard enough as it is."

If I was worried he hadn't gotten my gist, by the slight nod and small smile on his face, I realized he understood it and not only that, was thinking and feeling the same things I was.

"Is it true you're off the force?" he asked, apparently supposing a new change of subject was in order. He walked to the far end of the room and leaned down, opening a cupboard door. By the way he was turning his hand, I had to imagine he was unlocking a safe.

I took a second to answer. "Yeah, I retired."

He glanced back and me and frowned. "You were the best Regulator the ANC had, why would you do that?"

I wasn't sure how he'd take the truth. But, it wasn't like I was about to lie to him. "I failed, Quill. I should have taken you into custody that night but I didn't. I allowed my personal feelings to get in the way and I failed in my responsibility. I'm not the Regulator you thought I was...or I thought I was."

He stood up, gripping a small vial in one fist and a plastic bag in another. He was visibly angry. "That's a load of bullshit. You were the best and you still are the best."

I shook my head but he didn't allow me to speak. Instead, he approached me and grabbed my hand, pushing the vial into my palm.

"And as to your personal feelings for me, I appreciate you allowing them to get in the way."

Then before I could even realize what he was doing, his lips were on mine again, rough and demanding. The one kiss Quill and I had shared way back when had been sweet and this one was nothing like that, it was hot, and hard, almost angry. It was a side of Quillan I'd never seen before. I closed my eyes and reveled in the taste of him, the feel of him but realizing where we were and what had happened, I pulled away. There was a gap between us that would never be resolved. I was fire and he was water.

"This can't happen between us," I whispered and took a few steps away. "I would hate myself."

"I was afraid you'd say that." He handed me the plastic bag and his body language was all business, as if he'd shelved the emotional stuff and moved on.

"Quill," I started and wasn't really sure what to say.

He shook his head and it was clear he didn't want to talk about it. He pointed to the plastic bag. "Those will cancel the effects of the *Mandrake* and they'll make your withdrawals that much easier to combat." He paused a second or two. "I've given you enough *Mandrake* to last all week but if you stay on it that long, there's no telling how hard it will be to come down. I really should have given you only a three day supply."

"Quill, I'm a big girl, I think I know how to say no."

He nodded but it was unconvincing. "Don't ever let it out that I gave you those and don't let anyone know you came here. It's bad enough Bram knows." He was quiet for a minute and then faced me with pain in his expression. "Are you and Bram..."

"No," I interrupted. "I needed a ride. My car was totaled." I didn't have the heart to add that I hadn't wanted to drive my motorcycle dressed like a tart.

He seemed to be relieved, not that it mattered since he and I would never be anything, could never be anything.

"Can you give me any pointers on how to nab this guy, Quill?" I asked, realizing time was of the essence and I'd have to make my getaway soon.

Quill seemed lost in thought. "It's been quite a while now since I put Druiva away."

I swallowed hard. There was really only one answer I needed regarding the Druiva case. "Did you capture him while you were sleeping, Quill?"

Quillan faced me aghast. "Don't even consider it. You said it nearly killed you already."

I nodded, not completely giving up on the idea yet but it wasn't something Quill needed to know. No, I'd already given him too much information as it was. If he were anyone else, I would have considered the case compromised but I trusted Quill. Maybe I was stupid.

"So, how did you catch Druiva then?" I continued.

"We tracked him, day and night. We watched over his victims and waited for him to come to us. A *Dreamstalker* can't help but come back for his victims to finish them off. It's hard-wired into them."

He'd done basically the same thing we were doing now. Dammit, that wasn't what I wanted to hear because it didn't seem to me as if our approach was doing a damn bit of good.

"How long did it take to get Druiva into custody?" I asked.

Quill shrugged. "I don't remember for certain but I'd say a few days at the most."

Hmm, so our *Dreamstalker* was playing with us and I couldn't help but think it was waiting for me to succumb to slumber so it could use its strength in the dream state to kill me.

Quillan, apparently realizing I was lost in thought, tilted my chin up and gazed down at me. "I know you're contemplating defeating it in sleep. That's asking for trouble, Dulcie." He rubbed the pad of his thumb across my cheek. "The other thing you have to remember is that if it is a creature ingesting *Dreamstalker* blood, you don't know how much it's had. The more it ingests, the more strength and power it gets. You could end up dealing with something that morphs into a *Dreamstalker*."

Hmm, maybe it wasn't such a good idea then. So, we were stuck tracking it the old fashioned way. Well, at least I had *Gargoyle's Mandrake* to keep me alert and awake. The night was looking up.

I sighed and pulled his hand away from my face. "I gotta get going, Quill, before Bram sends the search party."

Quill laughed. "The search party of one, Bram."

I smiled sadly. "I'm not sure how to say goodbye."

He grabbed me and pulled me into his open arms. "This isn't goodbye, Dulce." He kissed my head and pushed me away from him. "Don't do anything to get yourself killed, okay?"

I nodded dumbly before glancing around. "Do us both a favor and find a new hangout. I don't want to know where you are."

"I'd reached that conclusion as soon as I realized you'd found me."

I stepped out from his embrace. "Thanks, Quill."

He neared the door before seeming to remember something. He paused a moment or two and then glanced back at me. "Am I still in your book?"

I swallowed. He was referring to a time when I'd been writing a historical romance and I'd modeled the character of the pirate hero after Quillan. It had been one of the more embarrassing times of my life when he found the word document complete with his name in one of my sex scenes.

I gave a little embarrassed laugh and thought about the fact that I'd retired that book and started the series about Bram. I glanced at Quillan's hopeful expression and felt myself doing something I hadn't done in a long time...lie. "Yeah, you're still in them. I couldn't take you out."

He beamed like a little boy.

NINE

After Bram dropped me off, I hurried up my front steps, unlocked the door and ignored Blue who was pawing at the kitchen door, wanting to be let back in.

"Sorry, Boy, but you've got to stay out there until I get back. Can't have you pooping in the house," I called as I hightailed it into my room and started unzipping my boots, pulling out the *Gargoyle's Mandrake* and the comedown pills Quill had given me. I hadn't wanted Bram to know what my little errand had been about so I'd hidden the evidence in my boots.

I peeled off my skirt and wadded it into a ball, throwing it in front of the door so I'd remember to put it in the trash on my way out. Grabbing a pair of jeans from my chest of drawers, I pulled them up and over my red thong underwear and snatched a sweatshirt, yanking it over my head, not bothering with a shirt. I finished my outfit with my blue and white tennies.

Dulcie O'Neil—from tart to bum in less than sixty seconds.

I eyed the vial of *Gargoyle's Mandrake* which I'd placed on the top of my dresser and took a deep breath. Now was the time of reckoning. I'd done a lot to obtain that tiny vial of *Mandrake*—I couldn't back down now although it would take everything in my will to go through with this—to break the ANC rules I put so much stock in. Before my brain started to buck at the idea, I reminded myself that this was necessary to save Sam and Jenny.

I held the clear vial up to my nose and shook it a few times, watching the opalescent liquid within slosh against the sides of the vial. Even though the cork cap seemed easy enough to open, that wasn't the case. Looks were almost always deceiving where Netherworld potions were concerned.

I shook my palm until a mound of fairy dust emerged. Then I blew the particles at the vial, imagining each sparkling prism digging like an earthworm beneath the cork, freeing the wards which were keeping the cork clamped tight. The cork began to spin to the left, the liquid within the vial bubbling up in anticipation. I grasped the cork and pulled it off.

The liquid inside turned to a deep emerald green as soon as it met the air and bubbles began forming along the sides of the vial, popping and hissing as more joined in the fray. The effervescence continued, little green bubbles rising up from the now gelatinous green goo, making their way out of the vial. As the bubbles sailed up from the vial and into the air, they began to bend and warp this way and that, expanding in size as they did so. Their dark green hue became lighter and lighter green as they enlarged, until they were the color of sea foam.

Once there were maybe twenty of them swirling around the room, I put the cap back on the vial and opened my mouth, inhaling deeply.

The bubbles seemed to recognize their cue and floated toward me, entering my mouth as they fizzed and burst against my tongue and teeth. Once the last one had migrated into my mouth, I clamped my lips together and swallowed. The taste was like cinnamon gum.

Gargoyle's Mandrake worked quickly. I'd never taken it before but I'd dealt with enough of it to know how to take it and what to expect. After a few seconds, it started to kick in and felt like a fizzing deep down in my stomach, like I'd taken a few too many Alka-Seltzers. Little by little that bubbling feeling began to work its way into my blood stream and I could feel the tingle carrying itself into my extremities. My fingers and toes began going numb and I stretched and clenched them, trying to counteract the bizarre feeling.

The intense exhaustion which had lately become my constant companion receded into the background of my body, a blissful energy taking its place. Pretty soon the exhaustion was only a memory and my body was acting like I'd just given it high octane; energy and pleasure coursing through me. I had to remind myself that I still had the weight of the Netherworld on my shoulders and I couldn't allow myself to get caught up in this blissful euphoria. I felt young, like today was the beginning of my life and I felt alive...more alive than I'd ever felt before. I wanted to shout, dance and sing all at the same time and trying to restrain that energy was next to impossible.

I grabbed my leather jacket and threw it over my sweatshirt, wedging my helmet underneath my arm. Luckily, there weren't any reported issues of driving while under the influence of *Mandrake* which was a damned good thing because I was needed at the hospital and glancing at the clock in my bedroom, realized I was already thirty minutes late. I had to keep myself from whistling, trying to continuously block the rampant feelings of happiness that encouraged me to evade my responsibilities. I couldn't afford to screw off, not when Jenny and Sam's lives were still in jeopardy. I locked the front door behind me and approached my bike, keys in hand.

I started the bike and had to suppress a ray of excitement as the engine purred beneath me. The stray thought that I could skip the hospital and take the bike for a joy ride struck me and I had to tear the thought apart. This fighting with myself was beginning to prove tiresome. Maybe it would have been better to be groggy and tired, after all...

Nah, better to be alert.

I gunned the bike and made it to the end of the street in record time. I silently said a prayer of thanks as I swung a right and made for the hospital, afraid my body might try to play the role of hijacker and head for that joyride.

En route to the hospital, I was struck by how verdantly green the lawns were. The song of a swallow echoed through the sky and it was the most melodious and wonderful sound I'd ever heard. The azure blue of the sky was in perfect harmony with the royal purple of the Morning Glories covering Old Man Jonas' chain link fence and together, they were the epitome of beauty. I felt an indescribable sense of contentment—that I was one of Nature's children and I was in seamless balance with my surroundings.

Upon reaching the hospital, I could say that the drive over had been the most enjoyable I'd ever taken. Nature was so perfect in her imperfections and the world was such a wondrously magical and special place. It almost made me want to cry.

"Get a grip, Dulce," I chided myself as I pulled into the Splendor Hospital parking lot. I noticed Knight's silver BMW M3 Coupe parked just outside the receiving doors so I parked alongside it and killed my engine. Taking off my helmet, I watched Knight step out from behind the driver's seat. It seemed to take him a second or two to actually recognize me and once he did, his gaze flickered between my hair and the Suzuki, as if he wasn't quite sure which one should get the privilege of being first discussed.

But, I couldn't really say I was that interested—instead, I had to keep myself from running up to Knight and throwing my arms around him in reckless abandon while forcing my mouth on his. The sudden desire to kiss him was overwhelming and I had to mentally scream at my feet to stay rooted in place.

Knight was just so…incredibly beautiful. He'd always been gorgeous, don't get me wrong, but this was different. He was absolute perfection and his body radiated a whitish glow, gleaming like a prism when the light hit him at a certain angle. His features were still the same—sun-kissed golden complexion, hair as dark as oil, face chiseled as if by Michaelangelo. I had to wonder if I was actually seeing him in his natural state or if this was merely a side effect of the *Mandrake*. Guess I'd never find out because it wasn't like I was actually going to ask him—talk about blowing my cover!

"I was wondering where the hell you were," he began in an annoyed tone. He pulled his attention from the Suzuki and focused it on my hair. "What the hell happened to you?"

I laughed and the sound was like bells ringing through my ears. "I've been doing research," I answered, figuring I could tell Knight everything minus the part about Quill and the part about the *Mandrake*. Everything else was fair game.

"Research?" he repeated skeptically. "And that research required you to color your hair?"

I approached him with a cheery grin. He seemed taken aback—an eyebrow raised in question. "Yep, I had to. I got a lead that took me to downtown Sanctity—you know, the bad parts."

"Go on," he said, crossing his arms against his chest.

I didn't even realize I was staring at his chest until he cleared his throat. I offered an embarrassed smile before turning back to my story. "The only problem with the location was that there were wards in place which meant I couldn't use magic and I wasn't about to go into a situation like that as Dulcie O'Neil, prior Regulator who has enemies up the wazoo." I smiled again, finding the word "wazoo" especially funny.

"So, you had to dye your hair?" Knight finished for me.

"What, don't you like it?" I asked, running a hand through it, which got caught in a curl.

Knight eyed me suspiciously before shaking his head. "No, I like the way you looked before."

One good thing about Dulcie on *Mandrake* was that criticisms bounced off me as if I'd magicked myself a "sticks and stones" barrier.

"And what the hell is with the bike?" Knight asked, his voice rising again in anger.

"Suzuki DL 650," I answered proudly and patted the seat. "She's pretty freaking fast."

Knight shook his head before bringing his incredibly perturbed expression back to me. "Have you lost your mind?" he asked. "You barely survived the accident in the Wrangler..."

"Hey, I had little time and even less money," I snapped, suddenly pleased that the cantankerous (as Bram would say) Dulcie was still in there somewhere. "And I'm not worried about the *Dreamstalker* coming after me. I'm not planning on sleeping."

Knight eyed me but said nothing else, instead turning and starting for the hospital. I jogged up to him and grabbed his arm, forcing him to a stop.

"I thought I was on duty tonight?" I asked. Knight had been on all day and into the evening—I was supposedly there to relieve him, or at least I'd thought that was the plan.

Knight glanced down at my hand that was still gripping his bicep and I dropped it. "I figured you might want company," he said and eyed me as if to reiterate the question before he started forward again.

"Sure, "I began, secretly very pleased to have his company. I'd been wondering what I was going to do all night and day. While there was no other place I'd rather be, other than keeping a watchful eye on Sam and Jenny, victim-sitting wasn't exactly thrilling. "I'd love some."

Knight stopped walking, turning around to eye me suspiciously. "Are you okay?"

"Yeah, I'm fine, why?" I answered, suddenly worried that I was being too uncharacteristically nice. The *Mandrake* needed to remain my little secret, with no one the wiser. I'd have to play my cards more strategically.

Knight shook his head. "You just seem too energetic, too happy."

I laughed and it was a tinny, fake sound. "I'm probably losing my mind from the lack of sleep." Then I eyed him just as warily, suddenly realizing that he looked freshly charged, as if he'd been sleeping for a millennia. "What's your secret? Why do you look so well rested?"

He shrugged and started for the hospital entrance again, me right beside him. "Sleep is my secret."

My mouth dropped open in disbelief. I'd now been awake for over three days and two nights with only an hour and a half of sleep to go on. Meanwhile, Knight had been sleeping all along? "You've been able to sleep?" I demanded,fury in my tone. He just nodded self-assuredly. "You haven't been scared of what might happen to you if the *Dreamstalker* attacked?"

He turned to face me and smiled broadly. "Nope."

I shook my head, suddenly incredibly angry with the fact that I'd gone through hell and back just to avoid sleeping and yet he was as well rested as a bear coming out of hibernation. "I don't understand you—are *Loki*s safe from *Dreamstalkers*?"

Knight cocked his head to the side as if he was considering it. Then he shrugged and smiled again. "I don't know. I guess we'll find out."

I grumbled underneath my breath and realized the giddy feeling of complete and total bliss was now absent—hmm, maybe it had been a short term effect of the *Mandrake*. I still felt amazingly alive and awake but I no longer had the feeling that I was living in Utopia which was just as well because I wasn't living in Utopia—I was living in Splendor which was about as nice as a troll's asshole.

The hospital doors slid open and granted us entrance. As soon as we entered the foyer, I nearly walked headlong into Dia and had to stabilize myself against her shoulders while I muttered a quick apology.

"Girl," she started as she recognized me. Recognition gave way to a smile which erupted into a full blown laugh. "Your hair! What the hell were you thinking?"

If I had a dollar for every time someone asked me what the hell I was thinking regarding my hair, I'd have...three dollars.

I continued forward, as if the elevator directly before us would provide solace from the relentless hair jibes. "I really don't need to hear it from you too," I ground out.

Dia glanced at Knight as she turned around and escorted us to the elevator. "What the hell was she thinking?"

He chuckled. "She wasn't."

I hit the call button and refused to look at either of them.

"Honey, you look like you're wearing a fright wig," Dia continued and I made the mistake of glancing at her. She made a face as if she'd eaten something foul. "That is *not* a good look for you."

Knight laughed again as the elevator's bell dinged, announcing its arrival. He held the elevator door for us as I walked inside and barricaded myself in the corner. "Okay, enough, I get it. I look like crap. Point taken."

"Ah, stop feeling sorry for yourself," Dia began.

"Instead of teasing me, you both should be thanking me," I interrupted.

"Why's that?" Dia demanded, crossing her arms against her chest as she tried to stifle another laugh. She was successful and ended up just shaking her head at my...fright wig.

I threw my hands on my hips, thinking they both deserved a little sass. "Because I destroyed the one thing I love about myself, my hair, so I could run recon for both of your sorry asses."

Dia didn't look impressed. The elevator doors closed and she hit the button that would take us to floor three. "And?" she prodded.

"And I found out a crapload," I answered, rubbing my knuckles against my left breast as if to say I was the shit. "But, before we get into that subject, how are our patients holding up?"

Dia shrugged. "So far so good."

"Sam?" I started, glancing at Knight.

"Nothing new to report," Knight finished. "Trey is watching her now."

Dia faced him. "Have Shirley and Travis been moved yet?"

I didn't wait for Knight's response but turned toward him, the demand for information in my eyes. "Update please."

He stepped out of the elevator, keeping the door from closing as Dia and I followed suit. "We've ordered Travis and Shirley to be moved from Moon General to Splendor. Otherwise, it's too difficult for Dia to travel back and forth. We thought the *Dreamstalker* might throw us a curve ball."

I nodded—that made sense. Since Dia was playing tracker for the victims, it would make her job a hell of a lot easier if the victims were all in the same place—especially since Moon was at least two hours from Splendor. I could only imagine the reason we hadn't reached this conclusion earlier was due to the fact that *Dreamstalkers* usually worked in linear patterns, killing their victims one at a time, from first attacked to last attacked. And going by that pattern, it would mean that Jenny would be next, followed by Travis and Shirley and, finally, Sam. Since I was now convinced that this creature wasn't a full-blooded *Dreamstalker* but a creature drinking from a full-blooded *Dreamstalker*, the idea to move Shirley and Travis was that much better since this creature was unpredictable. Who knew who he'd target next?

"Good idea," I said.

Knight faced Dia again. "And to answer your question, they should be arriving any minute. We've freed up the third floor so it's just Sam, Jenny, Travis and Shirley. And we've got security all over this hospital, especially on the third floor."

Just as he finished his statement, a cop walked past and nodded his head in salutation. Knight paused just beside a hospital room; the door closed. He faced me. "This is Jenny's room, do you want to check on her?"

I took a deep breath, afraid for what I might find. At this point, according to our deductions, Jenny was living on borrowed time. I turned the doorknob and entered the room, immediately noticing the cop stationed beside the still form of Jenny. He glanced up at me and smiled warmly. I returned the smile and approached him.

"I'm here to relieve you for a bit," I offered.

The cop didn't make any motion to leave. "And you are?"

"Dulcie O'Neil," Knight answered from behind me. "She's with us."

The cop stood up, offering me a small smile of apology as he walked past. I turned to face Knight, about to ask for a little personal time with my childhood nanny but he nodded as if he knew what was on my mind.

"I'll be back in a few," he said, closing the door behind me.

I felt almost uncomfortable as I approached Jenny—as if I didn't know what to say after not seeing her in over fifteen years. I stood above her and glanced down at her sweet face—there didn't appear to be anything wrong—no *Dreamstalker* attacking her dreams. She appeared to be sleeping peacefully. And that was bizarre—at this point, I would have thought she'd be battling for her life, not appearing as serene as Sleeping Beauty.

"Hi, Jenny," I started and my voice seemed alien somehow. "It's me, Dulcie O'Neil."

Of course she didn't say anything but I had to wonder if she could hear me, if my words might offer encouragement. I grasped her hand and squeezed it.

"I'm going to make sure you get out of this, Jenny. I work in law enforcement with the Splendor ANC," I continued. "I bet you never thought I'd end up a cop, did you?"

I laughed and eyed the dawn as it broke through Jenny's window, the yellow rays of the sun absorbing the mysterious darkness of night. Somehow that visual gave me strength and renewed my fervor. With the *Mandrake* pumping through my system, I was suddenly confident—I knew we could take this guy down.

"I know you're afraid, Jenny, but we're going to catch this creature."

I heard the door open and I glanced behind me at Knight. He smiled before gently closing the door and starting toward me. His footsteps belied his great height and build and I felt myself gulp as he draped his arm around me and glanced down at Jenny.

"How is she doing?"

I shook my head. "I don't know. I mean, she seems okay—I don't notice any indication of a struggle which doesn't make sense."

Knight nodded as if he knew where I was going with my comment. "This thing isn't operating under the same rules other *Dreamstalkers* have."

"Dia seems convinced it isn't a *Dreamstalker*," I said and eyed him, wondering how he'd take the news that I didn't think it was a *Dreamstalker* either.

"Maybe it isn't," he said noncommittally and shrugged. "Dia is outside, trying to get a read on whether the *Dreamstalker* has been around lately or not."

"How is she able to track them?"

"I'm not sure exactly but apparently she can sense them as long as she's close enough to one. I think she said it has to be within one hundred feet or something."

"So if the *Dreamstalker* isn't nearby, she's just wasting her time out there."

He shook his head. "She can sense them both before and after they visit their victims. Apparently they leave a psychic imprint in the air."

"Ah, so that's what she's searching for now?"

He nodded and pulled up the doctor's swivel stool, taking a seat. He then motioned to the visitor's seat just behind me. "Have a seat, Dulce, we're going to be here for a long time."

I didn't argue but released Jenny's hand, gingerly placing it beneath her blanket before retiring into the visitor's chair with a sigh. I stretched my legs out before me and crossed them at the ankles.

"We're waiting on Anna's autopsy reports to see if it really was her heart that gave out," Knight continued.

"Even if it was her heart, who's to say that it wasn't the *Dreamstalker* who scared her to death?"

Knight shook his head. "It wouldn't follow true *Dreamstalker* death patterns. Death by slumber usually points to solidly functioning organs. It could just be that Anna had a weak heart."

I shrugged but wasn't buying it. "Knight, I don't think it's a true *Dreamstalker* either."

I waited for the words to sink in, for him to argue with me but he just faced me with no emotion. "And I imagine this new opinion came about from this lead you mentioned earlier," Knight started, raising a brow, as if he expected more from my story. "Who was it from and what was it?"

I glanced up at him. "You should know better than to ask me who my leads are."

He chuckled. "Yep, I should. What can you tell me, then?"

I took a deep breath, not even really sure where to start. "I found out there is a new form of street potion in the underground. It's blood."

"Blood?" Knight repeated doubtfully.

"Blood of the most imposing creatures of the Netherworld is finding its way onto the streets. Apparently creatures are drinking the blood and adopting the strength and power of the creature to whom the blood belongs. And the more they drink, the stronger they become."

Knight was silent for a few seconds. "Then this *Dreamstalker* could be..."

"Anything," I interrupted. "That would explain why Dia couldn't sense it during *Transcendence*. Because it never went through *Transcendence*."

I could see his brain spinning, building up possible situations and outcomes. "But, where you're concerned..." he started again.

"Whatever it is, it has a personal vendetta against me, that much is obvious."

He chuckled. "How many Netherworld creatures have you pissed off, Dulce?"

"Too many to count." I glanced up at him and shook my head. "Way too many to count. I need all my ANC files—I need to find out who did time because of me and who got out."

"I've been working with Elsie to transfer all the hard files to e-files. I told her to start with yours and if I'm not mistaken, she's already finished them. You have that iPad on you?"

Damn, it was sitting on my desk. "Left it at home but I can run back..."

"Take the BMW," Knight interrupted in a tone that warned me not to argue with him. "It's safer than your bike."

What was it with bossy men who did nothing but worry? It was enough I had to deal with Bram and Quillan. Now I had to add Knight to that list? "You do realize I used to be a Regulator?"

He shrugged. "Yeah, of course."

"I've been through lots worse stuff than taking my bike a few miles down the street to my house."

"Just placate me, will you?"

I clenched my teeth but didn't want to get into an argument, especially one as stupid as this promised to be. "Where are your keys?"

He smiled but tried to keep it to himself, probably afraid his gloating would cause me to rethink my position. He fished inside his pocket and handed them to me without a word.

"I need to check on Sam and then I'll head home," I said and stood up, starting for the door. I didn't wait for a response.

"Roger that," Knight called behind me.

As I entered the hallway, Trey suddenly accosted me and forced a manila folder into my hands. "What's this?" I asked, glancing down at it.

"It's all the info I could find on Shirley Mickelson, like you requested," he said and beamed, his chest held high.

I'd forgotten that I'd even asked for the information in the first place. "Thanks, Trey." I opened the folder and quickly scanned through the contents before facing him with a smile. "Looks like you did an awesome job. I'll take a look at it right away."

#

As soon as I stepped inside my door, I didn't waste any time and hurried to my kitchen table, opening the file Trey had given me. Knight and his iPad could wait a few minutes. As I searched through Trey's chicken scratch notes, I read accounts of Shirley Mickelson's personality, as told to Trey by her neighbors, family and friends. There was a full page of information on where she'd grown up and gone to school, when she'd wed, how many kids she'd had, awards she'd won...Holy Hades, Trey had been detailed in his research. I definitely owed him a lunch for this one.

After reading through more information on Shirley Mickelson than I'd ever wanted to know, I glanced at the last sheet in the file which was a list of all her home addresses.

And that's when I realized her connection to me—Shirley Mickelson and her husband had owned the house my mother and I had rented when I'd been in my early teens, before my mother had died and I'd moved to Splendor.

TEN

Anna Murphy had died from a heart attack. At least that's what the autopsy revealed. I, myself, still wasn't convinced that her death had nothing to do with the *Dreamstalker* or whatever it was that we were dealing with. My beliefs ran more along the lines that her heart had simply expired because she'd been too freaked out by everything that had happened to her. But, apparently, I was in the minority, because everyone else bought the whole "heart failure from natural means" diagnosis. I had to wonder if it wasn't just wishful thinking on everyone else's part.

It had been another two nights of recon missions at the hospital and we still had nothing to show for it. Time was slipping through our hands like sand and although Jenny's disposition had remained stable, the same couldn't be said for Sam's. If Sam hadn't looked good before, she looked horrible now—she'd lost weight, her skin was sallow and her eyes sunken. It was pretty obvious what was happening—the *Dreamstalker* (I'd decided to continue to refer to him as such simply because I didn't know what else to call him...course, son-of-bitch-asshole-who-needed-to-die also worked) was getting restless, no pun intended. He'd been planning on the fact that I'd succumb to sleep sooner rather than later and the *Mandrake* had thrown a huge wrench in his plans. So, now he was going for my jugular—he was going for Sam.

I'd stood by Sam's bedside twenty four/seven while Knight, Trey and Dia as well as the rest of both Splendor ANC and Moon ANC units scouted the hospital, searching for any sign of foul play. Of course, Dia couldn't detect the slightest sign of the *Dreamstalker* which cemented the fact that our *Dreamstalker* was anything but full blooded.

Dia had given up relying on her *Somnogobelinus* sixth sense as well—pretty much after I agreed with her wholeheartedly that we weren't dealing with a true *Dreamstalker* and she had, instead, resorted to tracking it the old fashioned way by interviewing hospital staff, watching hospital security footage and gathering clues, all of which yielded nothing.

I'd now been awake for over five days and my sanity was becoming compromised. Even though a never-ending stream of energy coursed through me, courtesy of the *Mandrake*, I could feel my body wilting behind a mask of vitality. I'd lost my appetite and couldn't remember the last time I'd eaten something worth a damn. I just snacked here and there, whenever my mind reminded my stomach that it had been hours, sometimes a day since my last meal. My clothes hung limply from my already lithe figure and dark circles had taken up permanent lodging underneath my eyes.

Dia had offered her sleep services numerous times but I'd flatly declined her offers, knowing the *Mandrake* wouldn't allow me to sleep, no matter how hard I tried. I almost regretted taking it...almost. I was down to my last two *Mandrake* doses and we still didn't have any breaks in the case. Panic dwelt in my gut and alongside the ever-flowing river of *Mandrake*-induced energy, I was surprised I hadn't had a heart attack, myself.

But, the state of my physical health wasn't the worst of it. The worst, scariest part of the whole damned situation was the fact that I was starting to hallucinate. I was seeing things that weren't there and things I shouldn't have been seeing.

The visions started a night or so ago, I thought—I'd lost track of time, and I'd been at the hospital, sitting at Sam's bedside when I'd heard a faint cooing sound. I glanced behind me and felt my heart drop to my toes as a baby crawled past Sam's open door and down the corridor. I lurched from my seat and ran into the hallway, only to find an empty corridor greeting me. There had been no baby—there'd been nothing at all.

Later that same evening, I went home to take a quick shower and feed the dog when Knight suddenly materialized in my living room—materialized as if he'd just stepped out of thin air a la Bram-style. He stood in front of me but said nothing, staring at me with unadulterated lust, the same expression I'd seen him wear on more than one occasion.

"What the hell are you doing here?" I asked as Blue whined and clawed at the kitchen door, wanting to be let in. But, I wasn't concerned with the dog at the moment, what I was concerned with was how the hell Knight had pulled a Scotty and beamed himself right into my living room.

Knight said nothing but continued to stare at me, only now a smile tilted the ends of his lips.

"Hello? Earth to the *Loki*," I continued, annoyed with his games.

He didn't respond but simply disappeared—back into the atmosphere from whence he'd come. I didn't even have the chance to ponder how completely bizarre the situation had been because moments later my phone rang.

I gripped the receiver, bringing it to my mouth before checking the caller ID as I opened the kitchen door and Blue came galloping in.

"Hello?" I demanded, petting Blue's head as he danced around me.

"It's me," Knight answered.

"Where the hell did you go?"

There was silence on the other line. "What?"

I sighed and it was full of frustration. "Two seconds ago, you showed up in my house uninvited and when I tried to talk to you, you just ignored me and left. Really nice, Knight, I don't have the time for this crap."

More silence. I pulled out the Alpo bag from my broom closet and walked to the back door, reaching down for Blue's bowl as I wondered if Knight had dropped off the line.

"Hello?" I insisted, placing Blue's food dish on the kitchen floor.

"Dulcie, is everything okay?" Knight asked in a concerned voice.

"Yes," I bit out, wondering why the hell he was playing games. We didn't have time for games. "Why do you ask?"

"Because I've been at the hospital ever since you left—I never came to see you."

Now it was my turn for silence—the only sound in the room was the tinkling of the dog kibbles as they dropped into the silver bowl. Blue devoured them hungrily as I wondered what the hell was wrong with me? First I'd seen a baby who wasn't there and now I'd imagined Knight? I was losing my mind—it was a sign that I had to get off the *Mandrake*. But, the very thought of abandoning the *Mandrake* suddenly made my gut clench and anger bubbled up within me. I couldn't go cold turkey, er, cold fairy. I couldn't stop taking the *Mandrake*, not now when Sam's life still depended on it. No, my resolution was firm—I had to crack the case and I had two days left to do it in; if no one else would help me, then damn them. I'd do it myself.

"Are you still there?" Knight asked.

"Yeah," I started, my voice echoing my muddled thoughts. "Sorry. I must have just...been confused, that's all."

He cleared his throat. "Dulcie, you need to sleep."

"I'm fine."

"Dia said she offered to give you a couple of hours and you turned her down...repeatedly."

Damn Dia and her big mouth. "I don't have time to sleep. Not when Sam's life depends on us finding this guy," I blurted out.

"Your health is suffering, Dulcie, you don't look good."

"To hell with looking good!" I yelled into the phone. "I don't give a shit about my hair or..."

"I'm not talking about your hair," Knight snapped. "I'm talking about the fact that you've lost too much weight, you aren't eating and you look sick." He paused. "And now it sounds like you're seeing things."

"Well, I'm sorry I'm focused on my best friend and not my looks," I spat out, ignoring the part about seeing things. I didn't have an excuse for that one.

"Stop turning this around on me, Dulcie. You know what I'm talking about."

"No, I..."

"Anyway, you need to take the night off. I'm going to send Dia over later and you'd better get some sleep, understood?"

"Don't send Dia over," I started, panic spiraling through me as I realized I'd be found out as soon as Dia realized I couldn't fall asleep. "I'm coming back to the hospital. I'm not leaving Sam by herself."

"Don't tell me what to do," Knight said in a steely voice. "I'm the head of this investigation and what I say goes. Dia is coming over tonight and you'll thank me tomorrow."

Before I could argue, he hung up.

"Cocky bastard!" I yelled into the receiver before slamming the phone down. Blue jumped about two feet and retired to the far end of the room, his tail between his legs. I put my hand out, trying to coax him back over again. "Sorry, Boy, I didn't mean to scare you."

He didn't make any motion to approach me and, instead, went back to his half-eaten bowl of kibbles and picked up where he'd left off, eyeing me suspiciously from time to time as if to make sure I wasn't going to wig out on him again.

I collapsed onto the couch and tried to concentrate on what to do next. I attempted to focus but my mind was beyond the point of concentration and into the realm of make believe.

A knock on the door grabbed my attention as irritation swept through me. Dia. Knight must have told her to stop by as soon as I'd left the hospital—what a piece of work he was. Well, they both were about to find out what a piece of work I could be. I stood up, marched over to the door and was about to lambaste Dia but the words died in my throat once I pulled the door open.

"Quill?" I asked, keeping the door open only a sliver as Blue came trotting over, probably intending to bite my visitor.

Quill smiled and shrugged his broad shoulders. "Hi, Dulce, can I come in?"

I narrowed my eyes, suddenly wondering if he was just a figment of my completely distorted imagination.

I reached out and pinched his forearm.

"Ow, what the hell did you do that for?" he demanded, and cradled his arm like I'd just hacked into it with a machete.

"So, you are real?" I announced, still eyeing him as if he weren't. "Because I've had enough visits from people who aren't there. So, if you aren't real then buzz the fuck off!"

He frowned, his brows knotting in the middle of his forehead. "Of course I'm real," he said and eyed me askance. "Are you okay?"

"I'm sick of people asking me that!" I bellowed. "Yes, I'm freaking as fine as someone could be whose best friend is dying!" I couldn't help but choke on the words.

"Dulcie, let me in," Quill said and his tone was compassionate, concerned. "I'm worried about you—obviously you're still on the *Mandrake*."

"Don't be worried about me," I said and sighed. "I'm okay."

Blue yanked away from me and poked his nose out of the door. Quill's lips broke out into a huge smile. "Hi, Blue, remember me?"

"I wouldn't do that," I began as Quill leaned down and put his hand on Blue's muzzle. The dog did nothing but paw at the door, as if he wanted to be let out. "Wow," I started, amazed that Blue hadn't tried to bite him, or at the very least, growled.

"Dulce?" Quill prodded again, glancing up at me as if to say he hadn't forgotten the fact that I was losing my mind, becoming completely certifiable.

I stepped aside and allowed him entrance, shrugging as I figured he was as real as he was going to get. "Come in."

"Thanks," he said and walked inside, offering me a cheery smile as Blue, all smiles and wagging tail, circled him. Quill leaned down again and wrestled the dog into a bear hug, rubbing his head as he did so. I guess it made sense that Blue would accept Quill considering Quill was the one who gave me the dog in the first place.

"He likes me," Quill said as he glanced up for my approval.

I just shook my head, my thoughts turning to more important issues such as the fact that Quill had taken a big chance in coming here. I glanced down, realizing I was still clutching the doorknob and poked my head out, checking both sides of the street to make sure Dia hadn't decided to visit at the most inopportune moment. No sign of her so I closed the door and locked it. "You shouldn't have come. How did you know I didn't have anyone from the ANC here?"

I watched him walk into my living room, glancing around as if to make sure everything was as he remembered it, that nothing had changed. It was sad almost—like he was ensuring I was the same old Dulcie he'd always known. I was sure he didn't need me to tell him things weren't the same and never would be.

"I've been watching your house since you got home," he answered nonchalantly before approaching me. He reached for my face and tilted it upwards, studying me. "You need to get off the *Mandrake*."

"I can't, Quill..."

He shook his head. "You're getting addicted, I can see it in your eyes. And now it sounds like you're hallucinating?"

"It's worse than it looks," I started, thinking of any excuse I could. "I just need a little more time, Quill."

"Dulce..."

"I only have two doses left and then I'm out," I said and smiled anxiously. "I don't imagine you'll give me more." It was more a question than a statement.

Quill shook his head. "Absolutely not. I'm still irritated with myself that I gave you any to begin with."

"Just give me a few more days, Quill, that's all I ask for. Sam would thank you," I added, almost guiltily.

He sighed and didn't say anything, as if he was internally arguing with himself about whether or not to trust me.

"Please," I began, wracking my brain for a change of subject. Finding one, I latched onto it like a life preserver. "Why are you here?"

"I've got information for you," he said simply. "Do you have time to talk?"

"No," I began. "I'm expecting someone from the ANC any second and it wouldn't be a good thing if you're here."

"When can we talk then?"

I chewed my bottom lip as I thought about the fact that I really didn't want to be home when Dia came calling—I needed to avoid the whole sleep situation. What better way than play MIA for a few hours?

"Meet me at the Hyatt on Clover Street in Estuary in forty-five minutes," I started, thinking Quill might be recognized in Splendor so it was too risky to be seen out and about. He'd been incredibly stupid coming to my apartment in full daylight.

"Thanks for looking out for me."

"Yeah, yeah," I grumbled and walked him to the back door. "Once you're checked in, leave an envelope for Cindy Jones at the counter with your room number in it." I mentioned the name Cindy Jones because I didn't want anything tying me to this meeting with Quill. But, knowing Quill, he'd check in under a false name anyway.

Quill nodded, observing me like a proud parent. "I've taught you well, Cindy."

I smiled sadly. "I learned from the best."

He didn't say anything more but opened the back door and disappeared around the corner. I glanced at Blue who sat down on his haunches and whimpered.

#

The Hyatt in Estuary was decently nice. I pushed aside the vertically striped brown and blue curtains from the window and glanced down at Estuary Park, watching a kid learning how to ride his bike as his parents hovered protectively.

I was suddenly struck with the thought of how different this situation could have been—how in another life Quill and I could have been in this hotel room together for completely different reasons—maybe we were vacationing or meeting for a lovers' tryst. He could have been drawing a bath for me while I chattered on about something that didn't matter, merely trying to draw attention away from my anxious thoughts which revolved around the fact that he and I were alone...

But, thoughts like those were pointless and I wasn't one of those people who saw the world through rose-colored lenses. I preferred the hard and oftentimes ugly reality that was around me, that I knew so well.

"I dug a little deeper into the whole black market blood operation that I told you about earlier," Quill started and took a seat on the king-sized bed. The comforter was the same drab brown of the curtains and the bed was piled with so many pillows, it actually looked uncomfortable. I pulled my attention away from the window, releasing the curtain and took a seat on a nearby chair, covered in a polka dot blue and brown to, yes, match the curtains and the coverlet on the bed.

"And, what did you find out?" I asked.

"There is *Dreamstalker* blood on the market."

I nodded, not finding the announcement at all surprising. "I figured. So, how is anyone getting it? The only two *Dreamstalkers* are still in prison."

Quill shrugged. "Apparently it's coming from Banshee. I'm not exactly sure how but that's the point of origination. Somehow the blood is passing hands in Banshee and ending up on the streets. But, *Dreamstalkers* aren't even the worst offenders. There's *Kraken* blood and some sicko has been selling Dragon's blood but calling it *Chupacabra*."

"Dragon's blood will kill whoever takes it," I said, my mouth dropping open.

"Yep," Quill said. "Not surprisingly, there have been lots of DOAs."

I said nothing more, my mind in a tailspin, too many thoughts colliding into one another. If Banshee Prison was the source of the blood, who was the one providing it? Was it controlled solely by inmates or something more sinister?

"Dulcie, let me help you with this case," Quill said with pleading eyes.

I immediately shook my head. "You know I can't do that, Quill. You aren't ANC anymore."

His jaw was tight. "Neither are you."

"I'm still working with them."

Quill stood up and came closer to me, glancing down with determination in his eyes. "Dulcie, you need my help. I got *Druiva* behind bars before—I can do it again."

I stood up and wrapped my arms around myself. I was entirely too close to him and the smell of his aftershave was causing a flutter in my stomach that needed to be eradicated a.s.a.p. "This isn't even a *Dreamstalker*," I said without realizing it. I could have kicked myself as I hadn't wanted to reveal the slightest hint about the case and I'd just mouthed the biggest one.

Dammit to hell.

"Interesting," Quill nodded, his smile revealing the fact that he'd realized my faux pas.

"No, it's not interesting and do me a favor and forget that I told you. I refuse to get you involved."

His body language said he wasn't going to back down. "You've just basically told me the guts of the whole case. You might as well come out with the rest.

I was quiet as I considered it. Quillan was an amazing cop and he had busted *Druiva* which meant his help would be that much more necessary. Apparently, I'd already made the decision to include him. I nodded, knowing I was defeated. "You keep all of these case details to yourself," I said.

"Of course."

My lips were tight. "Quill, I'm trusting you and I'm serious. None of this leaves this room."

"I know, Dulce, my lips are sealed."

I swallowed hard and turned toward the window again, almost like I couldn't face him, knowing I was breaking ANC rules. Knight would definitely have fired me from the case right then and there if he knew what I was doing. Hmm, or maybe he would have locked me up. I was never sure about anything where Knight was concerned.

"I'm pretty sure our killer isn't really a *Dreamstalker*," I started. "But it's something posing as one. And I'm sure I locked the bastard away years ago because all the victims have had something to do with me."

"What do you mean?"

I sighed, and glanced at Quill again, not sure where to begin. "The first two deaths were girls in my second grade class. My childhood nanny is now in a coma, my boyfriend from high school, my mother's landlady and now Sam."

"Your best friend," Quill said absently—it meant his mind was racing with thoughts—thoughts too fast for his mouth to keep up with. "Sounds like you're up to your ears."

I laughed but it was a dry sound. "You could say that."

"Do you have any idea who it could be?"

I glanced at the small, round table in front of the solitary chair. I'd put my backpack on the table and inside the backpack was the iPad. No one could tell me I wasn't prepared. "I started going through the files and writing down possibilities but there are just too many who have reason to hate me. I got a lot of assholes locked up, Quill," I said with a sad smile. "And a number of them have been released."

"So, we start from the beginning and go through contact after contact. Give me the list and I'll help you get through it."

It wasn't a bad idea, actually. Quill had been involved in every case, every step of the way. If there was anyone to have on my side, it would have been him. I glanced at the backpack and unzipped it, grabbing the iPad.

"You have to promise me this isn't going to come back to bite me in the ass," I started.

"Dulce," Quill warned, as if to say we'd already been through this conversation.

Well, I didn't care. He needed to know how important his silence was. "What you see in this room stays in this room."

He smiled. "That almost sounds naughty."

I shook my head. "I'm serious, Quill."

He sighed. "Dulcie, you can trust me. I would never do anything to hurt you, you know that."

I laughed acidly at his words. His disloyalty to the ANC had hurt me in ways he would never know. Even now I wondered if I'd seriously lost my mind that I was allowing him in on this case. The old Dulcie of just a few months ago would have bucked at the idea and, instead, probably tried to arrest him.

"This is going to be the extent of our liaison, you know that right?" I asked, eyeing him warily.

He nodded and dropped his gaze to his large hands. "I figured."

I turned back to the window and watched the boy on the bike take a tumble. He stood up, glanced down at his grass stained corduroys and started crying. His mother enveloped him in a bear-like hug and all was right with his world again.

"I'll accept your assistance with this case because Sam needs all the help she can get but after this, we go back to how we used to be," I said in a firm tone.

"Enemies," he finished.

I glanced at him. "I can't work double duty, Quill. Even though I'm no longer a Regulator, I still work for the ANC. I can't and I won't maintain a relationship with you, not after I know what circles you travel in."

He frowned and stood up, dwarfing me. "You maintain a relationship with Dagan and Bram," he began angrily. "How can I be any worse than they are?"

Dagan was a demon who owned an S&M club, Payne. There were few worse than he was. "I've never busted them for anything," I said but the excuse sounded just as flimsy to me as I was sure it sounded to him.

"You know they're less than model citizens," he said and he was so close to me, I could feel his breath on my head. I didn't dare turn around from facing the window.

"You're different," I started, trying to think of the reasons why he was different. What it boiled down to was the fact that Quill had been allowed into my inner circle and Bram and Dagan never had. Because Quill had burned me, I couldn't stomach the idea of maintaining any sort of connection with him. In this case, it was better to rip the Band-Aid off and scream with the pain but also be done with it.

"How am I different?" Quill demanded as he ran his hands up and down my arms.

"I really don't want to get into this right now, Quill. You're not going to like what comes out of my mouth."

His hands stopped rubbing my arms and he backed away. I took it as my cue to turn on the iPad and start sorting through the various creatures who might be our perpetrator.

#

Three hours later I was back at home and in the process of listening to an angry voicemail from Dia where she berated me for ditching her. I pressed delete and sank into my couch, wondering what to do with the rest of my day and evening. Knight wouldn't take it well if I showed up at the hospital, but I had to wonder if I really cared. Obviously I wasn't going to sleep anytime soon which meant I'd be better off at Sam's bedside than twiddling my thumbs at home, especially if the *Dreamstalker* decided to attack. If Knight wanted me gone, he could forcibly remove me. Course, I wouldn't have put that past him.

My mind was made up—I was going back to the hospital.

Besides, I had news for Knight. Quill and I had pared the list of suspects down to a mere twenty who could possibly be our *Dreamstalker*, based on two factors: whether I sent them to Banshee and if they'd either been released or escaped. Even though escaping from Banshee was beyond rare, it did happen. And from the research Quill and I had done into the ANC bios, there had been one escapee.

Even though the list of possible culprits was decently long, I actually felt good about the fact that we had a starting point, something to go on. I shook my head as I realized how helpful it would have been to have this list five days ago but there was no use in crying over counterfeit *Dreamstalkers* or the fact that it had taken us the better part of a week to even figure out the *Dreamstalker* was counterfeit.

I grabbed my backpack, my helmet and gave Blue a kiss on the head before putting him outside. I started for my bike and wondered how much shit Knight was going to give me.

Guess I was just a glutton for punishment.

ELEVEN

The Gods must have been smiling down on me because when I arrived at the hospital, Knight was nowhere to be found and Dia refused to speak to me which meant my time was my own. I took up residency next to Sam and held her hand as I prattled on about random things that really didn't matter. I just imagined if I were stuck in a coma, afraid for my life, there would be nothing I'd rather hear than Sam's voice encouraging me and telling me things were going to be alright. I could only hope she could hear me.

Sam didn't look any worse than she had the last time I'd seen her—course, I couldn't imagine it was possible for her to look any worse and still be alive.

After about thirty minutes, I got sick of hearing myself talk so I continued holding Sam's hand, but turned my thoughts inward. Even though Dia, Knight and now Quill had all said it would be a suicide mission to fight the *Dreamstalker* in sleep, the more I thought about it, the more I realized it was the only way. Otherwise, we were stuck in a perpetual holding pattern; neither the *Dreamstalker* nor we were willing to budge. And I knew what the bastard was waiting for—me to finally admit that I needed to meet him on his turf, in dreams.

I turned on the iPad and connected to the Internet, continuing my research into lucid dreaming. I had to imagine this was my answer—if I could gain control of my dreams enough to use magic against the asshole, I could kill him.

I grabbed my backpack and rifled through it until I found a pen and a pad of paper. Then I started jotting down the keys to lucid dreaming, hoping that in writing them down, I'd commit them to memory.

1. *Once I realize I'm dreaming, I can take control and alter the dream—changing things like the scenery, the characters, etc. (Note: maybe this would be important in case the Dreamstalker wants to meet me in his own territory.)*
2. *Pretty much anyone can learn lucid dreaming through motivation and effort. Spontaneous lucid dreams rarely occur. In order to create the lucid dream environment. I have to recognize the fact that I'm dreaming while I'm dreaming.*
3. *In order to learn lucid dreaming, dream recalling is imperative. Why? Because when I remember my dreams, I become familiar with them—their patterns. This way I can recognize a dream as it happens, thereby allowing me the opportunity to control it.*

I glanced up from my notebook and tried to remember the last dream I'd had—I couldn't recall dreaming at all when Dia had allowed me the sweet respite of an hour and a half. And the time I'd been asleep prior to that was when the *Dreamstalker* had nearly killed me. I wasn't sure if that was a good dream to go on—I mean, it had been pretty much controlled by the *Dreamstalker* entirely so I had to admit the answer to that question was a definite no.

Like a blast from a past that hit me like an anvil over the head, I remembered the first explicit dream I'd ever had about Knight—in it he'd helped me get over Jack, my ex-asshole. Even though I wasn't thrilled with the content of the dream because it was entirely X-rated, I forced myself to pay attention to it, to write down characteristics that might help me in the future. I had to practice, right?

I turned back to my notebook and continued writing.

Dream with Knight:

I was in my bedroom, naked in my bed. Jack was there and we'd been talking about the fact that he'd really screwed me up since our breakup— I could trace all my trust issues back to him. Jack had proceeded to seduce me and I'd been unable to stop him.

Then there was Knight. Knight told me to let go of Jack, to tell him he was now a part of my past.

I glanced up as I considered the dream—maybe it had been a pseudo lucid dream—I mean, I hadn't realized I was dreaming but with Knight's help, I was able to take control of the situation and force Jack into the background where eventually, he disappeared. Maybe I could do the same thing where the *Dreamstalker* was concerned?

Granted, in the Jack dream I required Knight's assistance but maybe none of that mattered, especially since Knight said he was only able to interrupt my slumber, not control it. So, did that mean I was responsible for sending Jack away? Maybe it had just been the power of suggestion? Hmm... I'd never really know because I wasn't about to ask Knight, not when the dream had involved him and his fingers in places I'd rather not think about...

The point was that I'd been able to take control in that dream so why wouldn't I be able to recreate that same ability?

I turned back to the pad of paper and continued writing, trying to shake images of Knight and the things he did to my naked body.

4. *How to take control of a dream: Dream Signs*
    a. *Usually the sleeper can figure out if she's sleeping by the fantastical elements in dreams—things like flying or seeing dead people. If I can figure out that these signs mean I'm dreaming, I can get control of my dream.*
5. *What to do if I start to come out of the dream: Spinning*
    a. *If the dream shows signs of ending like a loss of detail or vividness of the imagery, the technique of "spinning" can bring the dream back. Simply spin my dream body around like I'm trying to get dizzy. (Note: what the hell does this mean?)*

"Dulcie."

I glanced up and felt my stomach drop as Knight glared at me. I snapped my journal shut and shoved it back into the backpack before he had the chance to play detective.

"Hi," I said, not really knowing what else to say.

Knight didn't say anything or smile but tilted his head slightly in greeting. I couldn't help the nerves that short-circuited through me. I was uneasy—my sweaty palms were evidence enough. And Knight's silence wasn't helping. Then I suddenly remembered the information I had for him.

"I have a list of possible suspects," I started, my voice edgy. "We'll need to order blood tests for each one to see if they've been ingesting or shooting up *Dreamstalker* blood."

"Good," Knight said. He didn't appear to be as pissed off as I might have imagined. Or maybe the hurricane just hadn't made its way this far South yet.

I reached inside my backpack and produced the list of names, handing it to him. He didn't even bother glancing at it, but folded it in half and put it under his arm. "I'm hungry, care to join me?" he asked and I could honestly say it was the last thing I would have imagined to come out of his mouth.

Taken aback, it took me a second to respond. I glanced at Sam and wasn't sure I should leave her side. "One of us should watch her."

"I'll put Trey on it," he said quickly and poked his head out of the door, hollering down the hallway to Trey. He glanced at me again and his jaw was tight like he was holding something back. "We won't be gone long—I'll hit the drive through."

I didn't say anything else but stood up and grabbed my backpack, not wanting to leave the iPad unattended. Knight turned on his foot and started for the door, me right behind him. I wasn't sure if he was going to call me on the fact that I'd ditched Dia and wasn't supposed to be at the hospital but I figured I'd leave that conversation to him.

"Where do you feel like going?" he asked, as we walked into the elevator.

"I don't care. I'm really not hungry."

He nodded but it wasn't a nod that was in any way understanding—especially not by the fact that his jaw was just as tight as it had been. I had to wonder why he wasn't freaking out on me yet. This wasn't like Knight. Maybe he didn't want to cause a scene in the hospital?

"Wendy's it is, then."

I followed him to his BMW and pulled open the passenger door before he could open it for me. He eyed me discouragingly but said nothing. Once I was buckled in and we were driving down the road, I couldn't handle the silent treatment any longer.

"So, why aren't you yelling at me yet?" I demanded.

"Why did you think I would?"

"Um, because I know you too well."

He chuckled but it sounded forced. He came to the stop sign at the end of the street and hung a left. Wendy's was to the right.

"You're going the wrong way."

"I like the Wendy's closer to my house," he answered. Fast food was fast food. Wendy's hamburger patties were just as square here as they were in his neck of the woods, but, who was I to argue? Knight could have his little OCD tendencies—that was fine by me. I settled back into my chair, surprised by the fact that I hadn't been read my rights yet. Maybe this day was going to be better than I'd imagined.

"So, given the fact that the *Dreamstalker* isn't a real one, don't you think we should change the way we're going after it? Clearly the sitting and waiting game isn't working," I started, finding his silence less than thrilling.

He took another turn in the opposite direction from his house.

"And what did you have in mind?" he asked.

My attention was pulled from the fact that either Knight's sense of direction was seriously shitty or he was pulling a fast one on me. "I think we need to go after it on its turf," I said absentmindedly before turning to the more important subject. "Where the hell are you taking me?"

"Fighting it on its turf is a suicide mission," he began, apparently ignoring my second question. "We've already had this discussion."

"Enough with trying to avoid the real question here, Knight, where are we going?" He didn't answer but he really didn't need to once he turned down my street. The answer was pretty crystal clear. "Why are we going to my house?" I insisted.

He said nothing but parked in front of my apartment building and then turned to face me and his expression was blank. "We can do this the easy way or we can do it the hard way."

While I tried to understand what the hell he was talking about, my heart began pounding as it jumped to conclusions. He stepped out of the car and before I had the chance to think, he was at my side, opening the door for me.

"What is this about?" I demanded.

"Dulcie, step out of the car. We need to have a conversation."

"To hell with you," I blurted and undid my seatbelt as I jumped out of the car, attempting to sidestep him. His hand was like iron as it wrapped around my wrist. "Let go of me," I seethed.

He shrugged. "If you want to make a spectacle of yourself in front of your neighbors, I have no problem with that. If you want more privacy, then let's take it inside."

I gulped, suddenly afraid he'd figured out I was on something. What else could this have been about? Knight wasn't stupid. I said nothing but started for my apartment, with half a mind to sic Blue on him. At least the *Mandrake* was buried deep in my panties drawer. And it wasn't like I was about to admit anything about the *Mandrake* to him anytime soon. So, for now, my secret was safe.

I unlocked my front door and he pushed it open. I stepped inside the apartment and he closed and locked the door behind me.

"What the hell is this all about?"

He took off his coat and draped it over a chair by the door. "It's about the *Mandrake*, Dulcie."

I felt my heart drop to my feet. He knew. "What...what are you talking about?"

He laughed but the sound was bitter. "Enough. It wasn't difficult to figure out—you haven't slept in over five days; you look sick and you're hallucinating."

"So what? Those are all common side effects resulting from sleeplessness."

He scoffed at me, crossing his arms against his great expanse of chest. "And you expect me to believe you've been staying awake on caffeine?" he asked. "Please."

"You can leave now," I said as a pang of anxiety overcame me. He was going to try to get me to give up the *Mandrake*. I had one dose left and there was no way in hell I was going to let him take it from me. Beads of perspiration formed along my hair line and I could already feel them gliding down the small of my back. But, none of that mattered. What did matter was that Knight knew my secret and he was going to try to take me off the *Mandrake*. Or maybe he was going to arrest me?

He reached inside his pants pocket and produced a white pill the size of a dime. He handed it to me. "Like I said, we can do this the easy way or the hard way."

"What is that?" I asked, backing away from it.

"It's *Corel Root*," he started. "Direct from the Netherworld. It'll clear you out and speed up your withdrawals. You're going to be a hell cat to deal with for the next few hours but I can handle it."

I glared at him and shook my head. "I'm not taking that."

He shrugged and put the pill back into his pocket. "The hard way it'll be then."

Before I had the chance to respond, he lurched for me and grabbed hold of my waist, hefting me over his shoulder. I yelled and batted my ineffectual hands against his massive back but I might as well have been a toddler putting up a fight for all the good it did me.

Without even thinking, I shook my fist until a mound of fairy dust emerged, then I dumped it on him, envisioning him shrinking until he was mouse-sized. The fairy dust just shimmered on his shoulders in an array of ineffectual glitter and fell to the ground as he chuckled.

"Your magic won't work on me or have you forgotten?"

I had remembered but by that time, I'd already doused him. Not that it mattered now anyway—my magic might not work but my fists and legs would. I beat against his back repeatedly and then attempted to de-ball him with a well-aimed foot to his nads but neither approach was successful. He merely deposited me against the couch and even as I attempted to get up, he was on top of me, straddling and holding my legs down with his thighs. Now with my legs out of the fighting picture, I tore at him with fists and nails but he didn't act fazed and, instead, forced my arms down.

"I'm trying to help you, Dulcie."

"Like hell you are," I seethed. "Get off me!"

I'm not sure how he did it since his hands were busily engaged with holding me down, but he managed to pull the *Corel Root* from his pocket and before I could stop him, he had my lips pursed together like a fish. He forced the pill between them and slammed his palm over my mouth, preventing me from any chance to spit it out.

"Swallow it," Knight demanded.

Once the thing hit my tongue, it dissolved and felt like sand, spreading over my tongue and the back of my throat. A second or so later, nothing was left. I turned my head to the side, thinking I could spit out whatever was left but Knight wedged his arm between the couch and my face until I found myself glaring back up at him again. Figuring I'd lost the battle, I swallowed.

"There, I swallowed the fucking thing, are you happy now?"

He made no motion to get off me. "Now the fun starts."

"What the hell is that supposed to..."

Before I could complete my sentence, I was silenced by what felt like liquid heat coursing through me. It started as a gentle warmth, like drinking warm coffee. But the gentle warmth began to spread and the temperature increased until it felt like a furnace erupting within me. I thought for sure I'd become a victim of spontaneous combustion. I thrashed back and forth, trying to quell the flames even as they burned me from the inside out.

"I'm on fire!" I screamed.

"It's in your imagination," Knight responded coolly, his hands restraining me until I could barely wiggle against the couch.

I clenched my eyes shut tight and screamed as the pain ripped through me.

"Dulcie, just be strong, you will get through this," Knight's voice interrupted me.

I opened my eyes, which were now streaming with tears and faced him in ire. "I hate you!" I screamed. "You did this to me!"

I tried to push up from my position on the couch, straining against him, but he was like trying to move a boulder.

"This will last a few more seconds," he ground out.

Another firestorm coursed through me and I wailed out again, writhing in agony. Pretty soon my screams were reduced to whimpers as the fire started to die down, feeling more like glowing embers in my stomach. After another few seconds, the pain subsided entirely.

I blinked a few times and opened my eyes. "It stopped," I started in a coarse voice.

Knight nodded and sat up, stretching his arms out. "It's not over."

"What do you mean?" I insisted in shock. "I can't take any more of that pain."

He shook his head. "The pain is over but you're going to go through withdrawals—what would normally take days is going to take about a half hour."

"I didn't just go through withdrawals?" I continued, my voice betraying fear and anger.

Knight shook his head and sighed. "Nope, that was just the beginning."

I laid back against the couch, more frightened than I'd ever been. And it wasn't a rational fear, necessarily, it was more a fear that had to do with the *Mandrake* leaving my body, being forced out by the *Corel Root*. And the answer to my problems was suddenly obvious. I needed that last *Mandrake* dose, I needed it like nothing I'd ever needed before. I had to remind myself that physically, I wasn't able to take on Knight, I was like a fly to his lion. That meant I'd have to rely on my smarts, on my feminine wiles. And one thing I was more than aware of was the fact that Knight wanted me.

I couldn't help my smile as I realized I had a weapon that was entirely more powerful than brawn. "I'm okay," I said and laid my head back against the couch, my chest heaving with my elevated breathing.

Knight continued straddling me, staring down at me as if trying to figure out if I was trying to pull a fast one.

"I mean it, I'm fine," I repeated.

All I could focus on was getting my hands on the last dose of *Mandrake* and if I could catch Knight unaware enough, I could grab the Op 7 he always wore somewhere on his person. Then I could force him to let me take the *Mandrake* or risk being shot.

I tried to sit up and was surprised and pleased when he allowed me to. I glanced at him and smiled, realizing I'd have to do a convincing job of seducing him. I was hardly the femme fatale type but at that moment, I summoned any acting ability I possessed, hoping to channel Marilyn Monroe, Jean Harlow, or failing them, Madonna in the "Vogue" video.

"Thank you," I said and my voice was low, sexy if I did say so myself.

Knight eyed me askance.

"I mean, I couldn't have come off the *Mandrake* without you," I finished. I even dropped my head to maintain the illusion of apology.

He sighed before the beginnings of a smile lifted his lips. "I thought you'd give me a bigger run for my money."

He had no idea I was about to give him the biggest run for his money he'd ever had. He sat up and allowed me the freedom to sit so I sidled up next to him.

"I don't know how to thank you," I continued.

"You just did." He laughed, his eyes following me like he was a hawk.

I shook my head. “I mean really thank you.” He glanced at me with a funny expression. “I was worried you were going to arrest me,” I finished.

“I had half a mind to…I still do.”

I put my hand on his shoulder and used it to push myself onto his lap, until I was straddling him.

“What are you doing?” he asked warily.

“Something I should have done a long time ago,” I answered and propped his chin up. “I’ve been fighting my feelings for you, Knight,” I started and could honestly say it was the truth. “I’ve talked myself out of wanting you and into thinking you were a bad choice for me.”

He grabbed my hand and pulled it away from his face, his eyes narrowed. “Why is this coming up now?”

“Because you keep protecting me left and right,” I said and ran my finger down the side of his face, surprised by how soft his skin was. “At some point I have to realize you’re a good thing, right?”

“That doesn’t sound like the Dulcie I know.”

Inside I was beginning to panic, wondering if my plan wasn’t going to work. “I just went to hell and back in front of you.”

“I hope you aren’t embarrassed?” he asked and his eyes followed mine as I leaned into him.

“I’m not,” I said and brought my lips to his. His lips were full and when I kissed him, I felt myself getting lost in his taste. I outlined his mouth with my tongue and felt him growing hard against my thigh. I pulled away and glanced down at him.

“I liked that,” he said with a sincere smile.

The need for *Mandrake* was overwhelming me at this point but I quashed the desire, promising myself that I would have some soon enough. For now, I had Knight right where I wanted him and I couldn’t blow that, not for the world.

“Do you still want me?” I asked as innocently as I could. “I mean, after what we just went through?”

“Want you?” he laughed. “There isn’t a moment where I’m not thinking about you, Dulcie.” His voice petered off as he watched my hands move to the bottom of my tee-shirt. “Yes I want you,” he finished.

There was a part of me that suddenly felt guilty that I was doing this—the old me never in a million years would have stooped to this level and the little voice inside my head yelled as much but the *Mandrake* part of me told that part to shut the hell up.

I was winning—that was all that mattered.

I pulled the tee shirt over my head until I was clad only in my jeans and bra. Knight's eyes settled on my bust and I smiled, feeling my power grow. He was like mush in my hands.

"Touch me," I whispered.

He gripped either side of my waist and pulled me into him, until his face was buried in my chest. And then I felt his lips as they kissed the swells of my breasts. I reached around and unclasped my bra, sliding it down my arms as Knight pulled away, watching me.

"God, you're so beautiful," he whispered and grabbed my waist again, forcing one of my nipples into his mouth. I moaned out as soon as I felt his tongue and a deep throbbing started within me. I had to admit to myself that I wasn't acting anymore—the bliss ricocheting through me was as real as it was going to get.

I had to fight to keep control of myself.

"Take your shirt off," I demanded, wanting to know where his Op 7 was. Focus on the gun and I could control my wayward sexual desires.

He wasted no time in pulling off his shirt and before the beauty of his naked chest could entice me, I caught a glimpse of the holster around his waist. Today was my lucky day.

"Lie back," I said, and as soon as he did so, I leaned down and trailed his chest with my breasts, feeling the tickle of his chest hair against my nipples. I found his lips again and kissed them. His hands splayed across my backside until he found my ass and spanned each cheek with his palms, pushing me into his hard shaft. I could feel the edge of his Op 7 as it bit into my hip. I needed to get his hands out of the way, so I could grab the gun without interception.

I pushed his hands above his head, sitting up as I hovered over him. I kissed up and down his biceps, my breasts dangling in his face. He groaned and tried to catch them in his mouth to which I laughed, creating the perfect distraction for what I had to do next. I held each of his wrists in one hand and started back down his body, kissing and touching as I did so. My right hand was now inches from the Op 7.

I continued trailing my fingers down his body and stopped at his zipper. I toyed with the button of his pants and then trailed my fingers to the side, teasing him. Once I was a barely a breath away from the Op 7, I could imagine the feel of the cold steel against my palm. It was now or never. I must have made it a fraction of an inch closer to the gun before I found myself flat on my back, Knight atop me.

He laughed acidly as he glanced down at me. "Did you really think I wasn't on to you?"

"So, you just played into the game the whole time?" I shrieked at him and realizing he'd bested me, erupted into a fit of tears.

He shrugged and his expression was hard. "I figured I'd enjoy it while I could."

"You bastard!" I screamed.

"Where is the *Mandrake*?" he demanded and his voice was deadly, warning me not to argue with him.

"There isn't any left," I lied.

He stood up and gripped my wrist, forcing me up beside him. Then he pushed me toward my bedroom.

"I'm going to ask you one more time, Dulcie, where the hell is the *Mandrake*?"

"And I'm going to tell you one more time that there isn't any left!" I screamed at him.

He gritted his teeth and threw open the bedroom door, slamming it behind us. He pushed me against the bed and climbed on top of me, his eyes issuing a warning of their own.

"This is your last chance. Tell me where the *Mandrake* is or I'm going to cart your ass down to Headquarters and let the Netherworld deal with you," he ordered and added. "And how the hell will you help Sam in jail?"

I swallowed hard. There was no way I wanted to admit where the *Mandrake* was but there was also no way I was going to let him get me locked away where I'd have no access to *Mandrake* and even less access to Sam. Damn, the bastard had won.

"Why won't you believe me?" I insisted.

"Because every time you tell me there isn't any left, you blink repeatedly which means you're lying."

Then a feeling of absolute despondency and panic shot through me. "Please don't take it from me, Knight."

"Where is it?" he demanded again.

"If I tell you, what are you going to do with it?"

He smiled but there was nothing sweet about it. It was the grin of a hunter which made me the prey. "If you tell me where it is, I'll give you the option of whether you want to clean yourself up and be the law enforcement agent I know you are or whether you want to stay addicted to *Mandrake*."

It couldn't have been more perfect. He was going to let me make the choice. As far as I was concerned, the choice was already made.

"It's in my top drawer, buried in the back."

I didn't even have the chance to feel any sort of mortification as Knight approached my dresser, pulled open the drawer and started plowing through my panties and bras. All that mattered was the sweet release the *Mandrake* promised soon enough. He grasped the small vial and rather than approaching me, neared the bathroom so I followed him. He propped the toilet seat up and yanked on the cork of the *Mandrake* so hard, it crumbled in his hand.

"You son of a bitch!" I seethed.

I leapt for him as soon as I realized what he intended to do and was in the process of doing already. He held me off with one arm and dumped the reminder of the *Mandrake* into the toilet. The bubbles fizzled and popped as they met the water and he flushed them down.

I slammed my fists into his chest, screaming curse words even I couldn't make out. He grabbed my arms and forced me out of the bathroom and back into my bedroom, depositing me on my bed. But, I was up and out of his reach before he could say "boo".

"It was for your own good," he yelled back at me. "You'll thank me once you come out of this."

I wanted to clobber him, to slam his head into the wall. I started to wonder where these violent feelings were coming from but, sensing my chance, I wiggled out of his hold. I bee-lined for the door but he caught my arm and yanked me back into the room.

"I hate you!" I yelled and collapsed against my bed as sobs wracked my body.

"You're lucky I don't just cart your ass into Headquarters now and lock you up."

"I wish you would," I spat it back in his face. "Anything to get away from you!"

He grabbed my tee-shirt from off the floor, and threw it at me. "Put this on."

I grabbed the shirt and forced it over my head, covering myself up as humiliation consumed me.

TWELVE

After another two hours, the *Mandrake* had been cleansed from my body and I felt nothing but exhausted. My emotions ran the gamut from extreme relief over the fact that Knight had seen to it that I was no longer addicted to *Mandrake* and complete mortification and embarrassment over the fact that I, Dulcie O'Neil, had basically become an addict.

If I'd never understood or been sympathetic toward the plight of the addict before, I felt differently now. It was as if the *Mandrake* had completely taken over my life—and, really, it had. The idea that I'd nearly seduced Knight just for another fix was something that would live with me for the rest of my life...in infamy.

"I don't even know what to say," I started, staring out the window to avoid having to face Knight. He'd just witnessed something I would have been mortified for even Sam to witness. I was such a private person that the fact that I'd gone through something so personal in front of Knight...the thought was enough to make me want to throw up.

"Don't say anything, Dulcie," he responded in a soft, compassionate tone.

I felt a lump forming in my throat and I wiped away a few tears. "I'm completely mortified."

Knight stood up from where he'd been sitting at my kitchen table and approached me. I couldn't stomach the sympathy in his eyes and turned my back to him again. I shouldn't have inspired sympathy or pity in other people—that wasn't who I was. I was Dulcie O'Neil, the badass, hard-as-nails fairy who didn't put up with anything from anyone. At least, that's who I used to be and who I wanted to be again. Who I was now, I really didn't know.

I shivered against the warmth of Knight's hands on my shoulders. As if I hadn't berated myself enough, images of me straddling him with my boobs hanging out like a baboon in estrus coursed through me until I wanted to slap myself.

"Dulcie, just remember that everything you did, you did for Sam."

I shook my head as an acid laugh fell off my lips. "I first took the *Mandrake* for Sam, yes, but at the end, I took it because I had to, because I couldn't turn it down." I glanced down at my small hands which were now fists at my side. "I thought I could defeat it, Knight. I didn't think I'd get addicted to it—I thought I was stronger than that."

"Dulcie, you aren't giving yourself enough credit."

"Credit?" I repeated facetiously, turning around to face him. "Credit for what?"

"For forcing yourself to do something that runs counter to everything you believe in just so you could save your friend. Yes, you got in over your head but that's not what you should be focusing on."

I dropped my eyes, feeling the sting of tears again. I blinked them away. "I think you're giving me too much latitude."

He chuckled. "Probably true in most things but not in this case."

A tear escaped my eye and he wiped it with the pad of his thumb.

"Hey, none of that was you, Dulce, I know it so why don't you?"

"I guess I have issues when it comes to failing."

His smile was wide and my breath caught in my throat. He was so incredibly handsome and I wasn't sure what to think about this tender and kind side of him—it was a version of Knight that I could very easily lose myself in and that was a scary thought.

"Issues with failing?" he laughed again. "That's got to be the understatement of the day. I hate to break it to you, Dulce, but you aren't perfect."

I glanced up at him and wiped away more tears. "Believe me, I know I'm less than perfect."

"Well, whatever you are, you've got the best intentions of anyone I know," Knight said in an iron tone, as if challenging me to argue or disagree with him. "And I've said it before and I'll say it again, you're an absolute asset to the ANC."

I couldn't even stand to listen to him—an asset? When I was addicted to an illegal narcotic? "Knight," I started and when he glanced down at me, I wasn't even sure I could get the words out. "I would have had sex with you just to get that next fix of *Mandrake*."

He shook his head and raised a brow. "Do you think I would have ever let it go that far?"

"That's not my point. If you had allowed it to...progress, I would have too," I finished, apparently hell-bent on lowering his estimation of me.

His lips were tight. "You don't know that for sure."

"Yes, I do."

His smile was broader than it had been. "Then, damn me for flushing the shit so fast. I should have waited a little longer."

I couldn't help my laugh and shook my head at the absurdity of the whole situation. Of all the people to have witnessed me at my worst, of course it would have been Knight—not Sam; not some random person I couldn't care less about, but Knight. Sometimes life was a major bitch.

I glanced at him again and chewed my lip, not entirely sure what to make of the fact that I felt indebted to him and grateful. "You know if our roles were reversed, I would have arrested you?"

"Said in true Dulcie O'Neil form," Knight said and shook his head. "I knew you had to be in there somewhere."

I didn't drop my gaze. "I'm being serious."

"I'm sure you are but we both know you wouldn't have arrested me. You play a mean game but underneath it all, you have feelings, Dulcie, even if you don't want to admit them."

I was spared the need to respond when the doorbell rang, announcing Dia's arrival. The thought that I could soon be sleeping was like waking up on Christmas morning. Knight dropped his hands from my shoulders and grinned warmly again.

"I don't want to hear any more about this," he started. "You need to forgive yourself and move on. I want the old Dulcie back—the one who gives me a crapload of attitude at every turn and makes my life significantly more difficult than it needs to be."

I wiped my eyes for the last time. "I think I can manage that." Maybe it was due to the fact that I hadn't slept in over six days, but I just didn't feel like me. I felt like I was going through some sort of identity crisis and I didn't like it one bit.

Knight approached the door and put his hand on the knob, then paused, glancing back at me. "Dia doesn't know anything about what went on here earlier," he began. "I didn't think it was my place to tell her."

I nodded in silent thanks. Sometimes Knight could be so...nice (for lack of a better word) that it just threw me for a loop—especially when he could be such an ass at other times.

He pulled open the door and Dia walked in, offering him a cheery smile before her complexion blanched as she focused on me. I had an apology to make and based on her expression, I'd better make it quick.

"I'm sorry for ditching you the other day, Dia," I said and smiled sheepishly. "Can you forgive me?"

She frowned. "Well, I guess I already have considering I'm here."

"Thanks," I started before Knight cleared his throat and opened the door further.

"I'm going to let you two get to it. I need to get back to the hospital to keep an eye on things," he announced and then glanced at me again, his expression softening. "It appears my work here is done."

I smiled back at him, not sure what to say or where to start. "Thanks," I said simply.

"Any time, Dulcie, we're in this together," he answered, smiling before he left.

I was sad to see him go.

Dia faced me after watching him close the door and she looked amused. "Thought anymore about Tweety?"

I laughed as I considered it—yes, Knight was a cocky, arrogant, bossy pain in my ass most the time but I had to admit that he wasn't all bad and even though I didn't want to accept it, I had to face the fact that Knight seemed to genuinely...care about me.

"Yeah, I have," I said with a thoughtful smile. "I don't know what to think of Tweety but I'm thinking about him all the same."

"It's a start, Girl, and thank Hades for that because I thought I'd have to knock some sense into that stubborn head of yours!"

"Hey, I've got baggage," I explained with a laugh.

She arched her brows. "Really? You don't say?"

"Okay, enough, smartass," I finished.

"You ready to get some sleep?"

I nodded. "Amen to that."

#

I sighed as I glanced down at Sam, who didn't look any worse but also didn't look any better. Yep, we were definitely in a holding pattern, the *Dreamstalker* waiting for me to call his bluff and vice versa. Well, if I had it my way, he was going to call my bluff and we'd face off in dreamland.

"She doesn't look good," Dia said as she inspected Sam.

"She doesn't look any worse than she did earlier though." I said the words more for my own peace of mind.

Dia and I had been summoned to Sam's room by Knight who had yet to show up. What the meeting was about, neither of us had any idea, although I hoped it had something to do with the fact that our current plan of sitting and waiting was working about as well as BP trying to control an oil leak.

Even though I couldn't say I felt good by any means, I'd been able to sleep for two hours thanks to Dia and at least I felt sane again—no longer craving illegal narcotics, seeing random babies or lust-craved *Lokis*. My day was looking up.

"Dia," I started, knowing this would probably lead to an argument but I was going to broach the subject anyway. I was running out of time.

"Hmm?" she asked and glanced at me before her gaze moved back to Sam. "It's almost like everything is on pause."

"How so?" I prodded, wondering if she'd reached the same conclusion I had.

She shook her head. "Sam isn't any better but isn't any worse. Meanwhile, Jenny, Travis and Shirley all look decently healthy, albeit in comas, but healthy all the same. Whatever this thing is, he definitely doesn't understand how *Dreamstalkers* work."

"Or he's fully aware of what he's doing," I said, eyeing her to judge her reaction to my cryptic comment.

"Meaning?"

I sighed, long and hard, wondering if it was better just to blurt my possibly outrageous ideas or warm her up to them, one toe into the deep end at a time. Ah, screw it, I'd blurt. "The *Dreamstalker* is waiting for me, Dia, he's waiting for me to fall asleep so I can fight him on his ground."

Dia nodded but didn't say anything although her silence was response enough. She either thought I was nuts and wanted to refrain from commenting or she was contemplating the idea. Hopefully the latter.

"And I think you know what we have to do," I continued. "Sitting and waiting is getting us nowhere and pretty soon, he's going to grow tired of waiting for me and he's going to do something to Sam, something I will have to live with for the rest of my life and something I'll never forgive myself for."

Dia nodded again, her eyes traveling from me to Sam, back to me again. "You know Knight won't go for it, especially since it would be putting you into a very precarious situation?"

She had a point. Knight wouldn't go for it and knowing his steel disposition, it would probably take a miracle on 34th street to change his mind. But, I hadn't really bothered myself with the minute details concerning what Knight would or would not approve of. Instead, I focused on Dia. If I could make her see the truth in my reasoning, she could help me work on Knight. And, although I wasn't really sure how she ranked in the ANC hierarchy, I assumed that as acting Chief of ANC Moon, she was high enough up there that her opinion mattered more than a damn.

Before I had the chance to further work on Dia, Knight lumbered into the room, looking like a warrior come to slay a dragon. There was a stiffness to his composure that I hadn't seen in a long time and with the way he worried the pen in his hand, clearly something big was rampaging through his mind.

I tried not to notice how chiseled his face was as he brought his eyes to mine and studied me for a second or two, seemingly to deduce whether I truly had made it through the *Mandrake* ordeal successfully. I smiled in response and he just nodded. We'd just had a full conversation without uttering a single word.

"Ladies," he said in greeting, finally breaking the silence.

"*Loki*," Dia answered and winked at me as I laughed.

"I've got to make this one quick," Knight said, his tone and body language back to business. "I'm traveling back to the Netherworld...tonight."

"What?" I snapped as both Dia's and my mouths dropped open in perfect unison like choir members. "What the hell for?"

Knight faced me with the same stubborn set to his jaw I'd come to know so well. "The blood lettings in Banshee," he answered simply as if we'd be satiated with such a ridiculously short response.

"Um, can't that wait?" Dia asked as she eyed me again, her expression one of concern.

"Knight, in case you don't remember, we're kind of in the middle of a major case here," I added. "One that is bound to break any second..."

"I know that, Dulcie," he spat out and shook his head, like he was trying to get his temper under control. Hmm, something was up because Knight normally wasn't this trigger happy. Don't get me wrong, he was often the King of all SOBs but now wasn't the time nor the place. "Regardless, I'm leaving tonight."

I shook my head and sighed, almost wondering if I was having another bout of hallucinations and was just imagining that Knight was actually saying this crap.

"You can't just leave, Knight," I started. "What about the blood tests for the suspects? What about the *Dreamstalker*? Hello? What about Sam?"

He nodded but it was hurried and he even checked his watch as if to exemplify the point. "Wait until I get back."

"Wait until you get back?" I yelled, feeling myself finally losing it. "Have you lost your fucking mind?"

"Knight, the timing of this trip is very bad," Dia added as if she were trying to justify my outburst with reason.

Knight ran an agitated hand through his hair before facing us both again. His jaw was just as tight, his expression just as pinched as it had been a few seconds ago. That meant he wasn't about to give in.

"I know it seems like bad timing but the blood lettings in Banshee are tied to this case," he finished.

I glanced at Sam, anger bubbling up within me. There was no way in hell I intended to wait for Knight to return from this utterly useless errand when Sam's life was hanging by a thread. I glanced at him again and hoped the ire oozing from my body reflected itself in my eyes.

"We can focus on Banshee once we get this guy, Knight. There's no reason for you to go there now."

"It's not up for discussion," he bit out. "Just don't do anything drastic until I return." He started to turn for the door but apparently remembered something and glanced back at me again. "That's an order."

Yep, just like that, the asshole I'd come to know so well had returned and who the hell knew when the nice Knight would show up again? I had half a mind to dub him Dr. *Loki* and Mr. Asswad.

I shook my head and stared at the floor. How the hell could he think this was a good idea? Now of all times? It made no sense and seemed to run counter to everything I'd ever thought about Knight. If nothing else, I used to be able to say I respected him as a detective and as an ANC cop, but now I couldn't even say that.

"And when the hell will you be back?" I demanded.

"A few days."

Fury bubbled up within me like lava and I thought I might blow right then and there. Dia, apparently sensing my volatility, placed a consoling hand on my arm and faced Knight. "Sam might not have a few days."

Knight sighed and glanced at the floor. "My hands are tied."

I turned around, afraid if I looked at him any longer, I'd claw his eyes out. His hands were tied? His hands were tied while my best friend was dying? Well, damn him to Hades—there was no way in hell I wasn't going to do anything but the drastic. And he wasn't my boss so he could screw himself.

"This is insane," I announced angrily.

"I have to get going," Knight answered and checked his watch again. "I'm due at the portal in fifteen minutes."

It wasn't like you could get a flight to the Netherworld, since it existed on the same plane as earth, but in a different dimension. Instead, the Netherworld traveler had to make preparations with the Netherworld ANC and then the ANC would send strata-hopping worm holes, known as dimensional portals to see the traveler to his destination.

Before I could object, Knight simply turned around and left. I looked at Dia and we were both speechless for a minute or two before a big smile outlined Dia's mouth.

"Guess we no longer need to worry about getting his buy in?" she asked and threw me for a second.

Once I realized she was referring to my plan to meet the *Dreamstalker* in his own territory, I smiled. She was on my side.

I glanced at her and couldn't help but laugh, even though worry, disbelief, anger and confusion all consumed my immediate thoughts. "No, I guess we don't."

#

Three hours later, I received a call from Dia who asked me to meet her for dinner in the hospital cafeteria. She'd gone to her hotel room to shower and nap before returning for the evening. I was only too happy to join up with her because I assumed we were going to discuss moving forward by laying out our next plan—that plan being how to kill the *Dreamstalker,* part two. And as far as I was concerned, whatever Knight didn't know, wouldn't hurt him.

"Hi, Girl," Dia said as she entered the cafeteria and plopped her bag into the seat next to me. "What slop are they serving tonight?"

I laughed. "I didn't check."

Instead of going to investigate what "food" the hospital was serving, she pulled out the plastic chair next to me and sat down. She took a deep breath and faced me with a wide smile, her dark eyes sparkling.

"I have news for you," she started.

"Shoot," I said noncommittally.

She tapped her long fingernails against the cheap plastic table and took a long pause before facing me again. She should have been an actress. "Knight didn't go back to the Netherworld to check on the Banshee blood lettings."

My eyes went wide and I felt my heartbeat speed up. "What? How do you know?"

She smiled and pulled out a compact, opening it to check her lipstick. I couldn't help but admire her plump, pretty lips. She snapped the compact closed and faced me again. "One thing you'll learn about me as we get to know each other better is that I'm a good cop and the reason is because I'm nosy."

I shook my head, a small laugh escaping me. "You crack me up, Dia."

She shrugged. "Well, I am good for a laugh too but back to the point about being nosy— I don't take people on their word and Knight seemed way too evasive earlier today so I investigated."

She was right, Knight had seemed too evasive. "So, what, you got in touch with Banshee?"

She nodded before a flirtatious smile lit her lips and I had to wonder if an incredibly hot doctor hadn't just entered the room. I glanced behind me but didn't see anyone so I turned back to Dia.

"I, uh, knew one of the guards at Banshee," she said with a laugh. "And boy was that man a hottie."

"Moving on," I said, frowning at the expression of absolute bliss on her face.

She shook her head, as if she were dispelling the images of the hottie and faced me with an apologetic smile. "Sorry, couldn't help remembering the abs on him and his butt..."

"Dia!"

She laughed and held up her hand in mock surrender. "Okay, okay. So, I spoke with my contact at Banshee and asked what the deal was with Knight's visit and he said Knight never showed up. And not only did Knight never show up, he was never scheduled to show up."

She leaned back in her chair and eyed me as if she was allowing the news to settle in. I gulped as I wondered what the hell Knight was up to and furthermore, why had he lied to us, to me? After all he and I had been through most recently, I didn't want to admit it to myself but Dia's news stung. Before I had the chance to inquire further, Dia leaned forward again and broke the silence.

"So, I did a bit more researching and called some friends I have in the ANC Netherworld and I found out that Knight was called back to the High Court for questioning."

"Oh my God," I started, realizing how bad that could be. The High Court was the determining law of the Netherworld—if you were a Netherworld creature and screwed up royally in the U.S., you ended up in the High Court where they would pronounce your punishment and they definitely weren't known for being easygoing. No wonder Knight had seemed so perturbed and anxious.

"What the hell would Knight be investigated for?" I asked, my stomach still somewhere down around my toes.

Dia nodded, apparently she had all the answers. "One of my very good friends happens to be the stenographer for the High Court," she began. "And Knight's case began this afternoon, an hour or so after he left the hospital." Dia took a deep breath. "Well, my stenographer friend told me that Knight was being investigated regarding a case with the former head of ANC Splendor, Quillan Beauregard."

"Oh my God," I repeated again, not knowing what else to say, and slumped back into my seat. This was terrible. Worse than terrible.

"Apparently Quillan was involved in some underhanded dealings regarding street potions and during the initial examination, he was never apprehended," Dia finished.

I knew the story all too well. "I was there," I said simply, as if to announce the fact that I knew exactly what had happened that evening and didn't want a reminder.

"I know," Dia responded and I glanced at her in surprise. "I wasn't done with my story."

"Sorry," I muttered.

"So, my friend told me that Judge Churchill was pretty upset with Knight because he was supposed to show up with you, Dulcie."

I felt the contents of my stomach rise up to my throat. "What?"

"Apparently it was you they wanted for questioning but Knight went in your stead and demanded that you had nothing to do with the situation which is why you hadn't come with him."

I wanted to throw up again. Knight had covered for me—he'd known full well that it had been my fault when Quill escaped. The awful image of that evening sliced through my head like a shard of glass, the memories already replaying themselves—me realizing Quill had been allied with the bad guys all along; how I'd aimed my Op 6 at him but hadn't been able to pull the trigger; how my heart had ached over the fact that I hadn't been able to take him into custody and more so, over the fact that one of my closest friends had betrayed me.

I shook the vision from my head. I'd basically let Quillan go and Knight had known that all along. Knight had lied to the High Court to protect me.

"What...what happened to Knight; what was the verdict?" I insisted, my voice sounding as distraught as I felt.

Dia shrugged. "Don't know. The case isn't over yet."

I pounded my fist into the table and swore.

"Dulcie," Dia said, an expression of worry on her face.

"Do you know anything more about it?" I interrupted.

She shook her head. "I only know that Knight swore up and down that you had nothing to do with Quillan's disappearance. That it was on his watch and he failed in his duties."

I swallowed hard and didn't say anything more. Dia glanced at me and her lips were tight.

"And if he's lying," she started with a tone of skepticism in her voice. "He could face life in Banshee."

"Why...why didn't he tell me?" I persisted, as the realization that I might have ruined Knight's life crashed and burned within me.

"Obviously he wanted to protect you," Dia finished before standing up. "That's all I know."

I glanced up at her and nodded, dropping my attention back to my shaking hands.

"Now, you and I need to eat and figure out what the hell we're going to do about this *Dreamstalker*," she said but I couldn't really say I'd processed her words. I was still completely floored by the news about Knight.

I vowed that once the *Dreamstalker* was dead, my next stop would be the Netherworld. I wasn't going to let Knight suffer for my shortcomings.

THIRTEEN

An hour later, I'd made the rounds among my comatose patients and was now back in Sam's room. I pulled Sam's head forward and fluffed her pillow, being careful to lay her neck and head back down. A stray hair stuck to her lip so I secured it behind her ear, feeling like a mother tending to her sick child. As far as Sam's health was concerned, there was still nothing new. No attacks from the *Dreamstalker*...yet.

Dia paced back and forth in front of me as we laid out our plans. And luckily for me (or unluckily, depending on how you looked at it) Dia had finally come around to my way of thinking—that we needed to take the *Dreamstalker* on in dream territory rather than continue sitting and waiting and basically, doing nothing. In preparation, we added another cot beside Sam's, the empty cot for me—for when I met the *Dreamstalker* in the land of dreams.

"When do you want to attempt this?" Dia asked, casting me a worried glance. By "attempt this," she meant when did I want to go to sleep so the *Dreamstalker* could attack me.

"Tonight," I answered and my voice was surprisingly level, calm. "I'm tired of waiting."

"I'll need to act as sentry for you, Dulcie," she continued as she chewed her bottom lip and started her fifth stroll across Sam's room. "I'm not going to let you sleep with no one to protect you."

I shook my head—this was one argument on which I wouldn't yield. "You'll need to continue searching the hospital and the grounds, Dia," I argued. "If the *Dreamstalker*...I mean, when the *Dreamstalker* comes for me, that will mean he'll have to be close by. We can't afford to have you worrying about me when you could be focused on nabbing this guy."

"Do you have a death wish?" she demanded, facing me with her hands on her hips. It suddenly made sense why some of her friends called her Diva—she was a force to be reckoned with, for sure. I liked Dia—she took girl power to a whole new level. "If you're asleep and I'm not there to protect you," she continued, "whatever this thing is could take you out and no one would ever know it."

I had to smile at her histrionics but the smile left my mouth as soon as I remembered the peril I was about to throw myself into. "No, I don't have a death wish and I'm considering this from every angle. I need you to be out there on the frontlines, Dia, not babysitting me." I glanced down at Sam again before returning my gaze to Dia. "I can handle myself."

Dia glared at me, her hands still resting on her hips. "And you do realize that if we do it your way and something happens to you, I'm going to have to deal with Knight?"

Ah, yes, the little problem known as Knight. "We're both going to have to deal with Knight, and it's not going to be pretty."

"You won't have to deal with him if you're dead," she snapped and started on her next lap across Sam's room. "And if you're dead, that means I'm going to have to face him alone."

I couldn't help but laugh at how casually she referred to my death—almost like it was a given. "Are you afraid of Knight...Diva?" I asked, challenging her.

She stopped pacing and glanced over at me before a smile brightened her lips. "With the way you're able to get what you want from Knight and me, you should have been a lawyer," she started. "And to answer your question, yes, Knight is sexy as sin, but intimidating all the same. I really don't want to be at the receiving end of that temper, not to mention the fact that he's very high up in the Netherworld ANC." She began pacing again. "This could be a career-limiting move."

"Buck up," I said. "You're the head of ANC Moon, you can deal with a *Loki.*"

She shook her head again. "Dealing with an enraged *Loki* aside, I'm not going to leave you alone with the *Dreamstalker*, Dulcie."

Obviously my skills of persuasion needed some work. So much for being a lawyer. "Dia, do you really think the *Dreamstalker* is going to come anywhere near me if he senses you're protecting me in my sleep? It sort of defeats the whole purpose."

She was silent and I realized I had a good argument.

"No," I continued. "We have to set this up as if it were real—that I'm here watching over Sam and not able to deal with the lack of sleep any longer, so I succumb. End of story." I paused and glanced at her. "And you don't enter into that equation."

"Well, Miz, I've got it all figured out," she started, hands on hips again, about as Diva as she could get. "How do you propose I catch the *Dreamstalker* if I can't sense him? Or had you forgotten about that little detail?"

I smiled sweetly. "Didn't you tell me you were an amazing cop earlier today at lunch?"

She shook her head and laughed but it was a strained sound. "Oh, you're good, Girl, too good."

I wasn't as good as I would have hoped because a few minutes later, we'd reached a decision and it was a compromise to say the least. If there was one thing I hated, it was a compromise because, really, neither side got what they wanted. Our compromise entailed Dia stationing her best ANC person in Sam's room and keeping an eye on me once I fell sleep. Meanwhile, Dia would scout the hospital, searching for any sign of the *Dreamstalker*. At the first sign of struggle from my sleeping body, my sitter would alert Dia and she'd invade my dreams, forcing me to wake up.

While this might have sounded good in theory, what it boiled down to was the fact that I would have no chance to defeat the *Dreamstalker* because Dia would be there at the first instance of me tossing and turning. And I assumed that as soon as my sleeping body came into contact with the *Dreamstalker*, I'd somehow reveal it by a sound or clenched eyes, or something else. I could wind up meeting the *Dreamstalker* and never having the chance to tell him off at the very least. I'd be awake with nothing gained. And to make matters worse, the *Dreamstalker* would know Dia was involved and who knew in how many ways that would blow our cover.

But, no matter, in true Dulcie O'Neil form, I already had a plan to foil this little problem without Dia being any the wiser.

"So, we start tonight," Dia asked but before I had the chance to answer, my cell phone rang. I glanced down to see who was calling but the screen was blank—like the phone couldn't even register the call, probably denoting long distance.

"Gimme a second," I said, glancing at Dia as I brought the phone to my ear. "Dulcie O'Neil."

"It's me." It was Knight.

I felt my stomach drop and leaned a hand against the wall to support myself. "Knight? Where are you?" I asked, wondering if he was already back from the Netherworld.

"I'm at Banshee," he answered and the lie pierced me like a dull blade.

"Bullshit," I started. "I know you aren't at Banshee so drop the charade."

I chanced a glance at Dia who looked entirely too interested in the conversation so I started for the hall, in search of a little privacy.

"How?"

"Why did you lie to me?" I insisted and perched myself on a window sill at the far end of the corridor.

"What..."

"I know where you are, Knight, you were brought in for questioning to the High Court."

He was quiet for a second. "How did you find out?"

"Dia," I answered before it occurred to me that maybe she wouldn't have wanted him to know she'd blown the lid off his lie. Oh, well, damage done. "Why did you lie to me?"

"I can't talk about that right now, Dulcie," he said and his tone was all business.

I sighed, knowing he wouldn't be able to tell me anything more. The ANC could have tapped the phone lines and probably had. "Just tell me you're alright," I said in a soft voice.

He breathed out a long breath. "I'm fine."

"Are you going to continue to be fine?"

He was silent for a few seconds. "I don't know."

"Knight," I started, not even knowing what I wanted to say, there were so many emotions pounding through me.

"I can't talk now, Dulcie," he said and cut me off. "I was just calling to make sure you aren't going to do anything stupid."

Ah, here it came. "Knight..."

"Dulcie, promise me. Wait until I get back."

But, I couldn't promise him anything. Not when Dia and I had already made plans to go after the *Dreamstalker* this evening. And, like I'd mentioned earlier, I hated to lie...well, when I wasn't on *Mandrake* anyway. "I can't promise, Knight."

"Dulcie, I know what you're going to try to do and like I said before, you're going to get yourself killed."

But, regardless of what he thought or said, I was steadfast. "I won't let Sam die, Knight."

"But, you'll let yourself die?" he asked and his voice was as sharp as barbed wire.

"I wasn't planning on it," I answered truthfully.

"Dulcie, I'll be out of here in another day. They expedited my case and I was able to go first." He breathed out a sigh of pent-up frustration. "If I've never asked you for a favor before, I'm asking for one now. Don't do anything until I get back."

I swallowed hard. "If the *Dreamstalker* goes after Sam..."

"Please, Dulcie."

I tried to relax my jaw once I realized I was clenching my teeth. "By the sound of it, you still want me to wait for you, even if this thing attacks Sam?" I asked icily.

He paused and his silence spoke volumes. I knew the answer to my question before he even offered it. "I'm sorry but you mean more to me than Sam does."

Well, Sam meant more to me than anyone else did and she was the only family I had, even if she wasn't related to me. "If something happens to Sam, Knight, I'm going to do what I have to do."

"Sam can hold on for another day or so."

"You don't know that and furthermore, you don't know that you'll be back in a day."

"No, I don't, but if I had to guess..."

"It would still be a guess," I interrupted.

"Dulcie, please." Knight had never begged for anything and the desperation in his tone gave me cause for pause.

The more I thought about it, I wondered if maybe we could put it off for another night or so. I mean, if I were to go to sleep now, who was to say the *Dreamstalker* would even know it? What it came down to was the fact that I had to try it my way—meaning I couldn't promise Knight anything, not when Sam's life was at stake.

"Knight, I can't..."

"Dulcie!" Dia screamed.

I felt my heart drop as I pushed off from the window sill and landed on the floor. My body went into autopilot and I started running as quickly as I could for Sam's room. Dia came tearing out of the room and there was panic on her face.

"What?!" I yelled. "What the hell happened?"

"The *Dreamstalker*!" Dia answered and grabbed my arm, both of us hurrying for Sam's room. "He's here!"

"Dulcie!" Knight yelled into the phone. I hadn't realized I still had the phone up to my ear. Everything had happened so quickly and yet even as I was in the situation and responding, I felt like I was in a dream; like I was watching it from afar and everything was in slow motion.

"Knight, I have to go," I said, not recognizing my own voice.

"Dulcie," Knight's voice broke. "Dulcie, don't do anything..."

I accidentally dropped the phone, causing it to shatter, the battery sliding across the floor and coming to rest underneath the empty cot. A few seconds later, Dia's phone started ringing but I couldn't say I really processed it and based on the fact that Dia was staring down at Sam in horror, she didn't either.

Looking at Dia's expression, I was afraid to glance down to witness whatever was happening to my best friend. But, I had to. When I forced my eyes to Sam's face, my heart constricted as rage built within me.

She was sweating profusely and her lips were completely white—pressed tightly together as tears bled from her eyes. A spasm rocked her body and I didn't even realize I was crying until I felt the tears tickling my cheeks as they fell .

The *Dreamstalker* had called my bluff.

I was ready to meet him.

"Now, it has to be now," I said and glanced at Dia who nodded before bolting for the door.

"I have to get someone to watch over you," she yelled behind her.

I climbed atop the empty cot and looked at Sam one last time. "I'm coming, Sam," I whispered. "Just hold the fuck on."

Before Dia could return to witness what I was up to, I shook my fist until a mound of fairy dust materialized and clenched it tightly, not wanting anyone to catch a glimpse of the opalescent particles in my hand. Luckily for me and my plan, the man who would keep watch over me arrived before Dia did and once he stepped into the room, I called him over.

As soon as he leaned down, I threw the fairy dust into his face and imagined his mind a blank canvas, ready for my command. He flinched and tried to free his eyes and mouth of the dust at first but once the words left my mouth, he stopped fighting and merely stared back at me.

"When Dia leaves this room, you are going to fall into a deep sleep and will not wake up until either I tell you to wake up or..."I could barely finish the sentence. I took a deep breath. "Or I die."

The man just nodded and stepped away from my cot, standing against the wall like a Beefeater outside Buckingham Palace. I had one shot to take the *Dreamstalker* down and I wasn't about to take the chance of having this guy alert Dia if I started to look restless.

Dia came racing back into Sam's room and her attention fell on me. She glanced at the man in the corner and I could see the relief in her eyes. Little did she know her assigned watcher was useless.

"I'm going to need your help," I said, looking up at her. "There's no way I can fall asleep on my own. Not with all this adrenaline pumping through me," I added.

She looked down at me before focusing on Sam again. She winced and I didn't want to look at Sam to figure out why.

"Are you ready?" she asked.

"Yes, do it now."

"Close your eyes and try to imagine your mind emptying out until there isn't anything to focus on," she said and I closed my eyes until all I could see was the beauty of darkness.

Dia grabbed my hand and squeezed it tight. I wasn't sure if she needed to in order to help me fall asleep or if she just did it for moral support. Either way, I needed and appreciated the gesture and squeezed back.

Then I focused on infinity as hard as I could, feeling myself swimming in the pitch blackness before me.

#

I was in a cave.

I glanced up at the ceiling which suspended stalactites and mineral deposits. As soon as I glanced up, a drop of water plopped against my forehead, followed by one after another. The smell of stagnant water permeated the air, mildewy and dank. I shivered in the darkness and had to wonder how I was able to see anything within the cave because in my mind's eye it was pitch black. I felt another drop of water but this time it landed on the top of my head because I was glancing down at myself. Somehow in the darkness, I was able to discover that I was wearing next to nothing—short white shorts and a bright pink tube top. My feet were bare.

And that was when I realized I was dreaming because there was no way in hell Dulcie O'Neil would ever wear pink or a tube top.

Ha, not on your life.

"You're asleep," I told myself, suddenly feeling like there was something I had to remember but couldn't. Yes, there was something important—something I'd been focused on for what felt like days or maybe even years. It was something I once knew or I'd written down. And I needed this information to break through the illusion of this dreamscape.

Illusion of this dreamscape...the words rang through me until I no longer pictured the cave around me from my own point of view. I was suddenly projected outside myself looking in—merely watching a woman as she stood in the cave and tried to make sense of the situation around her. And that was when I realized the sleeping me had taken over.

I was in a dream but I'd just harnessed it; I'd taken control.

The woman in the pink tube top glanced around the cave again and the realization that this wasn't my manifestation occurred to me. Someone else had created this landscape. The fleeting thought that I could change the reality around me floated through my cloudy mind and it took me a second or two to completely register the thought as true. Just as quickly as the thought entered, the next one was swiftly behind it—the feeling that I shouldn't change the dreamscape—no, I needed to hide my powers. I needed to project the image of a vulnerable woman trapped and completely helpless.

I watched the woman take a precarious step forward and nearly lose her footing on the uneven terrain of the cave floor. She stabilized herself against the wall and the sounds of metal clanking against chain were suddenly thick in my ears. She glanced up, just as manacles materialized from the rock wall, growing like weeds on fast forward as they reached out and clasped the woman's wrists, pulling her arms away from her body. Seeming to rewind, they retracted themselves back into the wall, pinning her arms.

I could feel the cold metal around my wrists and had to force my heartbeat to relax, imagining myself slowing my breathing. The woman suddenly inhaled deeply, breathing in for a count of three and breathing out for a count of three as my heartbeat decelerated.

The chill of cold metal against my ankles caused me to glance down and I found my feet secured against the rock wall, the wall jutting into my back painfully.

Then, I was outside of myself again, looking in on the image of the woman in the cave. There was fear in her eyes as she attempted to free herself from the manacles but her fight was pointless. As she struggled, she pushed her long gold hair out of the way and I caught the image of pointed ears.

If I hadn't realized before that the woman was me, I realized it now. Apparently the dream me was a little slow.

"Dulcie O'Neil."

The voice was deep but I couldn't focus on it long enough to wonder if I recognized it or not. It was as if the cave were speaking to me, the voice bouncing through the depths of the cavern, reverberating into infinity.

"Who the hell are you?" the woman demanded, with a clenched jaw and emerald green eyes that blazed with anger and hatred.

"You took your sweet fucking time to get here," the voice continued, frightening in its body-less void. "You kept me waiting too long."

But, the woman didn't seem to care. Instead, she tried to make out his features in the darkness but the task was impossible. It was as if he were made up of the air around him, shadowy and dark. He was merely an outline.

"Show yourself," she insisted but was met with nothing but the darkness of the cave. Her head turned from left to right as she tried to find any hint of the shadow man, her eyes wide with fear and anxiety.

"You're nothing but a coward," she spat out and pulled against her manacles again.

There wasn't any response but a cold wind whipped through the cave, building in intensity as it gusted past the empty walls, moaning like the cries of ghosts coming from deep within the cave's inner sanctum.

"Show yourself, you fucking coward," the woman yelled again.

Suddenly the outline of a man was before me, delineated more finely than the shadow man, but still, his face and body were like black smoke, opaque where his eyes, nose and mouth should have been. Nothing about the specter hinted to his identity. I felt myself flinch, felt my heartbeat start erratically—as if it was pumping too much blood. The sudden thought that I had to get out of my head and back into playing the part of spectator met me. I fought against the roar of blood pounding in my ears and tried to bring the image of the woman back to my mind's eye. When her image met me, it was translucent but it needed to be concrete, three-dimensional enough that I could reach out and touch her skin.

I clenched my eyes tight and forced my mind to detail the image of the woman, until I could make out the folds in her shorts, the drape of her eyelashes against her cheeks. I had her fully in my mind's eye again.

"You call that showing yourself?" she snarled at the shadow and spat at him in disgust.

"You want to know who I am, bitch?" the shadow demanded.

"Are you deaf?"

The shadow laughed a thick and ugly sound. It ricocheted through the cave, echoing into a thousand repetitions until I wanted to clamp my hands over my ears. But, I couldn't—my hands were still firmly secured against the cave wall.

"How about a few hints first?" the entity asked but didn't wait for a response. "Six years ago you got me locked up in Banshee."

"You'll have to do better than that," the woman scoffed. "I've sent a lot of criminals to Banshee, you dumb shit."

The entity was suddenly up in my face, its hand wrapped around my throat, tightening its hold. I couldn't breathe and felt myself flailing against him.

Focus on her, I told myself.

Picturing the woman, she was suddenly before me, the shadow man's hand wrapped around her throat as he leaned into her.

"Domestic violence," the shadow started. "Beat the shit out of my stupid girlfriend. The next thing I knew, this pretty little fairy with her long gold hair was in my face, threatening to shoot me if I didn't cooperate."

And suddenly I remembered. I remembered it as if it were yesterday. Images of another time, years ago came pouring into my head like jumbled film reels.

The bastard attacked his girlfriend, yes, on the basis that she'd argued with him. He beat her up so badly, she ended up in Splendor Hospital for weeks. I wasn't even sure she was going to make it through the ordeal. But, she was a Swan Maiden which meant she could take the form of the swan and, when she did, the swan helped heal her injuries. Had she been any other creature, aside from a vamp, she wouldn't have survived. After I visited her countless times, urging her to tell me who did this to her, she finally squealed and I went after the bastard.

I called for backup as I left for her boyfriend's house which was in the middle of the projects of Splendor, in a seedy little dump known as The End Of The Road which was fitting because it was located at the end of the town limits of Splendor, situated at the base of a large mountain. But, even the beauty of Mount Magnus couldn't detract from the filth of The End Of The Road. Trash lined the dirt streets and the craggy outlines of burned-out trees with only crows as tenants gave the place a haunted, doleful feel, as if Nature had given up on the hell-hole.

The arrest, itself, wasn't difficult. I merely knocked on the ramshackle door and as soon as the bastard answered, I went into detached cop mode although I wanted to pound his face in. The smell of dog was thick in my nose which meant he was a were. Wolf or not, he was a masochistic son of a bitch, needing to feel like a big man so he beat up his swan girlfriend. It was doubly bad because Swan Maidens were known for being nothing but placid, beautiful and elegant in their subservience. Needless-to-say, I hadn't believed his excuse that she'd argued with him—swans didn't argue, they just didn't have it in them.

I detested men like him and it was all I'd been able to do to keep my temper in control. Even though it might have been hard to believe, my temper had actually cooled over the years. Back then, I was a firecracker and just about anything could and did set me off.

"Are you Osric Cassius?" I asked and my voice was cool but calm.

"Yeah," he answered and scoffed down at me, like I was anything but a threat. He was sorely mistaken. "Are you here to ride me in your hot little cop outfit, slut?" he snickered and eyed me up and down until I wanted to vomit right then and there.

"No, you asshole," I started, feeling my famous temper rising within me. "I'm here to arrest your pathetic ass for putting your girlfriend in the hospital."

It wasn't traditional cop lingo but I was new back then and not exactly traditional. Quillan had worked with me over the years on my temper and I'd come a long way.

Osric laughed and lunged at me. I pulled my Op 6 out and before he knew what to think, he was staring down at the gun, probably wondering if I was trigger happy and hoping the answer was no.

Like I mentioned earlier, the arrest hadn't been difficult, Quill had arrived moments later and we'd thrown Osric into Splendor's holding cells before the Netherworld had sent for him and days later, he'd ended up in Banshee.

Apparently, he'd been released.

Lucky me.

FOURTEEN

"Osric Cassius," the woman in the pink tube top muttered to the shadow that loomed before her.

"Ding ding, right answer, bitch," the shade seethed back, undulating as if the sound of his name on her tongue sent him into a state of ire.

"So, now that I know who you are, why won't you show yourself?" she continued, her voice icy cold. "If I remember correctly, you're an ugly son of a bitch."

The shade seemed to shake himself—at least that's how it appeared with the way the black smoke within the outline of the man began to shimmy this way and that. The sound of roaring wind blew through the cave although I could feel nothing but stagnant air against my skin. After another few seconds, Osric Cassius stood before me and he didn't look happy.

It was as if I'd traveled back to that night when I'd stood on his doorstep and taken him into custody. He was just as thick and stocky as I remembered, though the time he'd spent in Banshee hadn't been good to him. Tattoos traveled up his arms and legs and covered the right side of his face. His long, wiry brown hair splayed in shambles around his shoulders, greyed with time. But, his face captured my attention—the rage in his eyes and the permanent sneer on his lips.

He hated me; that was as crystal clear as the savage glint in his eyes.

"Dulcie O'Neil, we meet again and this time it's on my terms," he started with a smile that revealed a mouthful of chipped, yellow teeth.

"You aren't a *Dreamstalker*." The voice was my own but hearing it confused me for a moment or two as I had to fight to retain the distance between my sleeping self and my projected self in the dream. "You're a were."

"So, you remember me?" he asked and there was a tone of hopefulness to his voice, hopefulness that somehow he was still outlined in my memory— that he stood out from all the other criminals I'd busted and locked away.

The woman nodded and although I planned to focus on questions to ask this bastard; it was like someone had suddenly turned on a fan in my head because all my questions began lifting in the air, spinning around the walls of my mind like a cyclone. I shook the visual away and concentrated, searching for the answers I needed from him.

"You've been drinking *Dreamstalker* blood, where did you get it?" I thought the words in my mind and the woman in the dreamscape spoke them. I was getting better at separating myself from the dream me. I didn't know why, but I felt that was a good thing.

"What does it matter?" He laughed snidely before bringing his finger to the woman's nose and tapping for a count of three as he repeated: "You are dead."

"Dead?" she repeated, trying to continue her ruse of playing dumb, to throw him off the fact that she knew she wasn't dead, only sleeping.

He nodded. "Right now, you're living on borrowed time."

I gulped, I couldn't help it. But, I had a job to do and so far I was doing a damned good job of it—maintaining the illusion that he was in control, that I wasn't aware I was dreaming and in having that control, wasn't aware I could use my magic.

"Humor me," the woman said.

"*Dreamstalker* blood is all over the streets of Splendor," he spat out and took two steps closer, glancing down at her body as he did so. The look of lust oozed from his eyes. "And there's other creatures' blood out there too," he finished, his eyes concentrated on her bust.

The feeling that I had to keep him talking rammed into me but I wasn't sure why. It was like I was buying time, but to what end, I had no idea.

"How did you find all your victims? All the people who were close to me or tied to me?" she asked.

His mouth lit up with an ugly smile before it morphed into a mere fuming white line across his face. "I had six long years in Banshee and I spent every second of my time scheming about the day I would meet up again with Dulcie O'Neil." He wrapped his hands around the woman's throat and smiled again. "How I would kill her with my bare hands."

"I didn't ask about your sentence," she interrupted. He dropped his hands from around her throat as I breathed an inward sigh of relief. "Answer my question."

His jaw clenched and he bashed his fist into the side of the cave, causing rocks and debris to crumble to the ground. When he pulled his hand away, there was no blood or injury, which I guessed made sense since this dreamscape was his creation.

The woman flinched and I felt the same reaction in my own body.

"It wasn't hard to find out about you—pay the guards and they give information," Osric answered in a non-committed sort of way, like he hadn't spent years trying to garner the facts about me.

The woman's eyes went wide and I could feel her shock, my own. "You pulled my ANC file?"

He nodded, his disheveled hair obscuring half his ugly face before he pushed it back. “And I searched the Internet. Your information was out there, easy to get.” He snickered. “And it wasn’t like I didn’t have all the fucking time in the world to get it.”

I swallowed hard, realizing the corruption of the ANC wasn’t just limited to Quillan duping us all at Splendor Headquarters but, from the sound of it, Banshee had its own problems. I could only wonder how much higher up it went. That was, if I survived this whole ordeal.

Osric stepped away from the woman and ran a mitt-like hand through his hair as he walked toward the mouth of the cave and back again, as if his thoughts were racing with such intensity, he wasn’t sure what to say next and needed to pace just to expend some energy.

Before I could blink, his face was suddenly up close and personal with mine and his eyes radiated a deep, red luminosity, glowing with the fires of hatred.

“You destroyed my life, bitch! You sent me to Banshee for six fucking years and the guards had a field day with me. They beat the shit out of me on a daily basis but it was worse at night.” I could smell the decay on his breath and it was the smell of death. He brought his face so close to mine that I could feel the scruff of his unshaven face against my cheek.

“At night the guards and some of the inmates used me as their woman.”

Shock waged through me, from my head to my toes and I cringed, I couldn’t help it. I had no idea what Banshee was like—I’d never been to the Netherworld, but his story actually made me start to sympathize with him, and feel pity for him. I closed my eyes.

“Look at me when I’m talking to you!” he ordered and gripped the woman’s chin, yanking her head up at an unnatural angle until she had no choice but to look at him. “Now I’m going to do to you what was done to me, day...and night.”

And just like that, my former sympathy was washed right out of me and replaced with vehemence and ferocity. There was no way in hell I was going to let this disgusting bastard anywhere near my body. Before I could respond, his fist connected with my gut and I felt myself capsize as pain reverberated up my stomach, and culminated in an undulating throb in my head. I couldn’t breathe, and felt like I needed to collapse against the floor but the manacles kept me in place, searing my wrists as I lurched forward.

Osric grasped a fistful of my hair and pulled me up, pushing me against the cave wall. His face was in mine again, his breath assaulting my sense of smell until I wanted to pass out. "You can bet your ass that swan bitch of mine is dead—she was the first one I looked up once I was released."

I gulped. The *Swan Maiden* was dead. I could only hope she hadn't suffered but seeing the cruel look in his eyes, I had to imagine she had.

And, I was next.

Osric held his hand out and I watched in horror as the ends of his fingers began growing translucent, a dull grey filling in as the flesh disappeared. He flexed and closed his hands as steel sprouted from his fingertips, elongating into nasty blades. He laughed as my eyes went wide.

You're in a dream, I screamed to myself. *None of this is real.*

I had to beat the fear, to pull myself from thinking that I was actually experiencing this and to recognize it for what it was—fake, counterfeit, imitation –nothing but a sham.

My eyes slammed shut and when I opened them, I was the outsider looking in, the voyeur to the woman in the pink tube top. I breathed a pent-up sigh of relief. I was still in control.

"Nice, Osric Scissorhands," the woman laughed in a biting tone. "Looking for some hedges to trim?"

Osric's face blanched and seconds later, he was fuming—turning as red as a *Huber Demon*.

"You think it's funny now, Dulcie, but how funny is this?"

When Osric rammed his finger blades into the woman's arm, shredding her flesh, it was only a numbness I felt—not the true feelings of pain that the visual would have warranted. The woman screamed out and fell forward again but Osric held her up with a deep, sardonic laugh. He stabbed his finger blades into each of her thighs, ripping the blades in and out again as the gold of her blood dripped down the dull steel, staining the cave floor below. She cried out in agony but I only felt a fraction of her pain.

Suddenly, the manacles around my wrists disappeared and I wondered if my own subconscious had issued the command or had Osric seen to it? He watched the manacles break away without surprise so I could only imagine he'd been the release mechanism. And that was a good thing—I didn't like the idea of orders issued without my being aware of them.

The woman fell to the ground, landing in a pool of her own blood. There was a horrible smacking sound as her head hit the dirt and she just lay there for a minute or two while Osric stared down at her, smiling at his conquest.

He lifted his leg and landed a well-placed kick into her midsection. She doubled over and grasped her stomach, her eyes wrenched tight with the pain.

How the fuck much longer am I going to put up with this? I demanded as the pain began to sink into me, becoming ever clearer and more pronounced in its throbbing.

I've had enough, I answered my own question.

The woman was huddled over on top of herself, both her hands hidden from view. Glancing up, she made sure Osric wasn't paying attention and smiled as she realized his gaze was wholly riveted on her ass. She shook one of her hands only slightly, but it was enough to create the fairy dust in her palm that would serve up some payback. Once the particles appeared, she released her fist, the particles falling to the ground below. Allowing them to sink into the pool of her blood, she imagined a white light of wellness suffusing her, a light only she could see.

I could feel myself growing stronger, with the pain dying away as healing invigorated me. The blood was still pooled beneath me but no matter, my body was healing itself, replenishing itself with new blood to make up for the loss.

The woman stood up, unsteady on her feet but standing all the same. Osric watched her with surprise in his expression, even though he made no motion to stop her. It was as if he wanted her to meet him on his level.

"You want more, baby?" he crooned with a hideous sneer on his face. "Cause you're about to get some."

He pulled his fist back and smashed it into her face, sending her toppling backwards, and landing against a rock that wedged itself into her back. She cried out and rolled away from the rock but before she could try to get back onto her feet, Osric was on top of her, his hands tearing at her shorts with an urgency that frightened her.

"Get the fuck off me," she yelled and pulled her fist back, landing a blow to his temple. Her arm shook with the effort and Osric flew back about three feet, his back hitting the side of the cave wall. He fell forward and landed against the ground, shaking the dirt out of his hair as he stood up. He glared at her with complete and utter shock in his eyes.

She stood up and her chest heaved as she inhaled, her hands balled up in fists at her side. She was strong in this dreamscape, stronger than she would have been in reality. And now Osric was also aware of the fact.

"So, you've been holding out on me, haven't you, bitch?" he seethed. "Good, it will be more fun this way."

And suddenly he was flying towards me, his arm transformed into an axe as he swung it at my head. I felt my dream body suddenly pulled backwards as I imagined a pair of unseen hands, grasping me and pulling me out of the path of the axe. The back of my head hit the wall of the cave and stars danced before my eyes momentarily. I closed them and forced the stars to subside, demanding my unwavering vision to return. I tumbled to the ground and before I could take another breath, Osric was on top of me again, his hands digging into my thighs, trying to rip my shorts away from me.

"You aren't strong enough for me!" he screamed into my face and smacked me hard across one cheek. I could feel viscous blood as it languidly streamed from my busted lip.

"Then why haven't you killed me yet?" I yelled at him.

"I control this dream," he spat out and grasped the waistline of my shorts again. "And I haven't killed you yet because I have other ideas."

"How much *Dreamstalker* blood have you drunk, you son of a bitch?" I yelled while wrestling his hands away from my shorts.

"Enough," he shrieked down at me. "You're no match for me—I've got the power of the *Dreamstalker* in my blood and you are nothing," he spat at me and his voice was level, even. He threw my hands off his own and in a split second, reached for my tube top, ripping it in two. I glanced down at my bare breasts and felt the heat of humiliation burning my cheeks.

Before I could respond, Osric's eyes were all over them and a second later, so were his hands. The fact that his attention was distracted allowed me to focus on changing the dreamscape so I could throw him. I'd let him know he wasn't dealing with a weakling.

I imagined a field of poppies, orange and beautiful. The sun was shining and birds flew from cherry tree to cherry tree, singing their trills for spring. I opened my eyes and found myself blinking against the bright sunlight.

Osric seemed stuck in shock as he gazed around himself in amazement. It was break enough for me to scoot out of his hold and stand up, shaking my hand until a mound of fairy dust emerged. I threw it into the air, allowing it to rain down over me. I glanced down and smiled at the metal chastity belt I'd constructed for myself—ha, I'd like to see the son of a bitch get through steel. A similar steel band protected my breasts from his intruding hands and although I probably looked like some bizarre Amazonian warrior or straight off the set of *Mad Max*, I lacked only one small but vital detail.

I closed my eyes one last time and pictured my Op 6, heavy in my hands, and at the feel of the cold steel in my palm, I smiled.

I opened my eyes and watched Osric as he realized I'd turned the tables on him and this was my dreamscape. He snarled but didn't make a move for me. Instead, he got down on all fours and his back arched as bristly fur burst from his spine, covering his entire body completely. His rib cage busted out and doubled in size as his fingernails ripped open, growing into long, hooked talons. He glared at me as his nose flattened into the landscape of his now furry face, and, in its place a snout began protruding, his teeth falling out of his mouth as canine fangs replaced them.

He was bigger, broader, scarier than any wolf I ever remembered seeing and I had to wonder if it was due in part to the *Dreamstalker* blood coursing through his veins or maybe it was just an illusion granted by the dreamscape. Either way, I aimed my Op 6 at the wolf.

Before I could squeeze off a shot, there was a sound like the air inhaling itself and I watched in shock as the sky zipped open, spitting out a man. The man dropped from the heavens and landed with a roll on the ground, coming to stand with his back to me as he faced Osric.

"Leave her the fuck alone," he screamed and Osric growled, leaping for him. The man didn't even pause to get his bearings and, instead, with his arm raised high and grasping a sword, he met Osric and thrust the sword into Osric's side.

Osric screamed out in agony and shook his head, simply disappearing into the earth, leaving only his blood staining the ground where he'd vanished. In a split second, Osric reappeared behind the intruder, now in his man skin, and with his arm around the man's throat. He rotated the man until they both were facing me and that was when I recognized the intruder.

"Quill?" I demanded, dumbfounded, with a sinking feeling in my gut as I tried to figure out how Quill had inserted himself in this dreamscape. He had to have drunk the blood of a *Dreamstalker*—the answer was obvious.

Quill didn't say anything but blinked himself in and out of focus, disappearing the same way Osric had, and then reappearing behind him. Quill landed a foot into Osric's lower back and Osric went down with a cry of pain. But, after rolling onto his back and pushing up with his hands, he soared five feet into the air before he started coming down again, his hands drawn around a blade.

The tip of the blade was aimed at the top of Quill's head.

I raised my trembling hands, aiming the Op 6, and thought the words "*slow motion*" and before Osric's blade could impale Quill, I squeezed the trigger. Time sped up again and at the instant that the tip of Osric's blade met Quill's hair, the bullet from my chamber penetrated the blade and it burst into a thousand pieces.

Osric fell against Quill, minus his weapon, and they both rolled on the ground, yelling and punching one another. Realizing this could go on forever and not wanting Quill to usurp my fight, I imagined a thick wall separating the two, building brick upon brick as it grew in seconds, towering to an unimaginable height, the top disappearing into the clouds. Side walls and a rear wall were quick to follow and seconds later, Quill was confined.

I could hear Quill screaming on the other side of the wall, bashing his hands into the concrete ineffectually. Osric glanced at the wall curiously as I extended both my hands, aiming the Op 6 at him. Osric brought his attention from the wall to me again and I smiled, nodding at him.

"Come and get me, you ugly piece of shit."

And he did come for me, he charged me with all the fury of an enraged elephant. I wasn't sure if he noticed the gun in my grip or not but when I fired, the look of shock on his ugly face was priceless. He glanced down at himself, watched the bullet penetrate his stomach and looked back up at me in surprise before his eyes went slack and he fell on the ground, disappearing into the earth, hopefully never to return.

I dropped the gun and felt myself sinking as the meadow began crumbling beneath my feet, the pieces falling into a black void below.

"Quill!" I screamed, watching the bricks of his fortress falling down and disappearing into nothing as they met the crumbling earth below them. The entire structure fell down and dissolved. Quill was nowhere to be seen. I screamed at the sound of bark ripping apart and glanced at the trees as they cracked and broke into what looked like puzzle pieces, disappearing into the abyss. The yellow of the sun faded into a deathly black.

I was waking up, I could feel it. But, I didn't know what had happened to Quill and I didn't want to wake up until I knew he was alright. I couldn't wake up, not yet! I suddenly remembered something about spinning—about imagining the dream me spinning to maintain the hold of the dream.

I brought the image of the woman in pink to my mind's eye and imagined her turning round and round as if her life depended on it.

I blinked and everything was black around me; there was nothing left.

#

"Dulcie!"

I woke up with a start and sat up, fear pounding through me. I could feel someone tugging at my shirt and glanced to my right, into Sam's concerned face. I said nothing as my attention darted around the room, which was stark in its whiteness. A man standing in the corner of the room had the same expression I must have had—shock as he tried to register where the hell he was and more, what the hell was going on.

"Dulcie!" Sam yelled again and grabbed my shoulder, forcing me to face her. "What...why are we in the hospital? What happened?"

And that was when it all came pouring back into me—the *Dreamstalker*, the dreamscape, Osric Cassius...I'd beaten Osric, I'd won and...I glanced over at Sam again.

Sam was alive.

Tears gushed from my eyes as I jumped down from the cot and grasped her in my arms, holding her as tightly as I could. I never wanted to let go.

"Sam, it's okay now," I breathed. "You're safe."

She wrapped her arms around me and I could feel the hot wetness of her tears against my neck.

"I've had the worst dreams, Dulce," she started.

"Shhh, I know," I crooned against her ear. "Believe me, I know."

"Girl, you've got a whole truckload of explaining to do!"

Dia's voice was both angry and relieved. I turned from Sam and smiled at Dia as she dropped her expression of anger, even though I'm sure there was a part of her that was super pissed off with me. And it wasn't like I blamed her.

She approached me in two strides and I wasn't sure who reached for the other first but it didn't matter. We stood in the middle of the room, clinging to one another.

"It's over, Dia," I whispered, and she answered me with a hearty laugh.

"I hope to Hades I never have to work with your ass again."

I returned the laugh as I pulled away and smiled at her guiltily. "I'm sorry, Dia," I started. "But, I did what I had to do."

Dia just shook her head but her smile said she forgave me although she probably wasn't lying when she said she didn't want to work with me again. And I couldn't blame her on that count either. I did have a tendency to do what I wanted and needed to, whether it went counter to other people's plans or not.

"What's going on?" Sam demanded, her voice nervous.

Dia faced her and the smile on her face widened. "Girl, I don't have the time for instant rewind." Then she faced me again. "I was able to track the son of a bitch using my *somnogobelinus* senses after all."

I nodded, it wasn't surprising. "He'd been drinking a lot of *Dreamstalker* blood. Maybe the more he drank, the easier it was for you to track him." I paused for a second or two as my stomach started to drop. "Where the hell is he?"

"Dead," Dia answered and sounded surprised. "I found the son of a bitch in the basement of the hospital but by the time I got to him, he was already dead."

I nodded, remembering the fact that I'd shot him. It only made sense that since he'd died in slumber, he'd died in reality.

"Who was he?" Dia demanded.

"Osric Cassius," I answered and heard Sam gasp. I glanced at her and nodded. "I'll explain all of this to you later, Sam."

"I don't know the name," Dia interrupted.

I shook my head. "You don't need to—just another asshole I locked up a long time ago—another asshole with a vendetta."

She laughed but my mouth had suddenly gone dry as the memory of Quill interrupting my fight with Osric met me like a nightmare. Quill had been in the dreamscape which meant he had to be somewhere nearby and hopefully wasn't hurt.

I started for the door before glancing back at Dia and Sam. The guy in the corner seemed like he was still shell-shocked and I offered him a quick smile. "I have to go find someone, Dia," I began as she looked at me with a question in her eyes. "Can you check on Jenny and the others? I'll be right back."

"Dulcie!" Sam said and her voice was panicked.

I faced her and smiled. "Sam, I gotta go but I'll be back in a second. Everything is okay. Just listen to what Dia says."

Dia frowned at me before she glanced at Sam again. "She needs to listen to her own advice."

But, I wasn't concerned—I rounded the corner and ran down the hallway, stopping to glance in every room as I searched for Quill. There was no sign of him. I nearly ran headlong into a nurse as she made her rounds and I grasped her arm, my expression wild, I was sure.

"Have you seen a man around here—tall with wavy blond hair?"

She shook her head. "No, are...are you okay?"

I nodded and released her, not sparing her another glance but continued down the hallway, checking each room as I did so. I couldn't shake the thoughts that maybe something had happened to Quill when the dream world had disintegrated. Or, did something happen prior to that? Had Osric hurt him somehow? I didn't want to learn the answers. All I wanted to do was find Quill, healthy and alive.

I didn't wait for the elevator to take me to the second floor but, instead, threw open the door to the stairwell and took the stairs two at a time. When I reached floor two, I blasted through the doors and ran down the hall, glancing in each of the rooms, dodging nurses and doctors left and right.

There was no sign of Quill on floor three and now on floor two.

Luckily, Splendor Hospital wasn't a huge medical center—it only had the three floors and after I'd exhausted all three, I scouted the basement. Finding nothing that would lead me to Quill, I started my search outside. I had to make sure he was okay; that's all that was going through my head.

The light of the streetlamps lit my path and I searched the perimeter of the hospital, my gaze traveling back and forth from the manicured trees, to the bushes running the border of the hospital, to the benches that periodically broke the monotony of the landscape. There was no sign of him. I leaned against the wall to catch my breath and felt a scream growing in my throat. What did it mean that I couldn't find him? Had he already taken off? Or was it worse than that—was he hurt somewhere? Tears of frustration blinded my eyes and I beat my hand against the wall.

"Looking for someone?"

I glanced to the right and watched him step around the corner, bathed in darkness. I wanted to run to him and throw my arms around him and hold him tight but I knew I couldn't do that. Instead, I just stood there, staring at him.

"Thank you," I said breathlessly. "Thank you for risking your life for me."

He chuckled but the sound was sweet. "Anything for you, Dulce," he answered and pulled his jacket closer around himself.

There were so many things I wanted to say to him, so many thoughts and words flying through my head but I couldn't get my mouth to form around any of them.

"You take care of yourself, my little warrior," he said with another chuckle and simply walked back into the darkness from whence he'd come.

FIFTEEN

After a few hours I was able to get Jenny, Travis, Shirley and Sam discharged from the hospital and Sam drove us back to my apartment where I explained the whole *Dreamstalker* situation to her in finite detail, starting with the fact that all the victims were connected to me personally—down to the fact that our *Dreamstalker* had really been Osric Cassius and even though I struggled to get through it, I also told her about the *Mandrake* and the fact that I'd seen Quill again.

"Wow, if I didn't think you were truly my best friend before," Sam began, scratching Blue's ears as he sat beside her on the couch. "I definitely do now."

I laughed and nodded, watching the rain as it poured outside and channeled into little rivulets on my living room windows. "Yeah, I'd say we're definitely on this trip called life together."

I held up my glass of red wine and swished the liquid inside the glass while thinking about everything that had happened over the last week.

"So, I have to ask you, Dulce," Sam started mysteriously before a huge grin overtook her mouth. "What in the heck happened to your hair?"

I was silent for a second or two before a laugh took hold of me and wouldn't let go. My hair was now no longer black, but had migrated through a transitory purple only to end its journey as a flat brownish-grey.

Lovely, just lovely.

"About that," I started and faced her, watching Blue collapse atop her lap as she continued to stroke his head. "Could you fix it?"

Being a witch, Sam could whip up a potion that would wash the color right out of my hair. My attempts to get it back to its golden honey-blond with my own magic had been less than successful.

"Of course," Sam replied, taking a sip of her wine as the rain continued to trickle down my window panes. Sam put her glass on the coffee table and faced me with a sober expression. "No word from Knight?" she asked, snuggling into the blanket which she wrapped around her shoulders. We were both sitting on my couch, warm and toasty beside the space heater as the wind tore through the trees and the rain continued to pound outside.

At the mention of Knight, I swallowed hard. "No," I said, glancing up at her. "No word from him at all." Course, not having my cell phone since I dropped it on the hospital floor might've explained that. But Knight couldn't use that as an excuse for his lack of communication—he also had my home number.

She nodded. "Are you worried?"

"Yeah, I'm really worried." I sighed, as I thought about how worried I was. I didn't know much about the Netherworld but from what I'd heard, it sounded like a tough place—wild and uncivilized in many ways. And the idea that Knight had taken it upon himself to lie to the Court of the ANC was unbelievable.

"Why would he have lied to the High Court, Sam?" I asked rhetorically.

"Because he's in love with you," she answered, startling me.

"In love with me?" I scoffed. "Please."

She frowned and shrugged. "Someday you're going to have to accept the fact that you're a pretty awesome girl, Dulcie O'Neil."

I laughed and emptied the contents of the wine into my mouth, wondering how I felt about the possibility of Knight being in love...with me. I banished the thought away as soon as it entered my head—there was no way he was in love with me. Was it even possible for Knight to be in love with anyone? Then that thought led to another one—*had* Knight ever been in love with someone?

I didn't dare admit to myself how uncomfortable that thought left me.

"I just hope he's okay," I said in a small voice. "Wherever he is, I hope he's okay."

And I'd already told myself that if Knight didn't contact me or show up on my doorstep in the next three days, I was going to the Netherworld to tell the High Court what really happened, that Knight had just been protecting me and I was the one who had let Quill go.

Yes, I realized that in doing so, Knight could be tried for perjury but I hoped his intention of protecting me would be a lesser offense than allowing Quill to escape. No, that was my failure and eventually I'd have to face up to it.

Three days, that was all I was giving Knight...

"Well, if I didn't say thank you before," Sam started, shattering my thoughts of Knight. "I'm saying it now." She grasped my ankle and squeezed it. "Thank you, Dulce, for being such an amazing friend and risking your life for mine."

I just nodded, feeling tears springing into my eyes. Yes, Sam was my best friend and the closest person to me in the world. I reached over and hugged her for the nth time that evening. Even though she'd asked if she could spend the night because she was afraid to be alone, she'd merely beaten me to it—there was no way I wanted to be alone either.

I pulled away from her and there was an expression on her face like she was in the midst of pondering some involved subject. "Do you think Quill is happy?" she asked in a voice that sounded far away.

I cocked my head as I considered it. "No," I said, finally. "I think he's tried to make a bad situation as good as he can. He's been able to rise to the top because he's smart and he knows how to play the game, but as to being happy, no I don't think he is." And it wasn't a thought that brought me any sort of pleasure.

"I bet he was happiest when he was working with us at the ANC," Sam continued. "When you two used to flirt and argue and flirt and argue some more."

I made a face at her. "We never flirted!"

"Total lie, Dulce!" Sam laughed and Blue lifted his head from Sam's lap as if to say that he, too, knew it was a total lie. "Do you know that we all used to make bets on whether or not it would be a Dulcie-Quillan flirt day or argue day?"

I faced her with my mouth agape. "You did not!"

She laughed and nodded. "Yeah, we did. And I have to admit, the odds usually ended up being fifty-fifty, which never surprised me, knowing your penchant for arguing."

"Hey, I don't like to argue," I started but Sam's raised eyebrow snatched the words right off my tongue, defeating me. I smiled but there was unexpressed grief inside me as I thought of Quill, remembering the last words he said to me.

You take care of yourself, my little warrior.

His words had been easier to listen to than "goodbye" would have been, but they basically meant the same thing—neither of us knew if we'd ever see each other again. And although I didn't want to admit it, I ached to see Quill again because being around him reminded me of a time when things weren't so difficult—before I knew that friends could betray one another and before I knew what it felt like to be addicted to illegal narcotics. Seeing Quill returned me to an innocent time when he played the muse of pirate captain, when the Wrangler was still around and when life was overall easier.

"What are you thinking about?" Sam asked.

"Stuff I shouldn't be thinking about," I answered, noncommittally.

A knock on the door pulled me from my reverie and alerted me to the fact that Dia and Trey had arrived—we'd decided to have a little *Dreamstalker*-ass-busting celebratory dinner at my place. I stood up, Blue at my side, and approached the door, grabbing hold of Blue's collar when he started to paw the door while barking. Opening it with a smile, I faced Dia, who was drenched from head to toe, wearing a deep frown that clashed with her otherwise pretty face.

"I should have told you to pick up the food," she grumbled as she glanced at Blue. "Is he friendly?"

I shrugged. "No, not really."

She made a face and cautiously entered while Blue sniffed her twice and instantly lost interest, trotting back over to the couch which he jumped on, circled a few times and made himself comfortable.

Trey was quick behind Dia and offered me a happy grin. It seemed like nothing got in the way of a happy mood and Trey and I had to admit, I liked him the better for it.

"Hi Dulce," he said, when a huge, beaming smile spread across his lips as he spotted Sam. "Hi, Sam!"

Sam smiled up at him and waved while I helped Dia with the bag of Italian takeout, bringing it into the kitchen, where I plopped it up on the counter and started unloading the various dishes. Dia rifled through my drawers, searching for utensils and plates.

"Any word from Knight?" I asked under my breath, not wanting to alert Trey to the fact that there was a problem. Trey really admired and liked Knight so I didn't want to worry him unnecessarily. But, I had a feeling it might become necessary as time went on.

Dia faced me and sighed. "No, you?"

I shook my head and returned to the task of serving up each dish. "I'm scared for him, Dia."

She put a consoling hand on my shoulder. "He'll reach out to you, Dulcie, I'm sure he will. He's probably up to his neck in crap at the moment."

"He would call me, if he was able to."

"Just give him a little more time. It's been, what..." she glanced down at her watch. "Four hours since we heard from him last? He could be in court."

I nodded, she was right—maybe I was jumping to conclusions. But, there was a little voice in the back of my head that said Knight would have gotten in touch with me, no matter how busy he'd been. Especially when we ended our conversation with him knowing I was going to go to sleep in order to meet up with the *Dreamstalker*.

"I got the reports on the blood tests back," Dia started, distracting my thoughts from Knight, which was just as well because worrying about him wasn't helping me.

I glanced at her, wondering why the blood tests were even a consideration now. Obviously we knew who our *Dreamstalker* was or had been. "And?"

"More than half of them were on some sort of blood—*Kraken*, Were..." She glanced at me. "Fairy."

"What?" I demanded. "Fairy?"

There weren't a lot of fairies in the U.S. We totaled maybe ten and in Splendor, there were just two—me and the fairy hooker, Zara. And, needless-to-say, I hadn't been donating my blood. Damn Zara...

"Why do I have a feeling that's the next case we're going to be working on?" I mumbled.

Dia laughed. "Honey, I already told you I am *not* interested in working with you again. You about gave me heart failure this time around."

I smiled. "What if I promise to be a better team player?"

She just gave me a diva-like expression and refrained from further comment.

"Where's dinner?" Trey called from the living room. "I'm a hungry man!"

I laughed and shook my head, suddenly feeling grateful to be surrounded by my friends.

#

Two hours later, Dia and Trey left and I was doing dishes while Sam cuddled up on the couch, watching reruns of "The Tudors. "

"I just don't see how it's possible for an ordinary human man to be as hot as Henry Cavill is," Sam announced. "He's got to be the best looking guy I think I've ever seen."

I laughed but had to disagree—there was one man who I could honestly say was the be all, end all in the looks category as far as I was concerned and that man was Knight.

I sighed inwardly as I thought about Knight again, for the umpteenth time this evening. It was like I just couldn't eradicate thoughts of him, try as I might. I even promised myself that once I got a good night's sleep, of which I was in dire need, my next plan would be getting to the Netherworld and confessing that I was the one who screwed up in the apprehension of Quillan.

I couldn't let Knight fall on the sword for this one.

I finished the dishes and not wanting to watch TV, turned on my computer and thought about checking my emails. I hadn't checked them in days and had to imagine my inbox was at the point of overflowing.

I logged into Yahoo and scanned the various subject lines, pausing once I recognized another email from Barbara Mandley, the literary agent. I opened it and smiled at her announcement that although my book had a few areas that could be improved upon, she wanted to offer representation.

I leaned back as I thought about it. Wow, I'd be able to say I actually had an agent and that had to mean the road to publication had just opened its golden gates for me. This was maybe the start of a new life for me—one where I didn't have to work law enforcement any longer and could write for a living.

As exciting as the thought was, I also felt a bit sad since, if I made it in the big leagues, I'd probably have to give up my life in law enforcement. I had to admit that I actually did enjoy keeping the citizens of Splendor on the straight and narrow. But, I didn't have time to think about any of that now. I was getting way ahead of myself.

I considered sharing the news that I now had an agent with Sam, but I was so exhausted, I figured I could save the conversation for the morning. And Bram...Bram would be very happy to hear it as well. But, that could also wait. For now, I had some Zzzz I needed to catch up on.

"Oh my God," Sam started. "I just saw Henry's butt and it was totally bare. Dulce, you gotta come watch this one."

I laughed just as a frantic knock on my door captured my attention. I glanced at the clock and noticed it was just past midnight.

"Who the hell is coming by at this hour?" Sam asked, pulling her attention from Henry's hot ass. "And in the rain, no less?"

I shrugged and reached for the Op 6 which stood unattended on my kitchen table. I palmed the gun and wrapped my fingers around it, holding it at my side as I approached the door. Glancing through the peephole was useless because the light above my door had burned out and it was dark outside.

I opened the door and found Knight standing before me, rain trailing down the hard planes of his face.

"Knight?" I whispered, almost afraid he was another *Mandrake* hallucination that would vanish before me. Then I had to remind myself I hadn't taken any *Mandrake* in days which meant...Knight was here and...safe.

"Dulcie," he said it in the same tone, as if neither one of us believed the other was real.

And then I did something that was so uncharacteristically me, so completely alien from the old Dulcie O'Neil but something that had to be done, all the same. I laid the gun on the table beside the door, walked outside and gently pulled the door closed behind me.

"I missed you," I said and leaned up on my tip toes, wrapping my arms around his neck and I kissed him.

I kissed him like I'd never kissed anyone before, as all the anxiety and worry that had been building up within me dissolved into Knight's taste.

Knight was safe.

The words were like music to my mind.

Knight's tongue was in my mouth before I could think and I welcomed it. I ran my hands through his sopping hair and held him tighter. As if it wasn't close enough, he hoisted me into his arms and I wrapped my legs around him, deepening the kiss until I almost couldn't breathe.

And Knight. I'd never seen him like his—his eyes were closed, one hand splaying through my hair as the other held me in place. He pushed me against the closed door and pulled his mouth from mine, shifting the hair from in front of my neck as he trailed a line of kisses down my throat.

"Why didn't you call me?" I whispered. "I was worried sick about you."

He chuckled but didn't stop nibbling my neck. "You were worried sick about me?" he asked, amused. "I've been beside myself wondering if you were...alive."

I grasped his hair and pulled him away from my neck. "Knight, what happened at the High Court?"

He shrugged. "I don't know."

"What do you mean you don't know?"

He didn't answer but gripped my neck and forced his mouth on mine again. His passion was insatiable and I couldn't help the groan that escaped my mouth.

"God, I want you, Dulcie," he growled.

"I want you too," I started and that seemed to be enough for him because his hand was suddenly turning the doorknob, like he'd grown tired of freezing outside and wanted to get it on in the comfort of my bed. I put my hand on top of his. "Sam is here, Knight."

He dropped his head and I could see the sag of his broad shoulders. He glanced up and smiled but there was disappointment in his eyes. "I'm happy Sam is okay, Dulce, but at the moment, I could kill her."

I laughed and shook my head, before the need to know what had happened to him gnawed away at me again. "What happened at the High Court and what the hell were you thinking when you to lied to them, Knight? That was so stupid."

He shook his head and just gazed at me for a moment or two. "I had to do it, Dulce. They'd be easier on me than they would on you."

"Why?"

He grasped my chin, tilting it up again. "I can't think about that right now. All I can focus on is tasting you."

He kissed me with an intense passion, pulling me into him, until I could feel the hardness between his thighs. I wrapped one leg around his waist, wanting to feel him inside my own melting core. If Sam hadn't been on the other side of the door, I would have ripped my clothes off and told Knight to take me right then and there. But, Sam *was* on the other side of the door and the thought of her enforced my self-control.

"Knight, talk to me," I said, pulling away from him. "Are you ready to go inside?"

He arched a brow. "No, I'm not, but there's no use in freezing out here."

I smiled and palmed the doorknob, opening the door. I offered Sam a sheepish grin as she glanced at both of us. "Knight!" she said with a smile.

"Sam, how are you doing?" he asked and I couldn't help but notice that he had his hands clasped in front of himself to hide the raging....ahem....thing behind his pants and looked totally ridiculous in the process.

"I'm great," she answered and then looked at me again with a smile that I knew all too well. She turned off the TV. "I am getting pretty tired so I'll just retire in Dulce's room. Night guys."

"Night," I said and figured I wouldn't hear the end of it tomorrow. But, for now, I could concentrate on Knight.

We watched her disappear into my room and close the door behind her and as soon as she did so, Knight's hands were all over me again, his tongue in my mouth. I had to pry myself away again.

"You never answered my question, why would the High Court go easier on you than me?"

"Because I'm higher up in the ranks," he answered absentmindedly as his hands found my waist and he pulled me into him. "I've proven myself, so to say."

I frowned. "And I haven't?"

He smiled down at me. "You've proven yourself and then some, you know that. But that's coming from me—the Netherworld ANC hasn't worked with you and they don't know you, Dulce, but they know me."

I nodded, guessing that made sense but I still didn't like it and it didn't change my plan to make sure his name didn't get muddied in this whole situation.

"So, what happened with the case?" I demanded.

He took a few steps from me, pulling out one of my kitchen chairs and deposited himself in it with a sigh, as if he realized the sex stuff was over for the night. "I didn't stay to find out."

"You left in the middle of your case?" I asked, my voice dropping in disbelief.

"I didn't wait for the case to begin," he answered with a grin. "Once I knew you were going to meet the *Dreamstalker* on his terms, I left." He glanced at me and his gaze raked me from head to toe. "I couldn't focus on anything else, knowing you could be dying."

I approached him and sat down on his lap, straddling him. He wrapped his hands around my waist and buried his face in my chest.

"I'm not going to let you take the rap for me letting Quillan go," I whispered in his ear and started kissing his neck.

"You don't have a choice," he responded, his hands on either of my breasts as I began rocking myself against the hardness in his pants.

"The High Court is going to be pissed you bailed on them," I added.

He chuckled. "Pissed isn't even the word for it." He brought his hands back to my waist and dropped his head back as he closed his eyes while I continued to gyrate against him.

This wasn't an argument that was going to be won tonight. For tonight, I just appreciated the fact that Knight was safe, that Sam was alive and the *Dreamstalker* was dead. Tomorrow I could face all the other problems that had recently become my life—I could face the question of the illegal blood on the underground market and I could figure out what the hell I was going to do about the High Court.

Knight glanced up at me and his eyes glowed that eerie luminescence I'd first seen at Bram's party.

"Okay, big guy, what's with the eye glowing bit?" I asked, while rubbing my fingers against his incredibly soft lips.

He diverted his gaze as if he was embarrassed. "Are they glowing?" he asked.

I tilted his chin up and smiled down at him. "Yep and now there are no interruptions like Angela or Bram's party so you'd better tell me why."

He sighed and it spoke volumes. Anything Knight didn't want to inform me about, I wanted to know all the more. "It's something *Lokis* do," he said simply.

"That doesn't answer my question," I answered with a raised brow.

He chuckled. "Nothing with you is ever easy, Dulcie."

"No tangents either," I said with a smirk. "Nice try though."

He returned the smirk. "I'll tell you on one condition."

"Name it."

"Dinner tomorrow night, my house, eight o'clock."

I narrowed my eyes and smiled. "Done."

He grasped my waist and lifted me off his lap, placing me on my kitchen floor. Then he stood up. "Until tomorrow," he said with a smile.

"Wait a second," I started, my hands on my hips. "I just agreed to your condition."

He nodded. "Yes, you did, but it isn't tomorrow night at my house at eight o'clock, is it?"

I frowned. "But..."

"Dulcie, I know you too well. Between now and tomorrow night, there's a very good chance you'll talk yourself out of the fact that you and I are great for each other. So, rather than giving up my secret now, I'll tell you tomorrow...once you show up for our date."

I laughed even though I was annoyed.

He reached for me and placed a chaste kiss on my lips then pulled away, starting for the door. He grasped the handle and opened it, stepping into the darkness before he turned around and faced me again.

"And be sure to show up because this is one of my better secrets."

Then he closed the door behind him and left me in my living room with only Blue for company.

"What a..." I started.

Blue glanced up at me and shook his canine head before closing his eyes as he drifted back into doggy sleep.

H.P. Mallory lives in California with her husband and son, although she's also lived abroad in the U.K.

She enjoys traveling, snorkeling, antiquing and being a mom.

If you are interested in receiving emails when she releases new books, please sign up for her distro list by visiting her website and clicking the "contact" tab:

www.hpmallory.com

Be sure to join HP's online facebook community where you will find pictures of the characters from both series and lots of other fun stuff including an online book club!

Facebook: www.facebook.com/people/Hp-Mallory/10000124964376

Discover other titles by H.P. Mallory:

To Kill A Warlock (Book 1 of the Dulcie O'Neil series)
Kiss Me, Kill Me (Anthology with Dulcie O'Neil short story)

Fire Burn and Cauldron Bubble (Book 1 of the Jolie Wilkins series)
Toil and Trouble (Book 2 of the Jolie Wilkins series)

Find H.P. Mallory Online:
www.hpmallory.com
Blog: www.urbanfantasyauthor.blogspot.com
www.twitter.com/hpmallory

Made in the USA
Lexington, KY
03 June 2011